TANGO

Kendall dropped her eyes and shoved the sleeves on her dress back into place. "You don't have to say anything. I put you on the spot. I'm ready to go home now."

Joseph transferred his heat with the touch of his hand on her cheek. "I was hoping you would stay."

Cautiously, Kendall met his smoldering gaze.

"I was hoping you would stay all night. Let me prove to you how unimportant those scars are to me."

Kendall's mouth opened, but there were no words.

"You want to know if I can hold you all through the night? Hell, yes. All night. Stay with me, because looking at you—all of you—I see the most beautiful, sexiest woman in the world and I don't want you to leave tonight."

BOOK YOUR PLACE ON OUR WEBSITE AND MAKE THE ARABESQUE ROMANCE CONNECTION!

We've created a customized website just for our very special Arabesque readers, where you can get the inside scoop on everything that's going on with Arabesque romance novels.

When you come online, you'll have the exciting opportunity to:

- View covers of upcoming books

- Learn about our future publishing schedule (listed by publication month and author)

- Find out when your favorite authors will be visiting a city near you

- Search for and order backlist books

- Check out author bios and background information

- Send e-mail to your favorite authors

- Join us in weekly chats with authors, readers and other guests

- Get writing guidelines

- AND MUCH MORE!

Visit our website at
http://www.arabesquebooks.com

TANGO

Kimberley White

BET Publications, LLC
http://www.bet.com
http://www.arabesquebooks.com

I met flight attendant Ken Rose at a book signing in downtown Detroit. He answered my questions pertaining to the day-to-day functions of flying for a commercial carrier without hesitation. I hope I've done a fair job of fictionalizing a most courageous career.

ACKNOWLEDGMENTS

Plotseekers and Sisterfriends book clubs in Detroit have supported me from the beginning of my writing career. These groups are made up of dynamic sisters with noble goals. All my best.

For my writing associates: Glenn R. Townes, Natalie Dunbar, Karen White-Owens, and Angela Wynn. Rainelle Burton stepped in and adopted me, showed me the way to go, and then helped me start my new journey—thank you. If you haven't checked out their work, you're missing the bold new voices of the twenty-first century.

To my biggest fan and most dynamic supporter: Sylvia McClain.

Special thanks to the writing groups who have opened their arms and embraced me and my writing endeavors, attended my workshops, come out to my book signings no matter the weather, and supported me in any way possible: International Women's Writer's Guild, Detroit Writer's Guild, Ridgewriters, ArtServe Michigan, Detroit Women Writers, Great Lakes Bookseller's Association, and the Farmington Arts Council.

Most importantly, thanks to Chandra Taylor and BET Books. Without your belief in my work, I wouldn't be able to pursue my dreams.

Chapter 1

Dressed in full uniform, Captain Joseph Stewart made heads turn as he strutted through Detroit Wayne Metropolitan Airport. The gold wings gracing his collar shined as brightly as his black patent leather shoes. He walked with the regal stride earned by an ex–air force pilot with twelve years of service behind him. The crowd parted as he passed. Women added extra swagger to their hips in hopes of getting his attention.

Joseph held his head high underneath the cap of his flight uniform. He could be the poster boy for new pilots with the crisp creases of his dark uniform and shiny black shoes. A neatly trimmed mustache and close-cut hairstyle with gray specks at the temples were his most distinguishing features—besides his heritage. Being one of a handful of black commercial pilots in the industry, Joseph no longer acknowledged the brazen stares of travelers.

Joseph had learned to ignore prejudice in military flight school. He survived the hazing incidents all rookies were forced to endure. He'd fought with excellent grades and superb skills the racist remarks of his instructors. In the end, it had all been worth it because flying had become his dream in elementary school.

He pulled his luggage-on-wheels behind him onto the elevator. He rubbed his weary eyes as he waited for the elevator to transport him to the pilots' private lounge.

"Joseph." Gabrielle hopped into the elevator car before the door closed.

He sighed with annoyance. "Gabrielle, it's Captain Stewart and this is a private elevator—for pilots only." He pointed above her head at the sign confirming his statement.

Gabrielle stepped up to him, letting the door close behind her. "Captain Stewart, I noticed the roster says you're on layover and . . ." she hesitated while she adjusted the band of her skirt. "I have a few days off myself and I thought—"

"This is my stop." Joseph stepped off the elevator into a small gathering of pilots, eating lunch and awaiting the takeoff of their next flights.

Gabrielle tried too hard. They'd flown together about a month ago, and ever since she'd been trying to get him to take her out. As pretty as she was, he had no interest in her. With her figure-eight body, green eyes, and soft Italian accent, any man would consider her the embodiment of many boys' "flight attendant" fantasies.

Gabrielle looked to be much younger than his own forty years, which wouldn't have bothered him if she didn't act immature. He didn't have the desire to answer gossip amongst his coworkers about being involved with a flight attendant. He had worked hard to achieve respect amongst his peers and didn't want to jeopardize it by getting involved in an affair that might satisfy his loins but never his heart.

"Joe, over here."

He stowed his luggage in a vacant corner, placed his cap on top of the bag, and joined his friend.

"Just landed?" Russ shoved a shrimp into his mouth before he signaled the waitress.

"Just landed. Ran into a lot of turbulence landing in Chicago."

"That's not all you ran into. Gabrielle still hanging on your coattail?"

"I've let her know I'm not interested, but she doesn't hear it."

Russ used the back of his hand to wipe the corner of his mouth. "She'd understand if you found a Mrs. Captain Joseph Stewart. Put poor Gabby out of her misery."

The waitress appeared, saving Joseph from answering. "Can I get you something, Captain Stewart?"

He ordered a ham sandwich. Knowing that his doctor would have a fit, he added a house salad with low-fat dressing.

After the waitress left Russ asked, "I have three days at home. When are you up again?"

"Two weeks."

"How'd you swing that?"

"I've logged sixty-five hours in the air this month."

Russ nodded his understanding. Federal rules prohibited commercial airline pilots from flying more than one hundred hours in a month.

"Sixty-five hours already, huh?" Russ questioned. "You really do need to find yourself a wife or at least someone to help occupy your time. There is a world outside of airports and cockpits, you know. What are you going to do with all that time off, buddy?"

"I have a major report I need to file. There's a mandatory training seminar I've been too busy to attend. I'll relax a little. Catch up on things around the house. Take my motorcycle out."

"Boring." Russ chugged down a drink of soda. "Listen, the wife has to attend an art showing at the Museum of African-American History. It's supposed to be a big deal. She's sitting on a board at the museum and we have to make an appearance. Come with us. I know she can get her hands on an extra ticket—or two," he hinted. "It'll give me someone to talk to."

"Is that a reference to your fear that you'll be the only white couple there?" Joseph goaded his friend.

"It's a reference to the fact that I'll be the only man there who doesn't understand what the hell is going on. You know this artsy-fartsy stuff is not my bag."

Joseph laughed at his good friend's crass honesty.

"You don't have anything going on, do a friend a favor."

Kendall Masterson held the African fertility statue at eye level, scrutinizing her work. This represented a symbol that her ancestors had cherished and idolized. The history behind the carving was profound. A legend even accompanied the gathering of the wood for the creation of the god.

When she pulled the wood-grain statue from the packing crate upon its arrival at the Detroit gallery, the driver of the semi had snickered at the exposed breasts and oversize lips. She'd like him to see how majestic it looked now that she had spent weeks restoring it to its once natural beauty.

"Are you ready to send that piece to the Museum of African-American History with the others?" Greg asked, stepping up behind her.

She looked up to see that the gallery owner had joined her. "It's gorgeous, isn't it?"

He rubbed his forefinger over the braided cornrows of the statue. "I'd say it's one of the finest pieces of artwork I've ever seen come out of Africa."

Kendall fought back emotion. "You'll never know what it means to hold a piece of your history—the history that was denied my people—in my own two hands."

Greg agreed by squeezing her shoulder. He was fully aware of Kendall's pride in her African-American heritage and he respected her for openly displaying it. Never once had black-white race issues marred their relationship; she was the daughter he and his wife couldn't have. She had been responsible for opening his eyes to the richness of black history and expanding the gallery's acquisitions to honor it. "This entire show is going to be a tremendous success, and it's all because of the work you've done." He brought her hand to his lips for a kiss of appreciation.

"Thank you, kind sir." Kendall turned to wrap the statue in a dust-free white cotton cloth.

"Listen, I need to talk to you."

"Yeah, what about?" Kendall asked, still preoccupied with the fertility statue.

"The art collectors who will be at the showing want to meet the person responsible for all of this."

Kendall carefully placed the statue on her workstation before swinging around to face Greg. "Are you going somewhere we agreed you wouldn't go?"

Greg's eyes were buried in the puffiness of his full cheeks, giving them a soft innocence. "I need you at the show, Kendall."

"We agreed that I would restore this shipment to see if I could handle it. We agreed that we would sit down and discuss my working on a contractual basis for the gallery until I was one hundred percent again. That's all. You know I can't handle attending a showing this soon."

"Kendall, have a seat."

They sat together on the twin stools adjacent to her workstation. Nervous habit made Greg run his palms up and down the seams of his trousers. Kendall watched him, hoping that he was sweating enough not to ask the inevitable.

Greg lifted his chin, ready to scold. "I'm honored that

you came back to the gallery to help me out of this bind. No independent contractor could have done the job you did on these pieces." He paused. "Kendall, this is the best work I've ever seen you do. You're better than one hundred percent. You need to put the accident behind you and start living again."

At the mention of the accident, Kendall instinctively flexed her fingers. "I still have a lot of pain. I can't maneuver the way I could before."

Greg cocked his head in question.

"It took me twice as long to finish these pieces as it would have before."

"That's because there was so much detail—"

"The scarring causes me to get stiff after working too many hours. Sometimes the pain is unbearable."

"What did the doctor suggest?" Greg challenged.

Kendall glanced at the fertility piece. "Continued occupational therapy exercises at home."

"Yes, he said to continue your occupational therapy exercises on your own, at home. He ended the physical therapy weeks ago because you have full range of motion and use of your hands again."

Kendall felt no one understood the depth of her grief. She left her stool and circled the workstation. "You promised not to push me."

"I promised not to push you beyond your capabilities. You're more than capable. Your work is better than ever. I can't be an enabler."

Kendall crossed the room and started packing other artwork. "Are you my personal psychiatrist now?"

"I'm your friend—one of the only people who hasn't let you push them away. I'm your friend, but I'm also your employer and I need you at the show. You don't have to stay all evening. I'll introduce you, you'll say a few words, mingle a little, and then you can leave."

Greg, of all people, should understand she wasn't ready to face the public. Reporters would get around to asking her about the accident, her recovery, and her sister. "I don't think I can do it. Just considering it makes my palms wet."

"This show is for charity, your favorite—the Detroit Public Schools. With you there, giving the history behind the pieces and mingling with the buyers, the prices will soar. The gallery will help fund the public school art program, your commission will skyrocket, and yours truly—the gallery owner—will be very happy." Greg joined her at the packing crate. "I'm your friend and I'm asking you to do this for me—for the kids. For yourself."

Kendall looked into his soft eyes and saw the same worry and concern he'd harbored for her during her recovery period. He was correct. She had pushed everyone important in her life away once she regained consciousness and learned what she had done.

The pain during her hospitalization had been more severe than she could bear. She hadn't been able to speak without lightning rods of agony piercing her. When debilitating pain had delayed her entrance into therapy, the doctor equipped her with a pump so she could press a button every ten minutes to administer her own analgesics via the intravenous route.

The medications eased the physical pain but never the emotional.

Eventually Kendall had embraced the idea of therapy. She apologized to the physical therapist that had spent weeks trying to ignore her hostility and teach her to walk again. She worked through crying jags to earn autonomy. Once she could walk up four stairs independently, the doctor discharged her to home.

Once released, Kendall had still needed physical therapy and a homecare nurse, but at least she was at home where she didn't have to smile to avoid a referral to the psych department. Learning to walk again was relatively easy compared to trying to use her right hand again. The flames had caused extensive nerve damage to her right shoulder and altered her dexterity. For weeks she attended occupational therapy sessions—three days at the clinic, two at home.

Kendall had recently reached the conclusion of her therapies. The homecare nurse and physical therapist had released her. Occupational therapy was over. She still had regular follow-ups with her physician, but officially she was considered "healed."

During that awful time, Greg ignored her tangents and supported her until she was back on her feet. He dodged flying trays. Laughed when she cursed him. Refused to leave when she begged to be left alone. Made a key to her place when he had to call the police after not hearing from her for two days. The list went on for days.

Somewhere between her losing her dexterity and suffering the loss of a lifetime, Kendall's boss turned into one of the best friends she ever had. When he asked her to do something simple like attend the opening of a show, she couldn't justify refusing.

"I can't let you down."

Greg smiled behind a sigh of relief.

"Can you pick me up?"

The concerned eyes returned. "Didn't the insurance company give you a check to replace the car?"

"Yes."

"Do you need me or my wife to drive you to a dealership?"

Kendall busied herself by fiddling with the top of the packing crate. "No, I bought a Honda Accord."

Greg knew her too well. "You aren't driving yet, are you?"

"No."

"How have you been getting to work every day?"

"Taxi." Her voice wavered with emotion. She prayed he wouldn't venture further into the conversation. She couldn't drive—not now, not ever. The only reason she had the car replaced was to pacify the nosy insurance carrier. The shiny gold car sat at the top of her driveway where the dealership had left it. If she had been able to hobble outside fast enough, she would have had the driver pull it into the garage where she didn't have to look at it. When he brought the invoice and keys to the door, his hurried attitude kept her from asking that he move it.

Greg read her correctly and backed off. He sighed, showing his disappointment in her progress. "My wife and I will pick you up. It'll do you good to get out and meet new people."

Chapter 2

Kendall waited backstage determined to get through the showing at the Museum of African-American History with dignity and grace. Greg and his wife agreed to run interference between her and any reporters who might make name recognition and connect her to the fiery crash. He also promised she could leave the museum after her favorite piece had been auctioned off. She had the feeling that Greg would hold that piece until late in the show just to keep her as long as possible. Annoying, but with good intentions, Kendall couldn't be mad at Greg for trying.

Finding the dressing room in use by performers, Kendall joined them to straighten her hair and makeup. Dancers in elaborate costumes depicting their individual heritages bustled, getting ready to go onstage. The director appeared, clapping his hands together with a sharp ring that pierced Kendall's ears. "Show time! Let's move."

The women passed him in turn, waiting to receive the director's pat of approval on their backsides before moving on. It only took something as harmless as this to turn on Kendall's waterworks. Her sister, Raven, could have been a dancer. She had graduated from Detroit's Center for Performing Arts and gone on to Wayne State University. She was in her sophomore year—and still undecided on majoring in theater or dance—when the accident shattered all her dreams.

"Are you lost?" the flamboyant director asked.

"I wanted to freshen up in here if you don't mind."

"Not at all." He ran off after the girls.

Kendall sat at the brightly lit makeup station and pulled out her cosmetics bag. She didn't need much makeup to bring out her cheek structure—her short texturized haircut with frosty blond tips did that. She selected a transparent mocha lip coloring over the satiny red. Her bottom lip protruded farther than the top, giving her a permanent pout. The professional arch of her eyebrows made her brown eyes stand out, but she coated her lashes with black mascara anyway.

She put the cosmetics bag away and stood to examine her attire in the full-length mirror. For her grand coming-out Kendall had rummaged through her closet searching for a dress that would be elegant, yet simple and comfortable. With her stomach in knots she didn't need to worry about how to sit down without showing everything her mama gave her. Most of her fancy dresses ended up in a box marked *Goodwill Donations* because of their revealing nature. The permanent scarring on her right shoulder left her little choice of selection. She chose a full-length mauve gown that hugged her lower body and shielded the scars from view. As she assessed herself in the dancers' mirror she hoped no one would see past the polished exterior into her shaky soul.

"There you are." Greg rushed into the room followed by the producer. He turned and thanked the man, who ran off to check on his performers. "You're on after this number. The president of the museum will say a few words and introduce me. I'll be charming and then introduce you. Ready?"

"Ready." She held up two sets of crossed fingers.

Greg quirked an ear at the crowd's enthusiastic response to the dancers. "Did I tell you, you look stunning tonight? I'm proud of you."

Kendall squeezed his hand for strength.

"I thank you and the kids thank you."

"Don't get mushy on me, Greg."

The announcer's voice came over the sound system. Dancers trudged into the area, perspiring and not as spry as when they had danced out.

"Let's do this," Kendall said before leading Greg out of the room.

"Captain Joseph Stewart, I'd like you to meet—"

Joseph plastered on the same phony smile he had shared with the last six single women Russ's wife introduced him to. He let them chatter, noticing Russ's attention wavered also.

Bored to tears, Joseph interrupted. "Sara, excuse me." He slipped away to the bar, leaving his friend's wife to apologize for his behavior.

The lights went down again. Joseph propped his foot on the silver railing lining the bottom of the bar and ordered another drink. If not for the endless parade of single women Sara insisted he meet, the showing would have been quite enjoyable. A staunch fan of the opera, Joseph appreciated all the arts. He didn't know much about art history, but what he had heard thus far fascinated him. He fully intended to purchase a piece to support the Detroit Public Schools, where his own education began—Murray-Wright High School class of 1978.

Joseph sipped his drink and checked the time. Shortly, they would be allowed into the museum area to look over the pieces up for auction. Afterward the bidding would begin.

The procession of gruff male voices over the microphone was pleasantly interrupted. Joseph turned toward the voice. The woman onstage glowed underneath the lights. She swayed side to side as she spoke; nerves. Her head turned to the right of the stage. Joseph couldn't see whom she was looking at, but after a deep breath she faced the crowd and continued with renewed self-confidence. She educated them on the history of restoring the art. She spoke about the origin of the pieces. Her face lit up with unbridled enthusiasm as she told of the myth surrounding one particular idol.

Joseph leaned over to the bartender. "What's her name?"

"Kendall Masterson."

"She works here at the museum?"

"No. She's one of the gallery people." He stretched to the end of the bar and handed Joseph a discarded program book. "I think I saw her bio in there."

"Thanks." Joseph slipped him an extra tip.

Captivated again by the sweet timbre of her voice, Joseph clutched the program for later examination. Right now he wanted to take in every drop of the princess on the stage. Poised, educated, refined, and just a touch nervous, Kendall Masterson had what no other woman could get—Joseph's attention. Her neat hairstyle and subtle touches of makeup told him she was disciplined and spent her time focused on more important things than shopping and beauty parlors.

Joseph tucked the program under his arm and clapped as Kendall exited the stage. He wanted to meet this young lady, and he knew the person who could arrange that.

* * *

"Why?" Sara asked, still mad about his quick departure. "Ask him why he wants me to introduce him to Kendall, Russ."

Sara had the annoying habit of talking to him through Russ.

Russ popped an olive into his month. Joseph knew the routine; there was no need for him to speak.

Sara went on. "Did you adopt children that I don't know about? Why do you need a baby-sitter? I've tried to introduce you to some very nice women tonight—any of whom would be a perfect match for you—and you want me to introduce you to Gidget."

Russ snickered behind his martini glass.

"You don't want to do this, Sara?" Joseph asked.

Of course Sara wanted to be able to take the credit for introducing Joseph to the woman responsible for set-tling him down—if it came to that. She pressed her lips into a thin line. "This way."

Sara sauntered through the crowd in Kendall's direc-tion. As Joseph's punishment, she stopped and chatted with every available woman in the room on the way.

"Greg." Sara politely kissed the man standing with Kendall. "Kendall, how are you? You look wonderful tonight."

"Good, thank you."

Sara pulled Joseph into the conversation by the cuff of his black tuxedo. "Greg, Kendall, I want you to meet Captain Joseph Stewart. He flies with the same airline as my husband."

"Nice to meet you." Greg extended his hand.

Joseph returned the greeting and then embraced Kendall's hand while he searched for something clever to say. Her youth surprised him. Despite Sara's com-ment, he hadn't realized how young she was from his vantage point at the bar. The announcer had interrupted before he could recoup.

Kendall pulled her hand away. "I'm sorry, Captain—"

"Stewart."

She gave him a polite smile. "I need to check on the exhibit before the public is admitted. Have a nice time tonight."

Joseph watched as Kendall disappeared into the crowd followed closely by Greg.

"She is rather young," he conceded to Sara.

"Joseph, you know I was only giving you a hard time. She's very refined. Why don't you ask her out? It's very obvious that you're taken with her—shut your mouth, dear." Sara hid her laughter behind her pale hand.

"I haven't dated for a long time, but isn't she supposed to remember my name if she's interested?"

Sara gave him a lopsided grin behind knowing eyes and left to find Russ.

Joseph pulled the program book from the breast pocket of his tux. He flipped to the back and found a close-up head-and-shoulder shot of Kendall Masterson. The photographer pictured her in a haze-filled pink background. Bare shoulders, her hair longer and without the blond coloring, she held her head back in laughter. Although a great shot, the picture did not do justice to the woman he had just met.

Joseph checked the front of the brochure for the night's schedule of events. After the auction there would be cocktails and dancing on the lower level. Maybe he'd have a chance to make a better, more memorable impression with Kendall then.

He wandered over to the buffet table where Russ lingered.

"Sorry for dragging you here, buddy," Russ apologized with a snicker. "Sara told me what happened with Kendall.

I bet Gabby would be happy to lick your wounds—amongst other things."

Joseph loaded meatballs onto his plate. "Do you kiss your wife with that mouth?"

"Only when she lets me."

Joseph and Russ ate from the buffet. They were cornered when word spread that they were airline pilots. People always asked the same questions when they learned of their profession. Most wanted to know the dirt behind the pilots and flight attendants. Others asked for free tickets. Everyone inquired about near misses and crashes. One woman brazenly asked about a pilot's salary when Sara told her Joseph was single.

The announcer took the stage, saving Joseph from politely refusing to disclose his salary. While the man onstage spoke, Joseph moved away from the woman.

Guests could enter the exhibit hall. Joseph followed the flow of people traffic into the hall. He and Russ moved shoulder-to-shoulder checking out each art piece. As Kendall had promised, the exhibit was breathtaking.

Joseph spotted Kendall across the hall. He straightened his bow tie before moving in her direction. He walked up behind her as she fussed over a musical instrument displayed atop a marble pedestal. "Ms. Masterson."

Kendall swung around. "Captain . . ."

"Stewart. Maybe Joseph would be easier for you to remember."

Her face blushed with a hint of pink. "I'm sorry. I've met so many people tonight." She extended her hand. "Please call me Kendall." She fit perfectly inside the palm of his hand. His eyes went to hers; she blinked and stared downward, pulling her hand away. "Are you enjoying the exhibit?"

"I am, but I have to admit that I don't know much about art history. Do you mind showing me around?"

Joseph had made up his mind to challenge him for Kendall.

He considered their age difference. It would be rude to ask her age outright, but he definitely had some years on her. It didn't seem to bother her. Then again, she was showing art—doing her job. He hadn't asked her out yet. Before the night ended, he would. He just hoped he didn't embarrass himself.

"There's a legend that surrounds the gathering of the wood to make this piece," Kendall was saying. "The young man who—"

"Kendall," Greg interrupted them. He acknowledged Captain Stewart with a nod. "We're ready to start."

Kendall turned to Joseph. "I'm sorry. I have to run."

"Thank you for showing me around."

Greg led her away. "Maybe I can finish telling you about the legend after the auction," she said.

"Definitely," he called after her. "I'll definitely look for you afterward."

With what he had in mind, she'd be searching the crowd for him.

Chapter 3

"What are you doing? Russ, ask him what he's doing," Sara said, aghast.

Russ leaned forward in his chair to clearly see Joseph's face around Sara. "What are you doing, Joe?"

Joseph stared straight ahead, his eyes glued to the fertility statue. An older man held up his paddle, topping Joseph's bid. He didn't hesitate to discreetly lift a finger when the auctioneer called out another dollar amount.

"Do you know how much your bid is on that statue? Russ, ask him if he knows how much money he's spending."

Before Russ could ask, the older man up front bid again. Joseph countered with a thousand dollars more than the auctioneer requested. The crowd began to whisper. People pulled out their programs, flipping through the pages in search of the description of the statue.

Onstage, Kendall's mouth parted in surprised recognition of the man placing the bid.

Greg whispered across the stage, "Isn't that Captain Stewart bidding?"

Kendall sat mesmerized by the action. Afraid she'd miss one word or gesture of the action, she didn't answer Greg. The old man in front and Joseph were locked in a bidding war. The old man waved his paddle, becoming more frustrated with every bid. Joseph remained cool, wagging his finger in the air to signal his bid.

The old man bid again. His wife whispered angrily into his ear and snatched the paddle away.

The crowd turned in anticipation. The auctioneer asked for five hundred more than the last offer. His mannerisms said he was ashamed to ask for such an outrageous figure.

Joseph maintained his stoic expression. Sara tugged desperately at Russ's jacket; she'd given up on trying to stop Joseph herself. Russ told her to calm down—he was sure Joseph would be outbid.

Joseph had already spent two thousand more than he intended. He planned on picking up something to help the kids, but not take a chunk out of his retirement fund to do it. His eyes glanced in Kendall's direction. Retirement would be a lot more fun with a gorgeous woman at his side. He lifted his finger in the air.

The crowd gasped. Kendall's hand went over her mouth. Greg leaned over and whispered to her.

The auctioneer called for final bids. With visible relief, the man closed the bidding. "Sold"—his gavel slammed down—"to the man in the black tux. Congratulations, sir."

Greg helped Kendall from her chair. "Is Captain Stewart buying the statue or *you?*"

Kendall looked back as Greg pulled her backstage. A small crowd gathered to congratulate Joseph on winning the bidding war over the statue. He shook their hands and nodded politely, but his eyes were locked on her.

"The Detroit Public Schools can use that money," Kendall told Greg.

"They most certainly can. Let's go thank Captain Stewart."

Before Kendall could think up a legitimate argument, Greg dragged her from behind the stage in search of Joseph. She felt as grateful as Greg, but Greg hadn't spent time alone with Captain Joseph Stewart and couldn't understand her hesitation in greeting him. As they had walked earlier, he maintained his debonair attitude, never being anything less than a gentleman, but the way he stared at her made her breath quicken.

"Captain Stewart," Greg said, all smiles.

Joseph turned to the ladies crowding around him. "Excuse me."

The women blatantly rolled their eyes at Kendall as they walked away. She hadn't seen anything this shameful since her cousin's bridal bouquet toss when three women tussled on the floor for the coveted flowers. No wonder the man let his broad shoulders lead him through the crowd with a suave swagger.

Greg played the diplomatic role. "We wanted to thank you on behalf of the gallery and the school system for your generous donation."

"I like supporting the kids. Ms. Masterson talked with me about the fertility statue earlier with such enthusiasm that I had to see it in my home."

Greg missed the hungry glance Joseph threw Kendall's way. He pulled out a business card and handed it to Joseph. "I'd like to invite you to my gallery. Let me know that you're coming and I'll arrange for myself and Kendall to be available for your questions."

Joseph studied the card before tucking it inside the breast pocket of his tux. "I think I'll do that. I was telling Ms. Masterson earlier that I have very little smarts when it comes to art and its history."

"Feel free to take me up on my offer any time. If

there's anything we can do to thank you for your contributions tonight, let me know."

"Actually." Joseph smiled. "There is something you could do for me."

Kendall would kill Greg the moment they were in the car! How dare he agree to Captain Stewart's request for her to be his escort for the remainder of the evening? She scowled at him from the dance floor. Greg turned away.

Not that Joseph Stewart wasn't handsome, interesting, and the best slow dancer she'd ever met. The problem was that Greg had promised her she could leave after the fertility statue was sold. As she had suspected, the statue ended up being the last piece to go on auction. Now Greg had lent her out in an attempt to keep her from going home early.

Scowling in Greg's direction, Kendall tripped over her own feet. Joseph grasped her tightly around the waist to catch her. Once she stood steady, he did not release his grip on her hips. Kendall's hands rested on the lapel of his tux, and now that he held her tightly, she could smell his aftershave. She looked up into his seriously sexy eyes. His temples were starting to gray. Small pockets underneath his eyes hinted at his age. She supposed him to be married with children in high school, a homebody who loved his family very much. A person who tinkered on the weekends, worked hard during the week, and took his responsibilities very seriously. Before the accident Kendall had been seeking the comforts of a man just like him.

Joseph extended his arm and led Kendall off the dance floor. "Would you like a drink?"

"I don't drink." Not since the accident.

Joseph pulled out her chair. "How about punch or soda?"

"Punch."

Joseph excused himself and went for their drinks. Such a gentleman. Brimming with confidence. Handsome in a distinguished way, he had an air of wisdom about him. A natural flirt, too. And charming! His wife had better reel him in to home before one of the young availables snatched him up. Kendall blushed. With the way she was gazing in his eyes and hanging on his arm, she could be mistaken for one of the young availables.

Joseph returned with their drinks. "Would you like to dance again?"

"No, it's getting late. I'm going to have to flag down Greg."

"You came with Greg? I'm confused. I thought he was married."

"Greg is very married. He's my ride for tonight."

"I see. At least finish your punch before you run away from me." Joseph sipped from his glass, watching her with smoldering eyes over the rim.

Kendall crossed her legs and watched the couples on the floor. In her periphery vision, she could see Joseph's eyes roaming over her.

Joseph leaned forward and rested his hand atop hers. Warmth spread up her arm, blushing her cheeks. "Kendall, would you like to go out to dinner this week?"

"Dinner? I assumed you were married."

Joseph shook his head. "No such luck. I'm being presumptuous. I didn't see a ring, but maybe you're involved?"

Kendall's eyes dropped to the tabletop. Not since the accident. Her boyfriend at the time was one of the people she had pushed away with her abrasive, out-of-control behavior. She pulled away and folded her hands in her lap.

"Did I say something wrong? I didn't mean to offend you."

"No." Kendall shook away the memories. "You didn't."
Joseph waited. "Dinner?"

"Can I decide later this week? I might be very busy."

Joseph hid his rejection behind the rim of his glass.
Thinking quickly he said, "I'd be happy to drive you
home. I should be going also."

Kendall hesitated.

Joseph pointed to the dance floor. "I don't think your
boss is ready to leave."

Greg and his wife were laughing and dancing in a
wide circle, bumping into people with every step. She'd
never get him to leave. Joseph had been a perfect gentleman all evening and she needed a ride home. "If it's
not too much trouble . . ."

"No trouble at all. Do you have a jacket?"

Kendall gave him her coat check. "I'll say good night
to Greg."

Joseph helped her from her chair before going for
her jacket.

Greg's face beamed when she told him Joseph would
be giving her a ride home. She ignored his silent ribbing
and met Joseph at the exit.

"Are you ready?" Joseph placed her shawl over her
shoulders and extended his arm.

Kendall could definitely get used to being treated with
gentlemanly respect. Many women found the gestures
old-fashioned and even sexiest. Not Kendall. Being
treated like a lady would never offend her or become
outdated. Joseph made her feel like a princess all
dressed up and out on the town. She intertwined her
arm with his and let him lead her out of the museum.

Kendall's mind began to spin as they crossed the jam-
packed parking lot. She had to come up with a reason
for needing to sit in the backseat of the car. Caught up
in the glitz of the evening, she had forgotten this small

detail when she accepted his offer to drive her home, but now it smacked her in the face. She couldn't tell him that fear paralyzed her when she reached for the door handle of a car.

"Here we are." Joseph stopped in front of a fire-mist, metallic-red Benz SK 320. A beautiful gem of a car, its owner's love for it could be seen in the shining exterior. One problem: the car was a two-seater.

Kendall froze as Joseph pulled out his key ring, pressing a button that made the lights blink and the alarm chirp. He released her arm to open the passenger-side door. Noticing Kendall glued to the pavement shaking, Joseph turned to her. "Is something wrong? Do you not feel well?"

"I can't do this!" Kendall shouted before running full speed back into the museum. The rapid clack of her heels on the pavement echoed into the night.

Joseph made the car blink and chirp again before running after her. Inside, he couldn't find her anywhere. He moved through the crowd and spotted Greg going backstage. A flash of mauve disappeared behind the curtain.

Chapter 4

Kendall cried all night.

The next morning, Greg was ringing her doorbell. "I knew you would still be crying." He followed Kendall into the kitchen. "It's noon. Why are you still in pajamas?"

"The usual?"

"Yes, hit me." Greg found a seat in the breakfast nook while Kendall pulled an ice-cold bottle of Mountain Dew from the refrigerator. "You have to buy the Code Red." In order to preserve her flawless complexion, Kendall never drank carbonated soda but kept an eight-pack of bottles on hand for his routine visits.

Greg drank from his soda before he started. "Nobody knows about what happened last night except you and Captain Stewart."

"You know."

"I'm nobody." He touched her hand across the table. "You can't let this impede your progress. You don't know how proud I was of you when you took the stage. You made big strides last night—don't let a minor setback hamper your progress."

"My personal therapist again."

"If you want to call me that. I'm here for you whatever you choose to name our relationship. I'm not going to give up on you. Even if you give up on yourself."

"I have a sneaky suspicion that you're now going to tell

me why you're sitting in my kitchen instead of at the gallery."

"Absolutely." Greg chugged his soda. "I'm here to drive you to work. Get dressed."

Kendall shook her head vehemently. "Nope. I fulfilled our original agreement, plus more. I'm not ready. I still have things to work out."

"And you plan to do that by moping in the house crying in your pajamas? You'll heal quicker if you get back into your old routine."

Kendall grabbed a banana from the fruit bowl and began to peel it. "If you could have seen how foolish I reacted when Captain Stewart opened the door of his car—"

"That's in the past. You'll get over your phobia soon enough, but you have to keep taking forward steps. Listen, a shipment of jewelry is coming in from the same ruins where the fertility pieces were found."

"The tomb in Egypt?" Kendall's eyes lit up.

"The same tomb. I want my best person on it. You worked really hard on the art pieces. You can't let a stranger step in and take over."

Kendall contemplated the offer. Being back in the gallery again had stimulated her artistic juices. Greg knew what to say to pique her curiosity. *Jewels in the same tomb as the fertility idols.* She could only imagine how exquisite they would be.

"Same deal as before, Kendall." Greg checked his wristwatch. "The shipment is due to arrive in two hours. Would you like to be on hand when the crates arrive?"

"You didn't just find out about the shipment today. Coordinating something like this takes months to pull off."

"I planned to tell you at the museum. It was to be a surprise for your reentrance into the art world. I never guessed I'd have to use it as bait." Sure that she couldn't turn away from this project, Greg said, "Hurry and get dressed."

Kendall took a quick shower while Greg helped himself to lunch from her refrigerator. Jewels! She always wanted the opportunity to hold precious pearls and rubies in her hand. Tanzanite, diamonds—who knew what would be awaiting her in the packing crates? Knowing the precious gems could have been touched by an Egyptian king or queen gave her goose bumps.

Maybe she could make this work. Greg would drive her to the gallery. She'd labor over the jewels all day, keeping her mind off the crash. The workers would get used to seeing her come in every day and the whispers would cease.

Kendall wondered if her sister looked down at her with pride or distain. Much time had passed since the crash. She had mourned to the point of losing everyone close to her. She prayed for forgiveness every day. The culmination of recent events could be a signal from Raven that it was time to leave the house and regain some sense of normalcy.

Kendall expected to spend her day scolding truck drivers and digging through dirty crates, so she slipped on a pair of dark jeans and a pink T-shirt. She spritzed her hair until the tight curls snapped into tiny gold ringlets. No makeup today—she applied only a thin layer of clear lip gloss, lavishing her bottom lip with more. After slipping on her gym shoes she bounded down the stairs.

Kendall felt foolish climbing into the backseat of Greg's huge luxury car. As they traveled to the museum, passing drivers gave her funny looks. Greg shot her a pitying look in the rearview mirror. He held his tongue, which Kendall appreciated.

Riding in the car made her palms sweaty. She felt trapped—claustrophobic. She pressed the button on the armrest that lowered the window. Next came the nausea. Greg merged onto the freeway. He knew the signs of her carsickness as well as she did. He also knew that she could tolerate the freeway better than the surface streets. Purely psychological, he believed.

Kendall held her head out the window, taking deep breaths with her eyes closed. What had she been thinking about—accepting a ride home with Captain Stewart? She would have made a big joke of herself if he had seen this.

"How are you doing?" Greg asked, watching her in the rearview mirror.

She rubbed her stomach. Afraid she would lose the contents of her lunch if she spoke, she nodded her reassurance that she wouldn't jump out of his car.

"Are you going to be sick?" He cared dearly for her, but he didn't want to have to get his interior shampooed—again this month.

Kendall shook her head.

"Do the exercises the bereavement nurse recommended."

From the depth of Greg's concern, she guessed she looked ashen. She wiped her forehead and her arm came away wet. She felt cold, but was perspiring.

Greg watched her in the rearview. His eyes were on her more than on the road.

He had good reason to be worried. When he had brought her home from the hospital after the accident, she freaked out in the backseat. His wife climbed in back trying to calm her, but it didn't work. She experienced the same symptoms then—cold, sweaty, nausea, the shakes. She puked all over the carpet of his Lincoln. Something snapped inside her head and the only thought she could process became *Get out of the car.* Greg had just merged onto the freeway when she popped the lock up, pulled the door handle back, and jumped from the car. His wife had been frantic. Kendall remembered Madge yelling, "Stop the car, Greg! Stop now! Before a car strikes her! My God, the fall alone!" Greg remained calm enough to pull over. It took the better part of an hour to coax Kendall back inside the car. After that incident Greg engaged the child safety locks. Unless she sat in the front seat—which she still couldn't do—he had to open her door from the outside.

"I think it's passing," Kendall announced, willing the horrible memories away. She rested her head against the seat. She took deep breaths and counted to ten over and over again. She let the fresh air wash over her. She used imagery to place herself anywhere but inside a car. The nausea subsided. The trembling of her hands slowed to a fine twitch.

"Just keep doing the exercises. We're about there. Slow down your breathing before you hyperventilate."

Twenty long minutes later, they arrived at the gallery. Kendall rushed to the bathroom, totally embarrassed, to splash cold water on her face.

Greg stood waiting when she came out. He wrapped his arm around her shoulders. "Are you okay?"

"I'm fine. Sorry."

They moved down the hall to the private restoration room. The bottom level of the gallery held several offices that Greg had converted into restoration and cataloging rooms. Several were private, but most were fashioned after assembly lines. Workstations with bright lighting and the tools of the trade lined the large rooms.

They entered the private room Kendall used, and Greg closed the door behind them. "I don't know how much longer you'll be able to go on like this."

Kendall plopped down on one of the stools in front of her workstation. "If I could tolerate the car rides, things would be better."

"Better?" Greg questioned, taking the stool next to her. "How do you get anything done?"

"The neighbor sharing the house with me picks up my

groceries when he does his shopping. If I can catch him, he'll run my errands with his."

"You can't even go to the grocery store? Kendall, you do see that this has to be resolved."

She moved behind her workstation and clicked on the desk lamp. "When time passes—"

"How much time?" Greg rounded the workstation and pulled a business card from his wallet. "My wife and I were talking last night—this guy is good."

Kendall reluctantly took the card from his fingers. "A psychiatrist? You think I'm crazy?"

"No." Greg took her hand in his. "No, of course I know you're sane. You've suffered a traumatic event and you need help dealing with it. I know you don't want to see the hospital-recommended therapist; consider seeing this doctor."

"A shrink can't help me bring my sister back."

"No one can help you bring your sister back." Greg laid the simple truth before her. Raven was gone. Nothing and no one could change that fact.

Greg was her greatest supporter and he was watching her as if she was about to have a nervous breakdown right in the gallery. If he doubted her sanity, it would be only a matter of time before some doctor petitioned her parents for an involuntary admission into a psych hospital. Knowing Greg was trying to help, and not wanting to look irrational, Kendall didn't argue. She placed the card in her purse. "I'll think about it."

"Good." He squeezed her hand before releasing it. "Now that we've gotten all the dirt out of the way, let's get to work. I'll be in my office if you need me."

"I need more time," Kendall called as she watched Greg's stout body walk away.

She was lucky to have him as a friend. His devotion was unparalleled. She'd think about seeing someone to help her get over her fear of riding in cars, but she hoped time would heal her. When she had first left the hospital she wouldn't even go near a car. Only recently had she been able to tolerate riding in the backseat. She needed more time.

By early evening Kendall directed the gallery workers in the controlled chaos of unpacking the crates from Egypt. One crate held the jewelry Greg had told her about. The other crates held more artwork. She observed every piece of raw jewelry as it was cataloged and secured. Excitement filled her as she selected the piece she would start working on in the morning. For a brief time the accident did not take precedence in her mind.

"I think we're about done for the evening," Greg announced, entering Kendall's office.

"I hope this isn't a bad time."

Kendall and Greg turned together to see Captain Joseph Stewart filling the doorway.

"Captain Stewart." Greg rushed to shake his hand. "I wasn't expecting you to visit the gallery this soon."

"The people upstairs told me I would find you here." Captain Stewart moved over to Kendall. "Ms. Masterson, how are you?"

Suddenly aware of her disheveled appearance, Kendall dusted her hands together before greeting him. She found it hard to maintain the intense eye contact he made with her. She had hoped she would never see Captain Stewart again and she could forget how silly she must have looked running away from him. No doubt he would have questions about the night before.

"What brings you to the gallery, Captain Stewart?" Greg asked.

"Please call me Joseph." He turned his intensity back

on Kendall. "My reason is twofold. I wanted to see your gallery and I wanted to visit Ms. Masterson."

Delighted, Greg made a hasty departure. "Then I'll give you two a little privacy. Kendall can show you around the gallery when you're finished talking."

Kendall waited until Greg closed the door before she spoke. "I owe you an apology for running away last night."

"An apology isn't necessary, but I would like to know if I scared you in some way."

"No." Her eyes went to the tiled floor.

"Something upset you."

A minute passed while Kendall contemplated her answer. Joseph's stance showed he was a strong man, both cultured and patient. He stood in silence—not at all seeming uncomfortable by the awkwardness of it— waiting for Kendall to explain her actions from the night before.

She met the burning glare of his eyes and felt an instant connection with him. His lips parted slightly, as if he were considering asking his question again. Instead he folded his arms over the dark dress shirt covering his chest, widened his stance, and continued to wait.

"Captain Stewart—"

"Joseph," sternly, and then softly, "please."

"Joseph, I get very carsick. It's worse in small cars."

Disbelief flashed across his face. Kendall hoped he would accept her answer without further prodding. She hardly knew this man. Despite the fact that her body reacted as if they were intimate friends when he came around, she couldn't tell him about the crash and her life since.

Joseph dropped his arms to his side. "I'm glad that I didn't offend you. Now that we've taken care of that piece of business, you never answered me about dinner."

That easy, he accepted her explanation and didn't seem bothered in the slightest.

"Dinner?" Kendall remembered her dust-covered jeans. Joseph had managed to see her at her worst two days in a row.

"Yes, dinner. If you're worried about riding in my two-seater, I have a larger car at home I'd be happy to drive for the occasion."

"I don't know."

"If you ever want to see your favorite piece of art again, you'll take me up on my offer for a nice, quiet dinner for two."

The mischievous lift of his voice made her smile.

Joseph smiled with her. "Now that's the stuff dreams are made of." He brushed her chin with the pad of his thumb. The casual gesture set off fireworks in Kendall's stomach. "Dinner, Ms. Masterson?"

"I'd like that."

"Great. How long do you need to change?"

"Tonight?" Kendall did want to see Joseph socially, but she needed time to adjust to the idea of having a real date.

"Yes, tonight. I can't take the chance you'll change your mind. Besides, my time on layover is limited. I have to take advantage of every minute."

Kendall thought of how good Joseph had looked in the tux at the museum. She recalled the shivers that moved through her body when he stroked her chin. She looked up into his smoldering eyes and could come to only one decision. "Okay, tonight. Give me about three hours and I'll meet you at the restaurant."

"It'll be no problem to pick you."

"No," Kendall said too quickly, "I'd prefer to meet you."

Chapter 5

Joseph stood outside the restaurant dressed in a dark suit with sharp creases. The collar of his new shirt fit snugly around his neck. He added life to the dark suit with a pastel blue tie. The rain earlier that afternoon left small puddles on the sidewalk that threatened to tarnish his polished black wingtips.

He hated the idea of Kendall driving herself to the restaurant. He was her date. When he asked her out it became his responsibility to pick her up and see her home safely. Standing outside the restaurant waiting for her to drive up was something the younger generation did without hesitation. Not he. Joseph had been raised to treat a woman like a lady; if her behavior forbade him doing so, he didn't date her again. He should have insisted on picking Kendall up, but she looked hesitant about accepting his invitation. After the incident the night before, he didn't want to risk her turning him away.

Kendall told him that she became carsick in smaller cars and that was what made her run away. He didn't want to call her a liar, but he certainly had trouble believing that was the depth of the problem. When he'd looked back at her standing in the parking lot, she looked pale and shook like a leaf. He called her name several times before she responded. The way she ran away and hid—running to Greg for comfort—Joseph's sharp perception told him there was something more behind the entire incident.

A yellow taxi pulled up to the curb slightly in front of where Joseph stood. Out stepped Kendall in a conservative red suit that showed the fullness of her curves.

"Kendall." Confused, Joseph rushed up to her. "I thought you were driving."

"My car gave me a little trouble."

"Let me get that." Joseph pulled a bill from his wallet and told the cabbie to keep the change. "You look stunning." He offered his arm and escorted Kendall inside the restaurant.

"Thank you."

Joseph stepped up to the host, who hovered over a large reservation book.

Having checked in before Kendall's arrival, Joseph said, "I'd like to be seated now. My guest has arrived."

"Yes, sir." The man nodded, his Japanese accent as heavy as when he had become a United States citizen twenty years ago. He turned his eyes to Kendall and in one long string of words commented, "Your daughter very pretty." With measured words, he added, "I like her meet my son."

Joseph stiffened with the double insult. If this had not been their first date, he would have swiftly put the rude man in his place. The man's words planted seeds of doubt in Joseph's head that grew at enormous speed as they passed through the restaurant, garnering stares from the other diners. Kendall didn't remark on the man's words. Maybe she thought of Joseph as a father figure or big brother and had accepted his offer of dinner in that spirit. Maybe Kendall had her sights set on a young man that walked with a practiced limp and chewed on toothpicks all day.

"This place is spectacular," Kendall told him.

Still scorched, Joseph held his tongue while they followed the demure Japanese woman past life-size aquariums into the main dining area. Although the place was full, the only sound to be heard was the background music that soothed the weary visitor along with the bubbling aquariums—letting the diners know they were as close to Japan as they could be in northwest Detroit. Tables of Japanese businessmen quibbled in their native language, pointing their chopsticks to emphasize their point.

Joseph thanked the server and waited for the woman to walk away before he questioned Kendall. "If your car gave you trouble you should have called me. I could have come for you."

Kendall's face reddened, half hidden behind the menu. "It was no problem for me to call a taxi, really. I know the driver."

"Still—"

The waitress reappeared to fill their water glasses.

Joseph picked up their conversation the second she walked away. "Kendall, I have to tell you I'm from the old school. It's disrespectful for me to allow you to drive yourself to a date I asked for."

The strange expression marring her beautiful features made him seek the cause. "The man at the door may have opened an area we need to discuss."

"What do you mean?" She fiddled with the pages of the leather-bound menu.

"I did mean this to be a date."

"I understand that."

Relief flustered him. He paused, gathering his thoughts while drinking his water. Kendall didn't say anything more about being mistaken for his daughter, so Joseph ignored the subject too. "The next time we go out, I insist on picking you up."

Kendall's eyes dropped to the tabletop, her face drained of color.

"I'm assuming there will be another date." Joseph rushed to save them from his mistake. "It would be smart to see how this night goes before pushing for another date with you. I'm sorry. Like I said, I'm old-fashioned."

Kendall nodded with a discreet smile.

"Would you like me to help you decipher the menu?"

"Please."

Joseph seized the opportunity to move his chair next to hers. Her red jacket dipped in the front, displaying the creamy soft place between her breasts. She crossed her legs and her skirt rose, giving him a tiny peek of her firm thighs. She wore a delicate perfume that tantalized him, making him lean closer as he read aloud in Japanese. He held a menu between them while he recited the dinner choices, explaining the ingredients for each item. She listened intently, taking his suggestion for her main dish. He liked the fact that she was open to sample the sushi. To him, it meant that she was willing to learn and grow—experience new things, trusting him to do right by her.

"You speak Japanese?" Kendall asked with amazement twinkling in her eyes. Finally, Joseph had found something that impressed her.

"I learned in the air force. I was stationed in Japan for three years. I had to learn the language or walk around completely unaware of what people were saying to me. I don't like being vulnerable. It's not smart. Especially when you're on foreign soil."

"You must have seen most of the world. Do you speak any other languages?"

Joseph drank from his glass before answering. He hoped to build up the suspense and pique her interest in him. "Japanese, Italian, Spanish, and a little French."

"I'm impressed."

"Are you sure you wouldn't like to try a glass of wine?"

"No, I don't drink—ever."

"I suppose I should take a page from your book." The doctor allowed him a maximum of one glass of wine a day. He never drank while flying the commercial airplanes, so tonight he'd allow himself two glasses of wine. He found he needed them to help him relax. Being near Kendall did things to his body he hadn't experienced in quite a long time.

"Tell me about some of the places you've gone."

Joseph placed his glass on the table and began telling her of his first time traveling abroad. The waitress came with their food as he finished.

"Taste." Joseph balanced a beautifully sculpted piece of sushi on his chopsticks.

"This is sushi?"

"This is sushi. Why are you scrunching your nose? You haven't even tasted it yet. Don't back out on me. Try it, I promise you'll like it."

Kendall blinked twice at the suggestive tone of his voice.

Joseph smiled. "C'mon."

Kendall allowed him to slip the chopsticks between her lips. She closed her eyes and chewed slowly. "It's slimy."

"It's supposed to be. How does it taste?"

She opened her eyes to answer him. "It's good."

"See?" Joseph said, delighted. "I told you."

The banter remained light as Kendall sampled the different types of sushi Joseph had ordered. They made a mental list of the ones she liked and the ones she didn't. This gave Joseph hope that she meant to visit the restaurant with him again.

They had become comfortable with each other by the

time Kendall asked about the auction. "Joseph, why did you buy the fertility statue?" Her eyes asked a different question.

"To impress you."

A faint laugh from Kendall. "You're very straight-forward."

"I wouldn't want to start this relationship on a lie."

Kendall brought the chopsticks to her lips. The sushi dropped to the table.

Joseph cleaned up the mess. "Let me show you." He took the chopsticks and instructed her on how to hold them between her fingers as she would a pencil. He covered her dainty hands with his. Her hands were as soft as he expected them to be. Her fingernails were short and manicured with white tips. A silver bracelet dangled from her wrist; one ring with a small ruby graced her left hand.

"Is this right?" She looked up into his eyes.

"Almost." He slipped his arm over her shoulder and underneath her opposite arm. He made a circle around her by joining his hands with the chopsticks in her right hand. He lingered in his instruction. He helped her lift the food from her plate and carry it to her mouth.

"I did it."

Joseph sat back and watched Kendall bounce up and down, laughing at her accomplishment. She could find joy in the simplest of things. Another endearing quality. He thought of the limitless possibilities her open attitude would enable them to try. He had learned so much in his life from his travels and wanted someone to share it all with.

"I'm embarrassing myself again," Kendall apologized.

"No, you're not. I'm staring because you're gorgeous when you laugh."

Kendall ran a nervous hand through her tight curls. "Let me try on my own."

Joseph rested his elbows on the table while he gave her verbal instructions. He focused on every feature of her profile. Once he got over the fact that she appeared to be too young for him, he saw the flawless caramel skin and huge brown eyes that completed her beauty.

Kendall's pretty face suddenly contorted into a mask of horror. Her right hand began to twitch. She dropped the chopsticks, and sushi fell into her lap. She shook her arm wildly, knocking over Joseph's wineglass.

"Kendall, what's wrong?"

She jumped up from the table and ran toward the exit. Reminiscent of the night before, Joseph went after her.

She disappeared in the ladies' room. He would not be deterred; he stood outside the door knocking and calling her name.

A woman stepped out. "The young lady says she'll be right out and that you should return to your table." Joseph thanked her, but lingered outside the door until another woman exited, giving him a glare of disapproval.

The waitress was at their table cleaning up the spill when he returned. "I'll bring you another glass of wine." She nodded with a slight dip and shuffled away from the table.

Joseph turned his chair in the direction of the ladies' room, his view obstructed by hanging plants and bubbling aquariums. He was halfway through his glass of wine when he flagged down the waitress. "Please check the ladies' room for my dinner date. Do you remember what she looks like?"

"Yes, sir." Nod, dip, shuffle away.

Too anxious to wait for the waitress's return, he followed her to the ladies' room.

"I'm sorry, sir. She gone."

Joseph rushed to the host lording over the big guest book. "Did you see my date leave?"

The man's face wrinkled in condemnation. "Date?"

"Yes, my date. Not my daughter. Do you have a problem with that?"

The man shook his head.

"Did you see her leave?"

"She had me call a cab and went outside to wait."

Joseph groped around inside his wallet and gave the waitress enough for the tab and tip before running outside.

The taillights of a taxicab turned onto the main street.

Chapter 6

Taking the muscle relaxant prescribed by her doctor made Kendall sleep later than normal on the sunny Saturday morning following her dinner date with Joseph. The heat dried the puddles of rain and left behind rays of hope that didn't stretch far enough to reach Kendall. She only took the medications when the spasms in her right hand set off a cramping of her entire arm. Working at the gallery again had preoccupied her mind enough to decrease the frequency of the spasms. Last night she was having such a wonderful time when the uncontrollable twitching started, ruining the evening. As she had feared, it was too soon to return to work and start dating.

Kendall forced herself to climb out of bed and dress. She cranked up the volume on her stereo and began to clean her home.

"There is life in you yet!" Max exclaimed when Kendall opened her back door to him. Equal in height and stature—even possessing similar brown eyes—the two neighbors were often mistaken for brother and sister.

"What are you doing out there?"

Max propped a dirt-covered shovel against the side of the house. "One of the people sharing this duplex has to do the yard work. Come out. I want to show you what I've done."

Kendall followed him around to the side of the house. They stopped in front of the newly planted bushes.

"I like it," Kendall said. "The landlord paid for the supplies, didn't he?" She crossed her arms over her chest.

"Yes, he did."

"Good."

Max liked to work in the yard and the landlord gave him a free hand. Last summer, Kendall discovered that Max bought and paid for all of the supplies he used to improve the property. Both renting a side of the two-family home, neither had a vested financial interest in the property. Kendall demanded the landlord reimburse her neighbor.

"Want to come in for lunch?" Kendall asked.

"Let me change and I'll be right over."

Kendall made two chicken Caesar salads and two glasses of iced tea with lemon.

Max tapped on the door frame before he walked in. "Someone has been painting the town the last two nights." He shook the Italian dressing. "Do you have anything other than fat-free?"

"No, and why are you adding dressing when there's already dressing on it?" Kendall joined him at the table.

"There's never enough dressing. Where have you been the past two nights?"

"I had to speak at an art auction and I had a dinner date last night."

"Dinner date? I was beginning to wonder about you. Who is the man that finally got you out of the house on a social occasion?"

Kendall ate her salad as she told Max about her date with Joseph. Omitting the details surrounding her hasty departure.

"I'm happy to see you getting out again." Max downed

the last of his iced tea. "I better get going. Lunch was delicious—as usual. I'm on the way to the grocery store and cleaner's, do you have anything for me?"

Kendall rushed to the laundry room and gathered her cleaning.

When she returned, Max was pulling her grocery list off the front of the refrigerator. "If I bring the ingredients, will you make me a lasagna tonight?"

"Of course. What's the occasion?"

"Big date with someone I met at work."

She handed him her laundry bag.

"And how about a Caesar salad?"

"You got it."

"Be back soon." Max disappeared out the back door.

Kendall had no idea what she would do without Max next door. He didn't venture far from home for long periods, so he was always available to run her errands. He never complained or tried to coerce her into coming along. They had developed a nicely flowing routine that worked for the both of them.

Kendall had moved into the suburban duplex years ago. Max had greeted her on the front lawn the morning after. Their conversation clicked and they decided to go on a driving tour of the neighborhood. Since that initial meeting they had shared many tragedies.

The first test of their friendship came the night Kendall heard banging on the walls next door. A crash and the sound of breaking glass followed. She threw on her robe and raced to his back door. They had swapped keys in case of an emergency.

Kendall entered Max's flat with caution. The house had been destroyed. She found Max lying on the sofa crying. His face was bruised and bloody. He refused to tell her what happened. Kendall helped him treat his wounds and stuck around late into the night while they cleaned his place. By morning, Max confessed that he had feelings for a man and believed the man was on the same page—until Max moved on him and found himself on the receiving end of the man's fists.

The incident scarred Max for months. It had been his first attempt at admitting his feelings for another man. It took him thirty-one years and a broken marriage to even acknowledge that he was homosexual.

The next hurdle in Max's life was to tell his parents about his sexual orientation. They banished him from the family. Max spent the entire year in a deep funk. He didn't come out of it until Kendall returned home from the accident.

When Max asked Kendall to cook dinner for his date that evening, she wanted to grill him with questions. Knowing Max, she decided to wait until he brought up the subject and gave details. He would in his own time. They never pushed each other, but were there when needed without vacillation.

Kendall was in the kitchen that evening putting the finishing touches on Max's Caesar salad when the phone rang. She snatched up the cordless and secured it to her ear with the use of her shoulder. "Max, I'm almost done. Now stop calling me so that I can finish."

"Kendall, it's Joseph Stewart."

The baritone voice on the other end of the line made her drop the wedge of Parmesan cheese she was grating into the bowl.

"Are you still there?"

"I'm here." Kendall sat at the table in her breakfast nook. "It seems I need to apologize again."

"Why don't we relax with each other and stop the apologizing? I don't expect you to be perfect and I hope you don't expect that of me either."

Kendall agreed.

"In light of the way our first two encounters ended I have to be blunt and ask if you're interested in spending any more time with me."

Kendall's stomach did a roller-coaster-ride flip against her rib cage. She pictured Joseph standing outside the Japanese restaurant with the evening sun casting a shadow on his regal silhouette. The dark suit had made his mocha skin glow. The gray specks at his temples made him appear sophisticated.

Joseph was a far cry from the young men she had dated in the past: the men searching to learn her income—and share a chunk of it. He didn't wear baggy pants where the crotch hung low between the knees. Not once had he made a reference to spending the night together promising the hottest sex she'd ever had.

Articulate and worldly, Joseph made her feel like a lady. He offered his arm and opened doors, becoming upset when she wouldn't allow him to pick her up properly for their date. He shared the adventures that made up his life. He juggled confidence with conceit, never appearing too stuck on himself to care for another. She knew the man's comments about her being his daughter upset him, but he maintained his composure with finesse. He respected her strength, but would act without hesitation as her protector if needed.

"You know, Joseph, I am interested in seeing you again."

"I have a suggestion. Can I bring dinner to you this evening?"

Kendall looked around at the sink full of dirty dishes and panicked. After abruptly ending their precarious attempts at dating twice, she couldn't refuse him. They negotiated enough time for her to clean up before his arrival and then she gave him the directions to her home.

"Why are you rushing me out?" Max asked as Kendall pushed him out the back door. They both carried platters.

"I have a date coming."

Max turned to her with a smile. "We both have dates? Maybe the two oddballs of the neighborhood are getting themselves together."

Kendall helped Max set a romantic table in his dining room before hurrying home to get ready for her date.

"I still have a half hour before my date arrives," Max said. "Go get dressed and I'll start setting your table."

Kendall kissed his cheek. "You're a doll." She sprinted up the stairs, leaving Max to his work.

Dining at home should be a simple affair, Kendall told herself as she leafed through the clothing filling her closet. She'd gone through the rack three times and still hadn't made a choice. With one last pass through, she decided on following her first thought: keep it simple. She pulled a casual evergreen dress over her head. Immediately upon looking in the mirror she knew she made the right choice. The color accentuated the yellow-gold coloring of her hair and made her eyes look exotic and mysterious. She dabbled at her vanity table, sparingly using makeup to highlight her strong features—her eyes and pouty bottom lip. She stepped into a pair of brown mules but tossed them aside, afraid she'd trip and make a spectacle of herself again. Sticking with the casual theme of the night she chose white tennis shoes and anklets before running downstairs to check on Max's progress.

"Max!" Kendall stopped short at the bottom of her stairs. "This is gorgeous!"

Max turned from the mantel and smiled at her approval. The decor of her peach and green living room took on the mystical glow of the many candles casting a shadow off the aquamarine walls.

Max followed her into the cozy dining area; the room's size only allowed a table that seated two. Peach was the prevailing color scheme for the room—peach carpet, embroidered high-back chairs, paintings with a hint of the color. The lighted curio along the wall held prized art pieces she had restored herself. Max had transformed the room into a romantic sanctuary with an elaborate table setting complete with more burning candles.

"Where did you get all these candles, Max?"

"I fished out what I could find of yours in the storage room. The rest come from my collection." He placed his hands on his waist. "I want them back—if you don't burn them to the nubs tonight."

"Thank you so much for your help." She graced him with another kiss to the cheek.

"I have to get going." He hurried off. "Good luck!"

"Good luck to you, too," Kendall shouted before the back door closed.

Chapter 7

Street lamps shone on the sign pointing out the subdivision, WUTHERING HEIGHTS. The quaint neighborhood's homes were in keeping with its namesake. The upwardly mobile lived in this suburban Detroit neighborhood. Only fifteen minutes to the center of downtown or the culturally diverse Southfield where major businesses flourished, the sub housed single and married couples on the rise in their careers. The sub had been showcased on local news programs countless times, and Joseph had even seen it highlighted on a program that named it the best place to live in America. The rents were moderate—with Michigan currently having the fourth highest price tags in the country, moderate meant very expensive.

Joseph knew the location of the subdivision as soon as Kendall told him the name. He drove directly to the quiet neighborhood, but found himself lost in the tangle of cul-de-sacs and one-way streets. He checked the address on his notepad against the one on the home to his left. He was on the right street now.

Joseph lived fifteen minutes northwest of Kendall and twenty minutes west of the airport. The geography formed a perfect triangle. The setup was perfect for dating Kendall. His future was laid out along easily accessible freeway lines. He pictured landing a 757 and rushing from the airport to see Kendall after a particularly grueling flight schedule. He came to his senses just as he pulled up in front of her home.

Joseph paused, puzzled when he saw the gold Honda parked in the driveway. As he approached, he noticed the sales tags still glued to the window. He wondered why Kendall would be catching a taxi with a new car in her driveway. And why would it be giving her mechanical trouble already? Surely the dealership would haul it in and give her a free loaner until the trouble was resolved. Maybe the dealership was taking advantage of her. They probably saw the innocent-looking woman with big brown eyes coming and were trying to dupe her. He made a note to ask her about it. He'd be happy to intervene with the mechanics if necessary.

Joseph climbed the stairs of the two-family home. The two halves of the house were identical but distinctively different. New brick and tan siding made up the charming house. Kendall's neighbor's porch was lined with plants. Kendall's porch was consumed by a huge hanging porch swing.

Joseph juggled their dinner, careful not to get any spills on the front of his onyx button-down shirt. He rang the bell, straightened his belt buckle, and kicked his feet out—making sure the pleats of his black slacks hung evenly. He felt his chest flutter with nervous excitement.

As he waited for Kendall to answer the bell, he tried to remember the last time a woman had his nose this wide open. He hadn't had an interest in dating anyone in months, his last date being a fix-up with one of Sara's friends. Try as he might, he couldn't recall anyone who had piqued his curiosity and made his blood boil like Kendall Masterson.

The door swung open, catching him off guard. "Hi, it's me, Joseph Stewart." *What an idiotic thing to say! Does this woman have your mind that wound up?*

"I remember you." Kendall laughed at his formality. "Would you like to come in?"

Joseph stepped inside, his large frame dominating the foyer. "These are for you." He handed her a bouquet wrapped in green tissue paper.

Kendall buried her nose in the colorful assortment of flowers. "No one has ever given me flowers before."

"Really?" Joseph asked, genuinely surprised. "I would think guys would be lined up around the block waiting their turn to deliver you flowers."

Their eyes connected and Joseph couldn't release her from his grip. Her lashes partly closed, giving him a minute to fully assess her. The emerald-green dress she wore was simply designed but looked like a specially tailored designer outfit on her curves.

"Can I take that?" Kendall asked.

"For your being such a trooper with the Japanese food, I thought we'd have something more conventional tonight."

"What is it?" Kendall asked, reaching for the grease-stained bag he held suspended above her.

"Two burgers with everything and fries." He handed her the bag. "And I didn't forget the malteds."

"You did good," Kendall said, peeking inside the bag. "Come in."

Joseph followed Kendall through the peach and green living room. "Greasy burgers don't go well with the setup you have here. I should have gotten something else. I can go back out—"

"No, this is great. I think we've been formal enough with each other. Burgers and fries are okay with me."

They crossed into the dining room and Joseph's heart began to pound again. Latin music played softly in the background. The lights were dimmed and candles glowed romantically throughout the house. He inhaled deeply, the aromatherapy easing his tension. Tonight he wouldn't have to worry if Kendall believed this was a date or not. He dared to think that Kendall might be as attracted to him as he was to her.

"Do you want ketchup?" Kendall asked, heading for the kitchen.

"Mustard, please." Joseph checked out the art pieces in the curio cabinet. "I was very worried about you when you ran out of the restaurant last night."

Kendall didn't respond.

"Your arm was bothering you?"

Kendall returned. "I keep ruining our dates."

He held out her chair before sitting down next to her. "You didn't ruin our date. I was worried. You looked like you were in pain and then you ran away without a word."

Kendall added ketchup to her burger, purposely not giving Joseph any information.

"I didn't mean to pry." Joseph backed off, not wanting to alienate her. "I didn't know where you lived to come check on you. I called you last night, but didn't get an answer." His hand rested on her right arm. "Is there anything I can do?"

"No." Kendall pulled her arm away. "I don't know what got into me. My arm cramped up and then I was spilling your drink all over you. I guess I was too embarrassed to face you."

The blush to her cheeks meant she was embarrassed even now. Joseph smoothed over the incident. "I don't want to make a big deal out of it. I just wanted to know if there was a problem."

"No problem." Kendall said, but pain was hidden beneath her smile.

Not wanting to dampen the evening—if the date ended badly this time, there probably wouldn't be another— Joseph changed the subject. "Do I smell pie?"

"Apple."

"You bake?"

"I bake. Don't look so amazed when you ask that."

"I am amazed. Amazed about everything when it comes to you. What else do you have up your sleeve, Ms. Masterson?"

"Ah, that you'll have to wait and see."

"Sounds like a challenge I might enjoy."

After burgers and fries, Kendall and Joseph found themselves comfortable enough to move to the living room floor. They sat in front of the hearth eating warm apple pie. They spoke in hushed voices and stared into the cold fireplace as if a roaring fire were responsible for the heat jumping between them.

"What is that music?" Joseph asked.

Kendall showed him the CD cover of one of her favorite Latin bands.

"No gangsta rap?"

"Not for me. I like to tango."

"Tango? Really?"

"Do you know how?"

Joseph shook his head. "Never learned it. As you know, I'm a two-step kind of guy."

"You dance very well."

Their eyes met again and again. Joseph held Kendall captive as long as she would allow. He wanted to run his fingers over her tight curls, past the nape of her neck, to the middle of her back. He wanted to cover her body with his, bringing her as close into him as he could. He had never felt the urge to consume a woman before. It was strangely erotic and his body stirred to confirm the new feeling.

"Why the tango?"

"Why the tango?" Kendall's face lit up. "It's only the most romantic dance in the world. I watched a tango competition on television once, fell in love with it, and ran out to take a six-week course. *El tango del coraz'on.*"

"What does that mean?"

"The Argentine tango is about making a connection of the souls. It's a dance among three: the music, a leader, and a follower."

Joseph wallowed in her enthusiasm. "Like a solid relationship. Love, the man, and a woman."

Kendall's eyes flipped upward and he guarded his expression. He questioned if he had said something wrong. She looked small and in need of his comfort. He could see the need in the pout of her bottom lip.

"Go on, Kendall."

"There are Argentine tango dance clubs across the nation. You can find tango workshops and classes in all the major cities. Tangueros Atlanta holds *milongas*—a tango dance party—where teachers come from Argentina. I dream of going to Atlanta one day and dancing the tango all night. Montreal even has a twenty-four-hour tango party once a year."

"Really?" Joseph watched the excitement spread through her body. He had found a subject that allowed her to express herself freely. All the shyness of earlier had disappeared.

"Yes. The tango is intricate—"

Joseph watched her bottom lip move with the formation of her words.

"It's sensual—"

He wanted to brush her bottom lip with his thumb.

"It's complex yet beautiful."

Joseph felt parts of his body yearning to dive into Kendall and absorb her energy. "Why don't you show me?" He jumped up from the floor and offered his hand.

"It's been a little while for me."

"You're still better at it than I am."

Kendall accepted his hand. She took his hands in hers, their bodies less than a foot apart. She looked up into his eyes. "There are two forms of tango: the stage version and the social dance."

"Which are we doing?"

"We're doing the stage version. The social version is one hundred percent improvisation led by the man."

"Yeah, we better stick to the stage version."

"Okay." Kendall showed Joseph the correct placement of his hands and feet until the start of the next record: appropriately, a slower version of the previous song. "This is the basic step. Bend your knees. Frog step for-ward."

Joseph followed her lead.

"For-ward. Forward. Right. Slide together. That's pretty good. Let's do it again."

Joseph would gladly do anything that kept Kendall in his arms with a bright smile on her face.

"Don't look at your feet," Kendall instructed. "Look in my eyes."

With the meeting of their eyes, Joseph learned the sensuality and intimacy of the tango. His eyes burned into Kendall, looking away only to watch the movements of her full lips. Candles flickered as they passed. Growing familiar with the movements, Joseph brought their bodies closer together. Kendall was dainty and soft as she brushed against his solid frame. He smiled with delight at the emotions she brought out in him. With Kendall he felt happy and stress-free. Her innocence intensified his desire to protect her. He never imagined a simple dance could awaken him with such zeal. He silently vowed to take a tango class as soon as time allowed.

The record ended. Joseph did not release Kendall.

"You learn quickly."

Joseph seized the searing passion of the utopia the tango created for them. He pulled Kendall firmly to his chest, wanting to rip off the buttons of his shirt for their offense in keeping his flesh from touching hers. He parted his lips and descended to meet the provocative pout of her bottom lip. His raging heat brushed her face as he drew near. His lips were millimeters from hers when she turned and offered her cheek. Embarrassment made him release her and step back. Again he worried they were not on the same page.

Kendall cleared her throat. "It's warm out, would you like to sit outside?"

"Yes." Joseph could only utter one word. He wanted to kick himself. *She's moving me out of the house. She probably thinks I'm a dirty old man.*

Joseph followed Kendall outside to the porch swing. He placed his feet firmly on the porch and pushed the swing back and forth. "Are you warm enough?"

Kendall nodded. She had retreated into her shell of shyness and it was his fault for being too forward.

"I noticed the Honda in your drive, is it still giving you trouble?"

"Ah, no," Kendall stammered, "no. I took care of it."

"If you need me to speak to the mechanic or take it in with you I'd be happy to. Sometimes dealerships try to take advantage of pretty women."

"Thanks, but that won't be necessary."

Joseph could see by Kendall's wall of formality that he was treading where he shouldn't. He decided not to ask about the new purchase stickers on the window. "If you need my help, just ask."

"I will."

They rocked in silence. Joseph couldn't have ordered up a more perfect night to share with Kendall. A cool breeze pushed aside the day's stifling heat. The neighborhood remained quiet and serene except for chirping crickets. Joseph turned his eyes upward and thanked his stars he wasn't in his plane flying across the star-filled sky instead of sharing it with a woman who easily enchanted him. Kendall relaxed next to him. He placed his arm on the back of the swing and she shifted in his direction. His touch was welcome. He placed his arm over her shoulders with a feather touch.

"Kendall." Joseph held his breath. "Does my age bother you?"

"Your age? How old are you?"

Why did I bring this up? I really am out of practice. "I'm forty. I can see that you're much younger . . ."

Kendall answered his unspoken question. "Twenty-five."

Joseph wanted to whistle from both surprise and happiness. She appeared much younger—no older than twenty-one.

"Is it all right?" Joseph asked tentatively. He'd never been afraid to speak his mind and he couldn't start now with something this important on his heart.

"No, Joseph, your age doesn't bother me."

He pulled Kendall to him and she slid over without hesitation. Pushing the swing in silence, he contemplated how to ask his next question. "I tried to kiss you . . ."

Kendall's fingers picked at invisible lint on the skirt of her dress.

Joseph's stomach twisted. "Do you have a boyfriend?" *Boyfriend. Is that what they call it now?* He was striking out on being cool.

"No." Her voice dropped to a luscious whisper. "Not in a long time."

Joseph's stomach unwound but his mind reeled in confusion. "I tired to kiss you, but you turned away. Why?"

She hesitated. "Nerves."

Joseph's personal specialty was making his passengers comfortable with his abilities. One advantage of their age difference was the experience he could bring to their intimacy. He had long passed the days of trying to hurry and finish before the girl changed her mind. He no longer worried that he would be labeled a "two-minute brother" because he couldn't control his body. He knew the value of loving a woman a long time. He knew the rhapsody of hearing his name drip from a woman's lips as she reached ecstasy. Time had taught him how to find the places on a woman's body that needed stroking and licking.

Most importantly at this moment, he knew that a good kiss with the right person could be better than making love.

Joseph pulled Kendall closer. "That's all? Nerves?"

She nodded.

"I agree first kisses can be murder, but the best thing about it is that you only have to go through it once. And the more you do it, the better and easier it seems to get."

Kendall laughed, her lashes sweeping low and her face turning rosy red.

"There's a simple way to get over first-kiss jitters." Joseph used his fingers to turn Kendall's head to him. Without hesitation, he closed his eyes and pressed his lips to hers. His tongue reached her lips, parting them before his lips touched hers. He took the pouty bottom lip that constantly teased him between his lips and suckled until her breathing became rapid. He coaxed her bashful tongue and coerced it to taste him. He wrapped his arms around her, easily bringing her into his lap. When her guard dropped and she revealed the passion he knew her capable of, he changed the rhythm of his tongue. He showed her the fervor with which he would make love to her. He promised, through the eagerness of his lips, his enthusiasm to please her.

Kendall allowed him to taste the bitter perfume behind her ear and along her neck. With faint sighs she encouraged his fingertips and they moved along her spine. His hand moved to her thigh, caressing until she moaned.

Kendall's arms went around his neck. She gave him the ultimate thrill when she loosened his tie and nibbled on his neck. He felt the sudden engorgement between his thighs and moved Kendall's hips to ensure that she felt it too. Desire made him forget to be a gentleman when his fingers moved underneath the skirt of her dress and inched up her thigh.

"Joseph."

This part of dating was reminiscent of his young adult years. He had gone too far, too fast. "I'm sorry. I got carried away a bit, didn't I?"

She ran her hand along the buttons of his shirt. "We both did. No more apologizing between us, remember?"

Joseph nodded, his hand resting comfortably on her behind. She allowed him this show of possession without protest. They marinated in quietness, letting the emotionally charged moment between them settle.

Joseph kissed her lips. "I better get going, but I definitely don't want this to be the last time I see you. Layovers this long come few and far between for me. I'd like to take advantage of the time I have by spending most of it with you—if that's all right."

"That would be good."

Kendall walked him to the metallic-red two-seater Benz that had caused her so much anxiety a few nights ago.

"Go inside and lock your door before I drive off," Joseph instructed. He kissed her cheek and then her lips.

"Call me?" Kendall asked.

"Of course."

"Tonight?"

"Most definitely. Good night."

"Good night." Kendall ran up the stairs of her porch. She waved before shutting the door.

Joseph waited until she appeared in the living room window before he started his engine and backed out of the driveway.

Chapter 8

"You're home." Kendall burst into a wide smile when she heard Joseph's voice on the other end of the phone line; she'd been smiling a lot tonight. Including the time she spent dancing around her bed in her nightgown. Doing the tango and pretending she was still in Joseph's arms.

"I'm home, in my bed, in the dark talking to you. I have to admit this is quite an erotic experience."

Picturing him in an intimate pose across his bed broke down Kendall's erotic borders too.

"I haven't done this since I was a teenager."

"Done what?" Kendall shimmied under her peach sheets and extinguished the lamp next to her bed.

"I went on a date and came straight home to call the woman. I think I'm breaking the rules. Or is it your responsibility to follow the rules?"

"I think the rule book went out the window on my porch swing tonight."

Joseph laughed. "I guess it did. Since we've dispensed of that 'rule' nonsense, what are you doing tomorrow? Would you like to catch dinner and a movie?"

"I'd really like that."

"What time should I pick you up?"

Kendall's happiness was instantly overturned. Anxiety took control. She could never ride in that small death box he called a car. After the panic attack she had with Greg, she couldn't ride in the car with him at all.

Joseph went on when she didn't answer. "I remember you get carsick in small cars. I have a big—almost clunky—SUV I'll drive."

"I appreciate how understanding you're being. Actually, I have to work in the morning and I have errands after that, so it would be better if I met you at the theater."

Kendall was ashamed at how quickly she came up with the lie. Her desire to see him challenged her fear of being inside a moving car. When she had sat on his lap being seduced by the skill of his mouth, she didn't think ahead to the fact that more dates would follow.

"Kendall, I really don't feel comfortable with that. It's not the way you treat a lady. I asked you out; I pick you up and see you home. I have to insist on that." Joseph laid down his own set of rules.

A confident man like Joseph would hold to his convictions if it meant being domineering. Hardly faults, but unusual in this age. Kendall could see many power struggles in their future. She'd deal with that later. Right now Kendall had to decide if her fear or her growing attraction for Captain Joseph Stewart would win.

"Are we in agreement on this?" Joseph asked.

She trickled in some of the truth. "I don't know, I get really carsick."

"Is your reluctance about a busy schedule or about getting carsick?"

"Both." Kendall hit her thigh with her fist. Lying came too easy.

"I'll wait patiently for you to finish work and your errands. Before we get off the phone tonight I'll give you my cell phone number. I'll carry it all day so you can reach me any time. My SUV is much larger than your Honda Accord. If you can drive around town in that you can ride in my SUV." He added with a chuckle, "I don't think a little carsickness will scare me away from you. I'm a pilot, I'm used to people getting sick. The planes don't have those barf bags for nothing."

Kendall thought back to the scene in Greg's car just yesterday. She flushed with embarrassment when she recalled the ending to the first two meetings with Joseph. *Fear of desire,* she juggled in her head. The answer to her question came from the ultimate source: her sister, Raven. Kendall asked herself what Raven would tell her to do. Men like Joseph didn't come along with enough frequency that she could afford to throw him away. His kisses held too much promise. His touch made her feel lighter than she had since the accident had toppled her world.

"Kendall, I'm waiting for your answer. Dinner and a movie tomorrow?"

"What the heck is wrong with you?"

"Huh, what did you say?"

Greg took the sable brush from Kendall's hand. "I think it's time to take you home. You've been somewhere else all day. What's going on?"

A devilish grin lifted her pouty lip. "Joseph came by last night."

"Captain Stewart? Get out of here." Greg pulled up a stool. "That's why you've been walking around in a fog all day. You didn't get any productive work done today."

"Sorry." She began to clean her workstation for the evening.

"So you like Captain Stewart, huh?"

"I do. What do you think about him?"

A shadow passed over his ruddy cheeks. "I hardly know him."

"Uh-oh. I know that look. You seemed happy when he offered to drive me home from the auction."

"Yes, I was happy to see you making friends, getting out again. Look, I know Joseph's reputation—his good friend's wife, Sara, knows my wife very well—and he sounds like a good man."

"I hear a 'but' coming."

"But, he's a tad older than you."

Kendall stopped fussing over her station. "Say what you mean, Greg."

"Well, reputation is one thing, but intentions are another. If you're going out with Joseph to have a good time and get back into the swing of things, I say good for you. But I know you and I know your character. Dare I say I know a little about your hopes and dreams? If I know you like I think I do, you want marriage and kids. Where is this man's head in relation to all that?"

"Marriage and kids? We've had one date."

"So what? Do you wait until you've fallen in love with him before finding out where his head is at? What happens if you do get serious and marriage starts occupying your thoughts? What happens if you bring the discussion up then instead of now and find out that he feels he's too old to start a family?"

"Dating a man my own age doesn't guarantee he wants kids or even marriage."

"Don't get philosophical on me, Kendall. There is something else to consider. Joseph is older and a pilot who flies coast to coast, hardly ever at home—"

"Don't go there, Greg." Kendall snatched up her jacket and shoved her arms through the sleeves.

"I see it's crossed your mind. Did he get fresh with you last night?"

If she hadn't exercised self-control they probably

would have been in her bed until late this morning. "I don't think we should talk about this anymore."

Greg heeded the warning of her narrowing brow. He followed her to the door, shutting off the lights. "One last thing and then I'll shut up. You've gone through a lot the last year. It's normal to want someone to comfort you as you take control of your life again. Just be careful. All knights wearing shining armor aren't one of the good guys."

"Are you staying for dinner? Russ, ask him if he's staying for dinner."

Russ huffed and rolled his eyes. "I hate when she does that. I feel like a seal in a trained animal act."

Joseph laughed. "No, Sara, I'm not staying. I have a date tonight."

Sara zoomed into the den. "A date? With who?" She dried her hands on a kitchen towel as she dropped next to him on the love seat.

"Kendall Masterson."

"The young girl from the museum?"

"The young lady from the museum, yes. And, don't look at me like I'm a lech. Russ, tell her not to look at me like I'm a lech."

Russ spewed beer across the room, snapping his recliner to the upright position in laughter.

"Very funny." Sara jumped up to clean Russ's mess. "Well, at least you have a date. Do you want to bring her here for dinner?"

"No, thank you. I want to be alone with Kendall. She's rather reserved."

"She's been that way since the accident."

Joseph sat up. He shared a look with Russ.

"What accident?" Russ asked his wife.

"I don't know the details. I only know that she was involved in a personal accident of some sort that kept her away from the gallery for almost a year. Greg was frantic. Finding a trustworthy restoration architect who knows what he's doing is very hard, I guess. I believe it made the papers, because reporters were sniffing around the gallery so badly that Greg passed on several exhibits. The accident must have been bad, because he's really closemouthed about it. It's why he and Kendall are so close now." Sara stood up with her wet towel. "She didn't mention anything to you?"

"No, she didn't."

"I'm sure she considers it in the past. From what I saw of her work at the auction—and how stunning she appeared—she's back with a vengeance."

Joseph was vacuuming out his SUV in preparation for his date with Kendall when Sara's voice echoed in his head. *"Accident."* He thought of the strange behavior he had noticed and the inconsistencies in her conversation. She might be "back with a vengeance" but the trauma still had a hold on her life.

"Accident." What kind of accident? The possibilities were endless. Whatever it was wouldn't deter him from pursuing her. He only wanted to know what demons he might be up against.

Joseph grabbed the sponge from the bucket of soapy water and began to clean the outside of the SUV. He toyed with whether or not he should ask Kendall about it. He didn't know her well enough to ask such personal information. Then again, how else would he get to know her? He labored on a pilot's schedule. Soon he'd be up in the air, away from home for long periods of time. He needed some definition of the direction of their relationship before he sat in front of his instrument panel.

What could be the worst-case scenario? He couldn't even fathom how bad this situation could end up. Again, he recalled the inconsistencies. The incident with the chopsticks still baffled him. *Could this all be connected?*

Joseph grabbed the water hose and began to rinse the suds away. It had been such a long time since he dated that he supposed he could be erecting barriers to protect himself. He thought of Kendall's enthusiastic smile as she spoke of the tango. He could still feel the softness of her lips as he explored her mouth. He tucked away all negative thoughts. They had only a little time and a great deal of ground to cover. He'd ask about the accident if she alluded to it. Otherwise, it wasn't important to him.

At two o'clock in the afternoon, Joseph regretted having had the greasy burger and fries the night before. He'd been noncompliant with his doctor's prescribed diet from the very beginning, and today he feared his defiance would come back to haunt him.

"Captain Stewart, how can I help you today?" the nurse in the military-provided white uniform asked from behind the counter.

He cleared his throat and lowered his voice to ensure privacy. "It's time for my blood pressure check."

"Sure, let me grab your chart. Come right back."

Joseph had visited the office so many times the staff knew him on sight. They had long ago dispensed with formalities—other than those required by military law— and took him in like a distant relative. He opened the door and ignored the stares of those waiting as he showed himself to the room where the nurse would check his blood pressure.

He chose to sit in the chair used for drawing blood instead of the gurney this time. Maybe it would be luckier.

He removed his black leather jacket to provide an unobstructed arm for the nurse.

"Are you having any problems?" the nurse asked.

"None." He tried to sound cheerful and confident.

She checked his pulse at his wrist while she ran down possible signs of trouble. "Rapid heartbeat? Palpitations? Headaches? Blurred vision? Pounding in your ears? Swollen ankles? Trouble urinating?"

"No. No. Yes. No. Sometimes. No. No."

The nurse jotted down his pulse. "Yes to?"

"I have headaches once in a while." He rushed to explain, "It's the stress of flying too many hours, so I'm on an extended layover."

She nodded with a compassionate smile. "Yes, sir. And sometimes to what?"

"I wake up with a pounding in my ears, but it goes right away."

"Okay, sir."

"Did you write down that it goes right away?"

"I will, sir."

Joseph doubted that she would. He was a retired military officer, couldn't he have her court-martialed?

"Let's check your pressure." The nurse wrapped the cuff around his upper arm and pressed a button on the computerized machine on wheels. The cuff inflated while she chatted about the weather. It paused and pumped some more. Joseph knew this was not a good sign. Finally, the air leaked out and the machine announced its reading with a long beep.

"Let me grab the manual cuff."

I'm sunk, Joseph thought. If the machine read high the nurse always checked it twice by manual cuff. She silently checked the pressure in his right arm and then his left. She made a note in his chart and tucked it underneath her arm. "The doctor will be right with you,

Captain Stewart." She pushed the button shutting off the machine before she left the room.

Three pressure readings and a visit from the doctor? The *nurse's actions* gave him heart palpitations. He thought of sneaking past the nurses' station before the doctor arrived, but his rational mind knew this wouldn't help him in the least.

"Captain Stewart." The doctor bounded into the room.

"Dr. Bennis."

They shook hands before the doctor leafed through the chart. He sat on the rolling stool and propelled himself up to Joseph. "I'll be blunt because I know you're a man who appreciates that."

Joseph braced himself for the worst.

"Your blood pressure is through the roof. It's dangerously high. I'm talking risk of stroke and kidney damage if we can't bring it down and keep it under control. If your systolic were a few points higher I'd hospitalize you. It's that serious, Joseph. I can't possibly clear you to fly like this."

"Wait, Dr. Bennis. I'm at the beginning of a two-week layover, can't I bring it down before it's time for me to take to the air again?"

The doctor glanced over the chart at Joseph's frantic face. He hesitated before giving in. "I want to start you on antihypertensives. Take them religiously. Are you exercising? Following the diet I prescribed?"

"Not as closely as I should," Joseph admitted.

"That may be part of the problem. Working the number of hours you work doesn't help either. Take the pills. Exercise and follow the diet. Get plenty of rest and avoid stress. I'll see you back in two weeks and we'll see where we go from there." The doctor headed for the door. "The nurse will spend some time with you today going over all of this again. Prepare to be here awhile."

"Thanks, Doctor."

"Joseph, I won't hesitate to ground you if I think you're putting yourself or your passengers and crew in danger."

Chapter 9

"What's wrong?" Kendall immediately noticed the distress furrowing Joseph's brow.

"The traffic on the drive over was really bad." He didn't want to burden her with worries about his blood pressure and his visit with Dr. Bennis.

"Do you want to reschedule?"

He wouldn't waste one moment with her fretting over something that would soon rectify itself. "No, but we should hurry."

Kendall nervously rambled on about restoring a gem at the gallery.

Joseph checked his watch for the third time. She was stalling. "Excuse me, Kendall, but we have to be going if we want to make the movie."

"Yeah," she said in a faint whisper. "I guess we do have to leave now—if you still want to see the movie."

"Of course I do. Grab a sweater; it's always cold in movie theaters."

Joseph watched Kendall inch up the stairs. She worried that getting carsick would turn him off. He'd prove something that simple couldn't scare him away and this silly disagreement over dating protocol would end.

Looking shaken, Kendall reappeared at the bottom of the stairs. "I'm ready." Her voice quivered, too.

Joseph followed her out onto the porch. He waited patiently while she fumbled to lock the door.

"Are you all right?" Joseph took the jingling keys from Kendall and completed the task. Slipping the keys in his pocket, he led her to the Bordeaux-red Mercedes Benz SUV.

"You like red," Kendall remarked as he pulled her along.

"My favorite color. Can you imagine how I felt when you showed up for our first date in that red suit?" He cocked his eyebrow, adding a suggestive smile. He used the keyless remote to open the locks.

Faint tremors moved through Kendall. "I get very, very sick." Her voice quaked.

"It'll be fine." Joseph held open the front door of the SUV.

Her face quickly drained of color. "I, I—"

He rushed to pull her into his arms. "Kendall?"

"I can't do this, Joseph. I tried but I can't." She took off in a brisk run for her house. Frantically searching her purse for keys, she spilled the contents onto the porch.

Joseph followed after her.

"I can't find my keys!"

"Kendall, calm down."

"My neighbor has a spare set, but I don't know if he's home."

She wouldn't shut him out this time. Joseph grasped her shoulders and trapped her trembling body securely against his. "Calm down. I have your keys." He stroked her back, calming her.

"I'm going to have to cancel," she sputtered. "I need my keys."

"No. Come sit down." Joseph directed her to the hanging swing where he had first tasted her lips. He sat next to her, sweeping her into his arms. "Kendall, calm down.

I'm not going to force you into the car. I'd never make you do anything you didn't want to do."

"I'm totally embarrassed. I told you I get carsick."

"You can't get carsick until you're actually *inside* the car." He laughed, trying to make light of the situation. This problem seemed small when measured against his attraction for her.

"I guess you're right."

"You'll find that my greatest fault."

"That and lack of modesty." Kendall's laugh came out ragged.

"That too." He pulled her tighter against his chest and stroked her cheek with one long finger. "Is something else going on?"

"No," she answered too quickly.

He whispered, "You can do this, Kendall. Try again—for me. There are so many things I want to show you, so many things I want us to do together. You can't experience all I have planned for us if you don't conquer this fear."

"You don't understand how it feels."

"No, I don't. But I know you have a fighter's spirit, and a fighter wouldn't let this fear win." He lifted her away from him to emphasize his point. "I can help you through this. You can do it." He upped the stakes with a profoundly intense kiss that bonded them together against the phobia. "Do you want to try again?"

"I can tolerate the backseat better."

"You want to sit in the back and pretend I'm your chauffeur?"

"It would help." A shaky smile.

Anything to keep her from canceling. After making sure she wouldn't bolt on him, Joseph scooped up the contents of her purse. He stood with a flourish. "Your carriage awaits, Ms. Masterson."

Joseph had no idea of the sheer terror riding in a car

could give someone until he pulled onto Telegraph Road—a street known to local residents as "the race-track."

He lost verbal contact with Kendall. He glanced in the rearview mirror and did a double take. She looked worse than in the parking lot of the museum and worse still than in her driveway earlier. She had dropped her head between her legs. If not for her audible breathing and heaving body, he would have thought she had fainted.

"Kendall, are you all right?" Joseph asked, keeping his eyes on the speeding traffic.

"Pull over," she panted.

"We're almost there." Pulling over between the racing cars would be harder than driving the half mile to their destination. He would immediately jump out and take her in his arms, apologizing for not listening when she had tried to warn him about her fear.

"Pull over!" Kendall shouted. "Pull over!" She sat ram-rod straight, and the panic reflected in her eyes frightened him.

If he didn't pull over quick she would take matters into her own hands. He started making his way to the right-hand lane. When he pulled into the parking lot of a vacant party store Kendall jumped from the vehicle. She fell to the ground in a heap.

Joseph joined her on the asphalt. He'd seen this re-action in first-time flyers, but only once this severe. The time he had to radio for clearance to make an emergency landing. The man became so terrified that the flight attendants couldn't control him. The other passengers started to feed off his fear, and unfounded panic about the possibility of crash-landing rapidly swept the plane. On the verge of cabin chaos, the senior flight attendant entered the cockpit and apprised him of the situation. Within ten minutes they were preparing to land. Now that he thought about it, that was the day he had met Gabrielle: in the mist of chaos.

Joseph eased Kendall's head into his lap. He shushed her while outlining the bone structure of her face. Her breathing slowed. Her lashes fluttered as if she was completely exhausted. Passersby stared at them sitting on the ground in the middle of an empty parking lot.

An older couple in a burgundy Pontiac stopped at the curb among a chorus of honking horns. "Do you need help?" The woman on the passenger's side waved her cell phone in the air.

"We're fine." Joseph waved back. "Thank you."

Kendall covered her face with the flats of her hands. "This is just awful."

"No, it's not." Joseph helped her to sit up. "How are you doing?"

"I should have insisted—"

"I would have insisted louder."

They held each other's eyes. Joseph cupped her chin in his fist. "We're almost there. Do we admit defeat and turn back, or keep trudging ahead?"

"You're asking me? Don't you want to call me a taxi and speed off as fast and as far as you can get from me?"

"Why would you think that? Because you got carsick like you warned me you would? You can't get rid of me that easily, Kendall." He wrapped her in his arms. "Let me let you in on a little secret. Actually, it's not a secret to the people who know me."

"What is it?" She shimmied into the cubby made by his arm.

"I haven't found anyone as fascinating as I find you in too long to remember. My friend's wife, Sára—you know her—is always setting me up with her single friends. I've tried to go out with most of them, but there was never anything there. With you, I felt a connection the first time I saw you. My mouth almost hit the bar when you took the stage at the museum. I turned and saw you standing up there—nervous but determined to win over stage fright. Ever since that moment I knew you were someone I had to spend time with—get to know better. So don't think this little episode is going to make me run away."

Kendall watched him, disbelief and then relief clearly washing over her.

"What's it going to be?" Joseph asked.

"We go forward."

And they did, arriving at the movie theater not long after sitting on the pavement of the vacant party store. Kendall freshened up in the backseat before Joseph escorted her inside. He didn't speak of the episode again. He just opened the door and helped her out—as if having his date ride in the backseat were a normal occurrence. He held his head high, proud to be out with such a beautiful creature.

The premier movie theater in Southfield was jam-packed. Joseph's temper threatened to flare while standing in the ridiculously long Saturday night box office lines. The manager should have been aware that Saturday night was date night and the lines would be longer than usual. When they finally reached the ticket counter, the movie they wanted to see had been sold out. Joseph knew his exaggerated response had something to do with the news he had gotten from Dr. Bennis—plus he was worried about Kendall—but that didn't keep him from blasting the pimply boy behind the Plexiglas.

"Joseph." Kendall wrapped her arm around his, transferring her natural calmness. "It's okay. Let's see something else."

Her touch melted his anger.

The angry crowd began to rumble and the manager on duty was called.

"Let's go back to my place. Look what you've started." Kendall pulled Joseph away from the box office. "My neighbor always rents movies on Saturday night, I'll grab a few and we'll have a quiet evening at my place. We're both over our stress limit tonight."

"Okay," Kendall called from her kitchen. "You can turn on the movie now."

Joseph appeared in the doorway. "Let me get that." He took the tray of sandwiches from her and headed for the living room. "None of our dates have been ordinary."

"We have a track record that should be examined thoroughly."

They sat together on the sofa, Joseph placing the tray on the coffee table in front of them. "I'm very sorry for the way I acted at the movies. My temper got away from me."

"It's all right. Good customer service is impossible to find. But you can't let it get under your skin."

"You're right. I'll make it up to you on Tuesday. You've shown me your favorite thing—the tango. I want to show you mine."

"And what's that?"

"I'm an avid fan of the theater. Dance, stage plays—anything. My favorite is the opera. I'm a season ticket holder at the Detroit Opera House. Tuesday there's a performance you'd be particularly interested in seeing."

"Really? I have to tell you that I've never seen an opera or even thought about seeing one."

"That's okay. This will be a good one to cut your teeth on. *Tango Pasión* is opening."

Kendall sat up excited. "An opera about the tango?"

Joseph stepped to the foyer and pulled the playbill from his leather jacket. Kendall watched him go with a yearning heart. Fit and trim, tall and wide-shouldered, Joseph opened doors to her heart that were long closed. His brazen stride and assertive manner were an irresistible combination. Add to that the subtle sexiness of the way he stroked the lines of her face, and Kendall's body lit up with the heated fire of a Bunsen burner when he came near.

Joseph dropped down next to her. His thigh grazed hers. He could unintentionally touch her with the most intimate of caresses. He handed her the playbill. "Are you interested?" he asked with a hopeful lift at the corner of his mouth.

"Interested? Are you kidding?" She examined the bright yellow circular. An Argentine couple embraced cheek-to-cheek. The inset showed a picture of a man and woman gazing deeply into each other's eyes.

Memories saddened her. She could never get her last boyfriend to share her love for the tango. Darren had reminded her he was blue collar. His plans went no further than the weekend. The only things on his mind were hard work, cold beer, and rugged sports.

Darren had hung around for several months after the accident. His pity made her push him away. He couldn't handle the drastic change in her attitude. He tried and tried to comfort her, but he always seemed to say or do the wrong thing. He began to ignore the situation, hoping to keep the peace between them. He cowered to her every tantrum. He was always searching for ways to cheer her up and make her feel better. He shielded her from the wrath of her relatives, people who blamed her for Raven's untimely death. She couldn't deny that Darren was a good man with a good heart. It's why she had to push him away.

Guilt consumed Kendall during those dark days. She still hadn't forgiven herself for the accident. But then it was much worse. She verbally abused Darren, cutting his manly pride with the sharp edge of her tongue. She knew well of his sexual appetite and his promise to her father and used the information to destroy him. She taunted him mercilessly. She needed to feel desired. She seduced him, coaxing him to forget the promise made to her father. The shocked expression when he saw her grotesque scarring made her lash out at him. She admonished his manhood. She called him horrible names. She yelled and screamed and threw things until he stormed from her house, vowing never to return.

But Darren was a good man. He called when he arrived home to check on her. He called every day after that terrible fight. She ignored all the calls, opting to let the answering machine pick up the phone. Two days into her exile, Greg showed up with the police, threatening to break down her door.

Kendall hadn't spoken to Darren in almost a year. She thought of him fondly and hoped he had found a woman who treated him with the love he deserved.

Kendall's right hand began its violent shake, bringing her back to the present. She dropped the opera program to the floor. The pain gripped her, racing up her forearm with the sharpness of a lightning bolt. Her fingers twitched, each moving in a separate rhythm—a combination of stress and overuse responsible for the spasms.

She jumped up from the sofa.

"What is it?" Joseph sprang up, ready to pull her into the comfort of his arms.

Tears stung Kendall's eyes. She wanted to keep him around, but why would he stay with these endless crisis episodes clouding their time together? She raced up the stairs. "I'm not feeling very well. You should see yourself out. I'll call you tomorrow."

Joseph stood dumbfounded at the bottom of the stairs. He grabbed his jacket and draped it over his arm.

Things had been going well—everything considered—and now Kendall was throwing him out.

Sara's voice ricocheted inside his skull, *"Accident."*

Had he seen tears in Kendall's eyes? Her hand had seized wildly, causing her to drop the opera program to the floor. Was this a residual of the accident? He could help her if she let him. He couldn't understand why she chose to run away from him when faced with adversity. They had covered a lot of ground tonight. She didn't have to be embarrassed or ashamed of her affliction. Despite the depth of his attraction, they hadn't known each other very long. He had to respect her need for privacy. He debated for a moment more before he left.

Chapter 10

Kendall angrily tore open the bottle of muscle relaxants. She had begun to taper herself off the medication when the spasms returned as a force to be reckoned with. Never tainting her body with alcohol or drugs, Kendall despised this dependence on the painkillers. Needing the medication to control her body was a sign of weakness, divine forces "teaching her a lesson" for her part in Raven's death. She swallowed the pill without water, her right hand resigning itself to intermittent jerks. The medicine would kick in shortly and her hand would return to normal—until the next time.

Kendall splashed cold water on her face while mentally preparing to call Joseph with yet another apology and exaggerated explanation of her weird behavior. She searched for honesty behind her mirrored reflection. In her mind she said, *Joseph is a good man. Leave him alone to find someone normal who appreciates him.* Like Darren, he deserved better than what she could offer. Would she ever be able to offer a man a solid, nurturing relationship?

Kendall admitted aloud, "You're not ready." She closed her eyes to the truth staring back at her. This couldn't work. As much as she wished it could, it wouldn't. She and Joseph couldn't even date like normal people because she had to ride in the backseat with her head stuck out the window like a puppy.

She had tried her best—and failed. *The next time will be easier,* she reassured herself. She would avoid dating until she was completely ready. She was doing too much, too fast. Jumping in with both feet. She'd change her focus to the gallery. Maybe she'd ride along with Max the next time he went to run errands—just to see if she could take it. With practice, she'd learn to ride in the backseat without the uncontrollable urge to jump out of a speeding car.

Kendall dried her face and stepped into her bedroom. "Joseph!" She clutched her chest.

Joseph stood tall and proud, his massive body filling the bedroom doorway. He removed his hands from the pockets of his trousers. "I didn't leave." He stepped up to her with caution. "We've both had our bad moments tonight. I'm not going to leave until I know you're all right."

"I'm fine." She turned and tucked the jerky hand under her opposite arm.

Joseph stood inches behind her. She could feel his body heat move between them. "The government trained me to handle crises very well. A major airline puts me at the helm of a huge 757 on a daily basis. Why can't I get a fragile princess like you to trust me to help you?"

Kendall let his words move her body. She turned to him. "It's complicated."

"More complicated than flying a 757 with two hundred passengers?"

"Maybe," she whispered.

"Maybe. I'm finding that you're more complex than I ever imagined." He took her hand and sat with her on the bed. Again, he had made the most intimate gesture with unthinkable ease. "Does this have anything to do with the accident?"

Kendall's chest exploded. Shame, fear, and guilt mixed into a potent cocktail. His invasion of her privacy triggered a rage only outdone by the tears of raw terror. She refused to suffer the humiliation of crying in front of Joseph—he'd seen her at her worst enough times.

"Kendall, am I right? Does all of this have something to do with the accident?"

"Who told you about the accident?" Kendall snapped.

"I don't know anything except that you were in some sort of bad accident. Tell me what's going on."

Kendall studied his sincerity. His eyes blinked slowly, the tiny crescents underneath shifting every time. His gaze was lethal, bending her will to his desire.

"Talk to me, Kendall." He took her hand in his and waited patiently for her to disclose her horrible past.

"I was driving," she choked out. Admitting that much made her need a break before continuing. "My little sister, Raven, was in the front seat."

A vision of Raven's glowing face appeared before her. She shook her head, unable to continue.

"Take your time." Joseph put his arm over her shoulders.

"We were going to a concert at the Fox. Raven loved the Fox because of its history. She had been one of the organization's best fund-raisers when the restoration projected started years ago."

"I remember. It's a glorious theater."

Kendall nodded. "Because of her efforts she often received free tickets to concerts. We were on the way to see one of her favorite performers sing when it happened. I stopped at a light. We were singing and dancing to the radio. Neither one of us could carry a tune." A shadow crossed her face. "The rain poured that night, a big storm was predicted, but Raven refused to miss the concert. I could have talked her out of it—I'm the big sister. I didn't. I was as excited as she was—we didn't get to spend a lot of time together because of our schedules, but we were very close."

Joseph's fingers kneaded her shoulders.

"We were at a red light one minute, in the middle of the intersection the next. I don't know how many cars hit us before my car burst into flames."

Joseph's fingers froze.

"I shook Raven, but she didn't say a word. Blood dripped from her mouth and her head moved funny— like her neck was broken. A good Samaritan pulled me from the fire. People tried to get Raven out, but the flames were raging by this time. I tried to fight my way back to my sister. Someone grabbed me and pulled me away right before the car erupted in flames."

"They couldn't save Raven?"

Kendall shook her head, her eyes fixed on a spot on the wall. "The pain hit me and I passed out. I didn't know about Raven until I woke up in the hospital later."

"Were you badly hurt?" Joseph's arm lingered at her waist.

Kendall nodded. "Months of therapy to learn to walk again. Day after day of trying to regain control of my right hand."

"That's why you have the spasms."

"Homecare nurses and therapists for weeks."

"And a new fear of riding in cars."

Kendall dropped her eyes to her lap.

"That explains the new car in your driveway with the stickers still on the window. I understand so much better now." He pulled her within the circle of his arms. "You should have shared this with me from the beginning. I never would have pressured you like I did."

"You didn't do anything wrong. Greg has been telling me for the past year that I have to control my life, not let life control me."

"How do you live? How do you get anything done if you're afraid of being inside a car?"

"My neighbor, Max, helps me tremendously. Greg gets me back and forth to work. I spend a lot of money on taxis." She explained that she had only recently returned to work. She told him of her routine with Max. As she talked and he comforted her, her life became easier to share.

"I had no idea. I don't know what to say to make it better for you."

Kendall placed her hand on his thigh. "Your being here listening helps. I've never shared this with anyone."

Joseph reached across her body for her right hand. The tremors had resolved to intermittent jerks of her fingers. "Is it painful?"

"Very."

Joseph turned her hand palm up. He pressed his fingers to the center of her hand from both sides. He kneaded gently, tracing the lightning-rod-hot trail of pain away. He worked his magic on each finger individually, then in unison. She guided his touch to mimic that of the occupational therapist's movements. He learned quickly, taking charge of the situation.

Kendall marveled at the healing effect of his touch. The jerking stopped. The pain subsided. He pressed her palm to his lips. His hypnotizing eyes transported her into the best place she'd been in over a year.

Joseph laid her hand against his cheek and pressed it there while he leaned in for a kiss. His lips worked as gently and patiently as his fingers had. He breathed deeply, exhaling hot air into her ear as he lazily nibbled the lobe. His hand cascaded down the sleeve of her arm and back up again. He took her bottom lip between his teeth as he settled her down on the bed. He straddled her middle, pressing their foreheads together.

"Joseph."

"Yes?" He kissed each eyelid, in turn, until she kept them closed.

In darkness, his touch became more intense. She concentrated on the fierce sensations his touch sent through her body. His lips brushed her lashes. His tongue tasted her jawline. Hot puffs of air inside her ear made her body shift on the bed. His fingers danced along the length of the buttons of her blouse.

Kendall could feel her nipples respond to his teasing touch. "Joseph."

Joseph made her feel good and cherished and safe. His fingers opened the top button on her blouse. He paused to kiss her lips before fitting the next button through its hole.

Kendall's tongue probed his mouth when the last button had been undone and the flaps of her blouse separated. Joseph easily lifted her, moving her up on the bed. He loomed over her, his eyes fixed on the lace of her black bra. He glanced up and she could read his hesitancy in his mind. She inhaled sharply when he cupped both her breasts in his hands.

He massaged her nipples to erection before licking each through the lace. With one flick of his thumbs, he opened the front clasp. Glancing hungrily at her, he descended upon her chest.

Joseph had listened to her fears and did not condemn her. He used her body to ease her pain. Joseph was tall, dark, handsome, kind, protective, and irresistible. Kendall's thumbs stroked the gray patches at his temples. She moved to the crescents beneath his eyes. Joseph dropped his body down on top of hers. He shifted until their grooves fit perfectly. He moved against her, working her into a frenzy that made her open her thighs to him. He had the ability to release her fears and open her body with an incidental touch. The fervor of his seductive movements freed her mind, and worked wizardry on her body.

Joseph's long fingers found their way into the smoldering dip between her legs. His expert movements were confident of the pleasure he could bring. Kendall felt him pull her jeans down her thighs. He lifted himself enough to unzip his slacks and pull them an equal distance down his thighs.

Kendall felt one of Joseph's long fingers tug at the elastic of her lace panties. Two fingers grazed her tangled bush, ready to answer her call. His thumb pressed the button that made her tense. Her thighs fell open, daring to forget that she wasn't ready to take this huge step with him.

Joseph settled between her thighs. His bulge pressed harder, straining against the thin layers of lace and cotton preventing it from penetration. Kendall gasped when one of his fingers slipped inside her slippery entrance. The power of his probing fingers tempted her body. Somewhere deep inside, she summoned the ability to think. This had been a crazy evening with their emotions running full scale. Only minutes ago she had thought about telling Joseph she couldn't see him again. Now they were pressed together on her bed in heated agony about to take a giant step that couldn't be undone. No matter what her body felt, she wasn't ready mentally.

"Joseph," Kendall called next to his ear.

"Yes?"

"It's too soon. I'm not ready."

He stiffened, touched her nose with his. "You're not ready?" he asked through panting breaths.

"I don't want to go this far, this fast."

Joseph rolled next to her, working to calm his breathing. He took a moment to compose himself before speaking. "I understand."

"Joseph—"

"It's okay, princess." He worked to right her clothing, then his own. "You're not ready. I understand. I respect that." He forced a smile against the sexual tension racking his body. "Willpower."

Joseph's lips whispered next to her ear, "Only when you're ready."

Chapter 11

"Captain Stewart, welcome aboard," Russ greeted his friend at the door of the aircraft.

Joseph shook his hand as he moved past him. Dressed as he was, casually in jeans and a white sweater with his favorite leather jacket, Joseph's stride still turned the heads of women scurrying for their flights in the busy airport. A close shave that morning left his mocha-brown skin baby smooth. The twin gray specks at his temples looked like a dusting of talcum powder. An extra spring lifted his step, his smile so wide the muscles at the corner of his mouth ached.

"Saved you a seat up front, near all the action. I knew you couldn't stay away for long."

"I want to be home right now," Joseph said with a devilish grin that lifted his white sideburns. "Believe me, I didn't want to tear myself away from Kendall."

Russ propped his behind on the arm of the seat. "How long are you going to be in Atlanta?"

"Three days." Three long days away from Kendall. "I'm conducting the workshop on instrumentation at the flight school and then flying back as soon as possible to see Kendall." Joseph found his seat and clicked his seat belt together. There was something special he planned to do for Kendall, but no one would know about that until he completed his mission.

"Sara will be glad to hear you've got it bad. I better get going; some of us are on duty. Enjoy the flight, buddy." Russ straightened his cap and returned to the front of the plane to greet his passengers.

Joseph settled into the cushiony surface of his first-class seat. He placed the stereo headphones over his ears and listened to the soundtrack from one of his favorite operas. The woman hit the musical notes composing the song high, crisp, and sharp. Surely she had shattered many glasses during rehearsal. He relaxed his head back on the seat, letting his eyelids drift close.

A wide grin spread across his face when he thought of Kendall. Her body was so ripe, so luscious; he had lavished in touching her the night before. He delighted in her young body; the difference in their ages served as an aphrodisiac. The things he would teach her! He could tell by her hungry response to his teasing fingers that their sexual experiences were worlds apart.

In the air force, Joseph had traveled to Europe—the women in that country were responsible for making a boy into a man. Iraq taught him the different life responsibilities of men and women and their roles in the bedroom. Back in the States, Joseph soon found that a uniform opened the door to as many sexual encounters as he desired. Instead of learning a specific technique or philosophy, he learned how to manage quantity. As much as a man wants to bed every pretty woman that crosses his path, he has to know how to manage his body to achieve this. Safety and stamina were his focus as he traveled the States as a young adult. He completed his sexual education in Japan, where he learned to relax and enjoy every second of the foreplay that led to the actual encounter.

By the time Joseph returned to the States, he had settled into a sexual comfort zone. His mission was not to conquer every perfect body or pretty face. As the years passed and he matured, he began to look for a woman whom he could spend his life with. His focus changed dramatically after getting tangled up in two relationships that were not healthy for him. Tina's physical attractiveness had him jumping through hoops. Every minute he stood in her presence, he couldn't believe he had won her over. He soon found out that Tina's talents were limited to grooming herself. Lisa followed. Lisa's single goal was to marry a flyboy. She rushed their relationship along, pulling him toward the altar. They never had a chance to develop honest emotions for each other. When he refused to be a part of her one-year marriage plan, she walked out.

Kendall possessed all the qualities he sought in a woman. This lady's intellectual depth at her age surprised him. Instead of rap she listened to Latin and Spanish music. Her dreams consisted of going to Atlanta to dance the tango all night. At twenty-five, she had already defined her career goals. She became excited about going to her first opera. Her peach and green house was tastefully decorated, making it instantly feel like home to him. In the back of his mind he had thought they would have to spend all their time together at his home because she would only have beanbags to sit on. She dressed conservatively. She was always a lady; he found her uneasiness with discussing intimate topics endearing.

He felt her physical and mental pain when she told him about her automobile accident. He tried to digest the gravity of it all. He couldn't imagine how he would deal with having to learn to walk again. It would drive him crazy to be trapped in bed for more than a day—unable to ride his hog or enjoy a drive in his drop-top Benz along the riverfront at Belle Isle Park. He gauged the effects the loss of his right hand would have on his flying career. Kendall had suffered through the possibility of not being able to continue the art restoration work she loved.

Worst of all, most unimaginable and mentally shocking was the guilt of shouldering the responsibility for your little sister's death. From the story Kendall told, Joseph didn't consider the accident her fault, but she did. The psychological devastation of the accident couldn't be categorized. Compared to that catastrophe, his life had sailed along smoothly. Kendall's inner strength amazed him.

Kendall didn't realize her tenacity. Sure, she had issues with being inside a car, but who wouldn't? After being trapped inside a burning car, watching your sister perish—Joseph shook his head at the tragedy of it all. At that moment, he knew he would do anything he could to help her cope with the stress of it all.

Helping her deal with the spasms of her hand would be easy. He had learned several massage techniques in his travels. Not to mention his knowledge of certain herbs that could be added to hot tea to soothe her weary body. The challenge would come when addressing the emotional scars. He knew big strong men in the air force who never recovered from seeing a dead body. He could only guess at the weight Kendall carried in her heart.

He hadn't planned to seduce Kendall last night. The moment came and it seemed to be what they both needed—release and acceptance. He gave her both and promised much more. Knowing that he could one day bring her body to ecstasy made him proud—but humble that she would consider giving him the honor.

Kendall had fallen asleep shortly after their make-out session. He hadn't done anything like that since high school. He didn't believe kids even made out these days. From his assessment, they kissed and hopped into bed. They never learned to enjoy the thrill of the hunt or the excitement of the wait. He would pursue Kendall at the pace she dictated. He'd chase her with romantic dates, flowers, and candy.

While Kendall slept, he had wrapped his body around hers and fallen asleep. He awoke before dawn, leaving her with a kiss. When she came downstairs this morning, she'd find his love note and a box of candy.

An aggressive touch made Joseph's eyes fly open. He snatched off his headphones, cutting the power.

Gabrielle leaned over the vacant aisle seat, her lips close enough that he felt her warm breath on the bridge of his nose. "Joseph."

"Captain Stewart," he corrected.

She slipped her lithe body into the seat next to him. "I couldn't believe my luck when I saw your name on the roster. How long will you be in Atlanta?"

"A few days." Joseph felt his muscles tighten. Gabrielle tended to be as annoying as she was beautiful.

"Good, me too!" Her hand went to his knee. "Imagine the things we can do together." Her thick Italian accent added an unmistakable sensuality to her words.

Joseph lifted her hand and placed it on her own knee. "*We* won't be doing anything together, Gabrielle. I'm flattered, but not interested. I can't say it more plainly than that."

She trapped his hand underneath hers and pressed it securely into the flesh of her thigh. Her long lashes blinked slowly, making her green eyes flash their "go" sign at him. "Why do you resist what you feel for me? You Americans make things too complicated. I'm attracted to you—you like my body." She emphasized her point by sliding her fingers over her breasts. "We are different in my country. If we are attracted it is okay to make love."

"You're right—our countries are very different in that regard. In America, we make love when we are *in love*. I don't have those kinds of feelings for you."

Gabrielle sucked her teeth in annoyance. "Then what

do you do when you want to have sex before you fall in love?"

"What do I do? Walk away. I don't sleep with women I don't have strong feelings for. I'm a mature adult. It's not about lust."

The senior flight attendant called for Gabrielle. Her sharp tone displayed her anger. Joseph remembered hearing the flight attendants complain about Gabrielle on their one flight together. She spent a great deal of time "tending" to the male passengers and very little of actually working.

Gabrielle sucked her teeth again. "I have to go, but I'll be back."

"I'm sure you will," Joseph said as he replaced his headphones.

"Kendall! Get down here and cook breakfast," Max shouted from the bottom of the stairs. "Wake up! Wake up! Wake up!"

Kendall came down the stairs, tying the ends of her robe together. "Why are you in my house shouting this early in the morning?" She brushed her fingers through her curls.

"I'm excited." He sang in loud operatic fashion, "Excited!"

"About what?" Kendall trudged off to the kitchen with Max on her heels. "And stop that awful noise. It's shooting right through my skull."

"Uh-huh."

"Here." Kendall handed him a pitcher of orange juice from the fridge.

Max worked on setting the table while Kendall started breakfast.

"My date went wonderfully, thank you for asking."

"I'm sorry," Kendall tossed over her shoulder, "I did forget to ask. I woke up in a grumpy mood."

Max rifled through the silverware drawer. "Could that be because you think your lover boy ran out on you without saying good-bye?"

Kendall dropped the frying pan on the front eye of the stove. "What do you know?"

"There's a note and a box of candy on the dining room table."

Kendall tossed him the spatula and ran from the room. Propped against the vase holding her red roses sat a large box of chocolates tied with a red bow. She pulled a neatly folded note from the box.

Dear Kendall,
    I enjoyed our evening.
    I'm off to Atlanta to conduct a training seminar.
    I'll call you before bed.
                            With care,
                            Joseph

Kendall ripped the bow from the box and plucked a juicy chocolate from one of the endless rows. She wandered back to the kitchen, humming.

"I see your date went well, too," Max remarked.

"It did and I'm going to tell you all about it, but first I want to hear about your night."

"It didn't end in me having a sparring match, so that's definitely a step in the right direction. This could really be the start of something with Dan."

Kendall fried eggs and bacon, boiled grits, and toasted bread for their breakfast. She listened contently as Max gave her every detail of his evening with Dan. An unusual premise, but a romance all the same. Kendall found herself daydreaming about her and Joseph. She sipped her juice as Max described the flipping of his stomach at Dan's touch. She felt the velvety texture of Joseph's lips when Max described his first kiss with another man. They were both entering into relationships that were foreign to them. Max was experiencing his first homosexual encounter while Kendall was falling in love for the first time.

Max scooped up his eggs with the edge of his toast. "Who was the man in the big red Benz?"

"Are you spying on me?"

"I have to keep an eye on my favorite neighbor. Who was the man?"

Kendall shared with Max the way she met Joseph. She gave him an abbreviated version of their short dating history.

Max peered at her over the rim of his glass. "He didn't leave until morning. That's out of character for you."

"He didn't?"

"You didn't know?"

"No, my hand was bothering me last night. I took the muscle relaxants and fell into a deep sleep." She conveniently omitted the part about allowing Joseph to partially undress her and toy with her body.

"He left early and returned carrying the box of candy. Minutes after that he sped off in the red Benz truck. Nice ride."

Kendall smiled at the trouble Joseph had gone to. Getting up early, shopping for a gift, returning, and then heading to the airport. She was sure he had to go home to change clothes and pack before leaving. In Joseph she had found a gem. There was so much she needed to do emotionally to be worthy of him.

Chapter 12

Joseph spent the morning reviewing the standard language of instrument flying. He picked out the new pilots in his class by the way their pens flew across the page trying to keep up with everything he said. The veterans watched him unblinkingly, their presence at the lecture purely for student recruitment and to obtain brownie points with the boss.

At lunch he learned a majority of the pilots attending the refresher seminar were the proud owners of "hangar queens"—planes that are in the shop for repair more than in the air. The pilots revered his experience in flying for the air force and a major commercial carrier. They hounded him with questions. Many begged to hear the steamy details of the pilot–flight attendant relationship. At this point in the conversation, he smiled and politely excused himself. Somehow people always got around to asking for the dirt.

After lunch Joseph spoke in detail of instrument approach. He concluded with proficiency exercises he was glad the majority of men grasped without trouble.

Joseph enjoyed the break that speaking at seminars allowed, but his heart was in the air. Taking command of a 757 or 767, soaring above the clouds with the sun reflecting off the gray steel giant brought him a calming peace he could only describe to another pilot. You had to be the one behind the wheel, speaking the jargon, reading the instrument panel to grasp the spirituality of it all.

He didn't take his responsibilities lightly—he never forgot about his passengers' or crew's safety. He made sure he had adequate rest. He kept his skills sharp by studying every piece of literature written about flying. He attended training classes religiously. He never mixed business with pleasure. When on duty, his kept his mind free of stress and remained focused at all times.

Joseph wasn't being honest with himself. He had ignored Dr. Bennis's orders regarding his blood pressure regulation—didn't that put his passengers and crew at risk? The thought made his head pound. Dr. Bennis told him to regulate his diet—he didn't. He should have limited fried foods and cut back on the tomato products. He couldn't do that if he wanted to continue to have dinner with Kendall. Because of his schedule, he often ate at fast food restaurants. The rare days he was at home for dinner, he couldn't cook and most times ended up ordering a pizza with everything.

Dr. Bennis told him to incorporate a regular workout routine into his schedule. Flying would make that hard, but not impossible. For a forty-year-old man he had an excellent body. He liked the outdoors. He often bounced his basketball down to the neighborhood high school and challenged the teenagers to a game.

The final part of the equation was tucked in his wallet. Pride made him refuse to have the prescription for the antihypertensives filled. He could beat this without medications. Once he started down that road Dr. Bennis wouldn't be able to discontinue the medicines and he'd be grounded for certain.

No, he knew his body. Exercise, rest, and a lot of Kendall were all he needed to get his blood pressure under control.

Joseph slid the key card into its slot, opening his hotel door. He planned to call for room service, shower, and jump into bed to catch up on television—in that order. After eating his dinner, he would call Kendall and ask if she liked the candy and flowers. He wanted to hear every detail of her day and confirm that they were on for the opera when he returned.

"Joseph?" Kendall sounded groggy.

"Expecting another man to call you at this hour?" he said lightly, but his gut wrenched at the thought of another man whispering sweet nothings over the phone line, trying to persuade her to let him come over to "talk."

"Only you."

"I called too late."

"No, I had a long day. I was waiting for your call when I nodded off."

Joseph cut off the bedside lamp, letting the darkness submerge his soul in calming peace. "It's been a long day for me, too. How did you spend your day?"

Joseph listened to the melodic timbre of Kendall's voice as she told him about her day at the gallery. Although he'd spent the night before with her, he missed her terribly. He listened intently, enjoying seeing the world through her eyes. He let the sound of her voice lull him into a stress-free zone saturated with erotic images of what was to come.

Joseph asked, "Are we still on for the opera when I get back?"

Kendall hesitated.

"Do you need to change our plans?" He desperately hoped not.

"Joseph, you've been so understanding, but it's embarrassing when I get sick. It's humiliating and I don't like you to see me that way."

"Are you canceling our date because you get carsick? Or is it because you don't want to see me?"

"No, I want to see you. I thought I would meet you at the opera house."

"I don't want that." Joseph sat at attention, the sheets falling around his waist.

Kendall remained quiet.

"I don't care if you get carsick. Since you do get sick, that's even more reason why I should see you to and from the theater."

"What you witnessed the other day is a mild reaction compared to other episodes I've had."

"Kendall, it doesn't matter. Really. The proper way for a man to take a woman out on a date is to start by picking her up. Knowing that you get carsick I would worry to death until you arrived. We can't let carsickness come between us. I can handle it."

Joseph used many arguments, but he could not persuade Kendall to change her mind. She kept emphasizing her shame. She had the idea that if she became *too* sick he wouldn't want to see her again. He tried to tell her it was the complete opposite: he wanted to be with her so badly that he didn't want to throw away any precious minutes.

Afraid that she would cancel their plans, Joseph finally gave in. "I have to tell you that I'm very bothered by this. We have to find a compromise we can both live with."

"We will. I'm making progress, I just need a little more time and a lot of understanding from you."

"I do understand."

"I considered not seeing you because of this, but I don't want that. I am really trying—"

"I know, I know."

"Then can I meet you at the opera and we work out something later?"

What could he do other than accept Kendall's ultimatum? He wanted to spend time with her, and that was more important than how they each arrived for the date.

Joseph huffed at how his day had played out. Gabrielle had clung to him no matter how hard he tried to get rid of her, and the one woman he wanted to cling to him he had to fight to earn permission to pick her up for their dates.

Chapter 13

Gabrielle managed to maintain her smile during the flight back into Detroit Metro Airport. She pushed the beverage cart up and down the aisle with one purpose in mind: pay Joseph back for humiliating her. *"Excuse me,"* she mumbled aloud, "Captain Stewart."

"I'm sorry?" the passenger asked.

Gabrielle wanted to tell the woman that if she had kept that whining baby quiet, she could have heard what was said. Instead she smiled. "Pretty baby."

Gabrielle finished her pass with the beverage cart and sought out a place of refuge. She needed to calm herself. Her brash attitude toward the people filling the seats was uncharacteristic. She loved her work and she loved her passengers.

She buckled herself into the rumble seat near the back of the plane. How dare Joseph deny every one of her attempts to begin a relationship with him? Knowing the male libido, she had even offered to sleep with him without any promises. It really hadn't been a risky proposition for her; she knew that once he fell into her arms he'd never be able to let her go. She never counted on him denying her.

The first time Gabrielle saw Joseph was when he emerged from the cockpit to subdue an irrational passenger. He took control of the situation, and within minutes emergency medical personnel had removed the passenger from the plane. Effortlessly he had used his brawn to pin the man in his seat. With compassion he tried to calm the man. She adored a man that could take charge. Paired with his good looks, his commanding presence stole her heart. The fact that he played hard to get only fueled her desire to have him.

But he was no longer playing hard to get. He boldly told her he wasn't interested. A man had never denied Gabrielle. Her looks opened all doors and sparked every man's libido. There had to be an explanation for Joseph's rejection.

Could there be a woman in his life? He spoke of love and lust—words learned from a woman. Gabrielle followed Joseph's romantic encounters closer than she tracked her own. She made friends with every flight attendant that flew with him. She dated pilots to gain inside information on him; the pilots at this airline stuck together like a fraternity. How could she have missed another woman flying under her radar? She had to learn if this was so and who this woman was.

Gabrielle put together a list of women—flight attendants that openly flirted with him or stared too long when he passed by. She considered other airport workers who salivated when he crossed the terminal.

Anger and hurt began to weave a tangled network of emotions inside Gabrielle's heart. She struggled with which issue to attack first. Should she seek out this woman and threaten her? She'd tell her to stay away from Joseph or else. She discarded that idea. The other woman wouldn't matter if Joseph still didn't want her. So, the first thing she needed to do was make Joseph realize how badly he wanted to be with her.

Gabrielle's spirits lifted. She knew exactly how to get to a man like Joseph. She had to attack his pride. His ego

boosts came at her expense. Chasing him gave him a
sense of power over her. She'd take that power away and
crush his ego in one swoop. He'd come begging for her
to give him a chance.

A wide grin separated her painted lips. *Oh, this will be
too easy,* she thought.

Determination fueled each of Gabrielle's steps. She
pranced down the hallway of the hotel with a confident
stride that rocked her behind. She glanced over her
shoulder with a toss of her blond mane and a huge smile
that lighted her green eyes.

The pilot followed behind her not suspecting that
what they were about to do was all part of her master
plan.

"You have the key, darling?" Gabrielle asked.

He leered at her. Too anxious to get the hotel door
open, he dropped the key to the floor.

Gabrielle knew he had a thing for her accent. She
spoke to him in Italian.

"What did you say?" he asked, flinging the door open.

"I said I want you so badly." Actually, she had called
him desperate and stupid.

"I want you, too." He pushed the door closed with the
flat of his hand and started tugging at his tie. "I've never
done anything like this before."

Gabrielle's eyes became question marks. All the married men said that, but if his nervousness was any
indication, this might actually be his first time cheating.

"My wife and I have a good, solid marriage. Just the
other night we went to a benefit at the Museum of
African-American History."

"It'll be fine, Captain—"

"Call me Russ."

Gabrielle sauntered to the bed and began to strip free of her uniform. If Russ's marriage was as good as he said, he wouldn't be with her in the hotel. She didn't want to be his counselor; she wanted revenge.

In only her thong underwear, Gabrielle approached him and began to unbutton his shirt.

Russ rambled on. "We danced and had a wonderful time. Joseph was there—you know Captain Stewart. He'll tell you we looked happy—my wife and I."

Gabrielle's fingers froze on his chest. She had no idea the two men socialized together. Knowing about Joseph's career and hobbies, she could see their paths crossing. This would work out better than she originally planned. With the way Russ rambled on, his guilt would lead him to spill a confession to anyone who would listen. And since Russ and Joseph were friends, he would be the first to hear about their rendezvous.

"You went to a benefit and Captain Stewart was there?"

"I invited him. He made an outrageous bid on a piece of artwork to get the attention of a woman."

Gabrielle's insides twisted. "Really?"

"I think it made the society pages."

She had the sudden urge to run to the nearest library and research the papers.

Russ's face paled. "Do you still have a thing for Joseph? You told me that was over—"

"I had a tiny crush on Captain Stewart." She reached for him. "But that passed as soon as I saw you."

"You won't mention this to him, will you? It could get back to my wife. She'd never understand."

Gabrielle snuggled into his chest, working to calm him down. If they continued to talk about his marriage he might change his mind about their tryst. "No one will know." She repeated the phrase in Italian.

"It turns me on when you speak Italian." His lips went to her neck.

Gabrielle uttered more foreign words as he lifted her into his arms.

Chapter 14

Captain Joseph Stewart stood tall and regal outside the Detroit Opera House wearing a black-on-black tuxedo with a look of deep concentration. He shifted the long black coat draped over his right arm to his left. The graying hair at his temples made his mocha skin more pronounced. He held his clean-shaven chin high. His eyes darted from one cab lined up in front of the theater to the other.

Kendall's heart pounded as the cabbie pulled up. She allowed herself time to gawk unabashedly at Joseph's handsomeness. Women did a double take in his direction as they passed on the arm of their own date. Pride filled Kendall: this distinguished man awaited *her* arrival. Her head swam with lust as she recalled the firestorm of his kisses.

Before stepping out of the cab, she checked her makeup one last time. The usual symptoms accompanied her on the drive, but using Joseph as her focal point lessened their severity. She added a final touch of lipstick as the cabbie inched up to the drop-off point. The usher opened her door and she stepped out. Before she could lift her hand to signal her arrival, Joseph was taking long strides in her direction.

"It feels like I haven't seen you in weeks." He greeted

her with a proper kiss on the cheek. "Kendall, you look spectacular."

He leaned into the window of the cab and settled the bill. "You wore red," Joseph said, extending his arm to her.

Kendall wrapped both of her arms around his, pressing her body snugly into his grooves. "It's your favorite color."

Joseph smiled his appreciation. "This way." He moved through the crowd to a secluded entrance into the Detroit Opera House. A small group of superbly dressed couples spoke in hushed whispers while they enjoyed cocktails in the private lounge. Dressed as they all were in coat and tails or lavish cocktail dresses, Kendall felt proud to be included in their elite circle. Instead of arriving at the palace on a carriage transformed from a pumpkin, Kendall had been delivered to the theater by taxi into the arms of the most handsome man she'd ever met.

Joseph chuckled. Leaning next to her ear, he said, "Your eyes are this big." He demonstrated by forming an O with his fingers.

"I've never been to anything like this before. I didn't even know this part of the Detroit Opera House existed."

They found a cozy corner with soft lighting to enjoy their drinks.

"I received many compliments on my date's beauty from the men at the bar," Joseph said when he returned with their refreshments.

"You always make me feel special." Kendall hid her blush by sipping from her juice.

"You should feel special, because you are."

After a few minutes of silence, Kendall thanked Joseph again for the flowers and candy. "It must be hard trying to have a relationship when you're in and out of town so often."

"I've never found anyone I wanted a serious relationship with, but I'll admit that being away from you on this short junket was torture."

Kendall leaned toward him, dropping her voice. "I know we spent time together the night before you left, but when I drove up to the theater and saw you standing there, it seemed an eternity since I had seen you."

Joseph's smoky gaze revealed the secrets of his heart. "I think that's a good sign."

They finished their drinks and Joseph asked if Kendall would like anything else. Her answer being no, they found their seats. The usher escorted them to a private box to the right of the theater.

"You didn't tell me you were a season ticket holder of box seats," Kendall exclaimed excitedly. "I feel like Cinderella." She sat on the edge of her chair, looking down at the patrons as they hustled to find their seats.

Intricate gold ornamentation decorated the high ceilings. Red velvet drapes cloaked the stage in mystery. The dim lighting of the theater solidified the romantic atmosphere. A low murmur of excited voices floated through the air. In minutes, dancers would grace the stage performing Kendall's most loved form of dance.

Joseph crossed his left ankle over his right knee as he took in Kendall's excitement. The corners of her mouth turned downward. He sat forward. "What is it?"

"Box tickets. It doesn't seem likely that you would hold box tickets for one person."

Joseph covered her hand with his on the armrest that separated them. "Are you asking me if I'm involved with someone?"

Kendall swallowed her first response. She was going to answer with a cool, aloof phrase that made it appear she didn't care one way or the other. She planned to slip into instant friendship mode as if she had no feelings for him.

"Is that what you want to know?" Joseph asked again.

Kendall held her chin high. She had suffered through the cab ride to the theater; she wouldn't let fear of the unknown make her back down. "Yes. I want to know if you're seeing anyone."

"Other than you?" Joseph toyed with her.

"Other than me, are you seeing anyone else?"

"And by 'seeing anyone' you mean what?"

"Joseph!"

He laughed, sitting forward to pull her back into his arms. "As much as I missed you while I was in Atlanta? I can't believe you have to ask me that. You are the only woman on my mind." He kissed the top of her head, inhaling the flowery scent mingling with her tight curls.

Kendall snuggled into his chest as the lights blinked, signaling the show would soon start.

The theater darkened. The crowd clapped conservatively. A line of dancers entered from stage right accompanied by the Latin tunes of the live band sitting in the orchestra pit. Kendall slid to the edge of her seat, where she stayed for the entire performance. When she became most excited, she turned to Joseph and explained the complicated dance steps. By midway through the show, Kendall felt sure that he had developed a new appreciation for the Argentine tango.

Authentic to the history of the one-hundred-year-old dance, most of the show took place in a brothel. Kendall's favorite acts were the ones that occurred in the mystical era of the 1920s. The tango had reached its peak popularity in this time period when widely explored in film and music. During the finale, the two lead dancers burned up the stage in a dazzling display of socialized tango. The program stated that the dancers would improvise the entire closing act. Kendall could not believe the intricate details were not rehearsed hour after hour. Having studied the tango on an amateur level, she couldn't fathom the possibility that these two actors-slash-dancers could pull off a flawless performance without one mistake. The moves were too complicated and too rapid for her to name. She sat on the edge of her seat, her mouth open in awe. She stood on her feet to applaud when the music stopped. She glanced back at Joseph, who was watching her every gesture with a broad smile.

"I don't think I've ever seen you this excited," Joseph said as the theater began to empty.

"Look, my hands are shaking." She held out her hands for his inspection. "And my heart is beating a mile a minute. That was thrilling!"

"I'm glad you enjoyed yourself."

Kendall settled into her seat, her mind still chanting the dance steps she'd just seen. The excitement of the moment made her want to call her old dance instructor and ask for a place in his next class. She wanted to dress in a sexy dress and be whisked across the stage. Her phobia had taken away so much of her life.

The usher appeared from behind the black curtain that ensured their privacy during the show. "Would you like me to have your car brought around, sir, or will you be staying for the next show?"

Joseph's gaze fell on Kendall. "I thought we'd go for dinner." He studied the excitement lighting her face. "Would you like to watch it again?"

"Can we, Joseph?" Her hands pressed against his chest, waiting his answer.

How could he deny her this joy? "Of course we can."

The usher acknowledged Joseph's decision before disappearing behind the black curtain.

Joseph sat contently through the next show. Kendall's delight was enough to make him enjoy it also. He slipped out briefly for a rest-room break. Kendall's eyes remained locked on the stage until he returned. During the performance, she took his hand and held it tightly. This mild show of affection thrilled Joseph as much as the dancers thrilled her.

If Russ and Sara hadn't invited him along to the museum auction, he would be spending his entire layover at home in front of the television. He would have taken his bike to the park or the beach. Probably studied his pilot magazines a great deal. No matter how he had chosen to occupy his time during the two weeks, he would have been alone. Fate had given him a chance at happiness.

Kendall glanced back at him and smiled. She looked scrumptious in the flaming red sequined dress that flowed to the top of her high-heel, satiny red shoes. Her short hairstyle accentuated her face, bringing out the sexiness of her large brown eyes. Joseph reached out and boldly ran his hand up her arm to rest on her shoulder. Instinctively, she leaned into his touch, her eyes still on the stage.

With one of Kendall's smiles, flying ceased to define his world. He loved flying—always had and always would—but Kendall brought something foreign, something good into his life. Kendall awoke male urges that he had long ago stowed away. Other than the occasional date and rare sexual encounter, he had abandoned the traditional desires of men. As his love for flying grew, he had discarded pieces of the American dream. Finding a wife and having children seemed impossible when he slept in a different city most every night.

Being with Kendall the past week made him rethink his philosophy. He understood that they hadn't known each other long, but what he was feeling had traces of permanency. The difference between their ages worried him. At twenty-five, she hadn't had many relationships by her account. Maybe she had decided to be a career woman. Here he was dreaming about settling down with a wife and kids and he didn't know where she stood on the issue. He had placed her in the role of a housewife, awaiting his calls from who knows where in the country while tending to their children.

Joseph knew they needed to have a serious discussion before he took to the skies again.

Kendall applauded the ending of the show. "Thank you for sitting through the show again."

"I enjoyed your company—and the show." Joseph stood and helped her on with her wrap. His fingertips danced across her shoulders and he felt a shiver cross her body. "Are you hungry? I thought we'd go for dinner at Tom's Oyster Bar or Union Street."

Kendall stiffened beneath his fingertips. "It's getting late. I should probably head home."

"You have to eat."

"I can make something when I get home."

"Sit down for a minute."

Joseph took her hands in his, sitting on the edge of his seat to bring them closer. "We've been here for over five hours, you must be starving. I am and I'm not ready to end this evening."

Kendall remained silent, casting her eyes down.

"I know this has to do with your fear of cars. I agreed to meet you here with the stipulation that we would work on a compromise. It's time to compromise."

"Joseph—"

He pressed his finger to her lips. "I want to help you deal with this. I don't want it to hamper us having a good time together. It would mean so much to me if you would let me be there for you."

She dropped her head. "You don't understand."

"No." He lifted her chin with a firm touch. "I don't pretend that I do. I can't begin to imagine the heartache and pain you've been in, but I can help you get through it. I want to be there for you. If we're going to have something special between us, you have to let me try." He watched as Kendall's will crumbled. "Let's go to dinner. You let me know if we need to pull over to the curb. We'll stop every time you tell me to. Even if it takes us three hours to get to the restaurant."

"You won't think I'm being silly?"

"Of course not." He signaled the usher. "I think I have an idea that will make it better. Will you give it a try?"

Kendall studied him for a long moment in which Joseph thought she might jump over the balcony and run away. He couldn't imagine a fear that held your soul captive. In his mind, he coaxed her to take a step toward recovery by accepting his offer.

The usher appeared. "Yes, sir?"

"Kendall?" Joseph gave a small nudge.

"Okay, I'll try."

Joseph took her in his arms. "That's all I ask of you." He glanced at the usher. "Please bring my car around."

Chapter 15

"Joseph, what did you do?" Kendall exclaimed, her heart racing with delight.

"I thought it would help." Joseph towered over her, looking down with a bashfulness that asked her acceptance of his efforts to make her life right.

She considered the wisdom behind the smoldering eyes. "I don't want to disappoint you."

"How could you do that? You could never disappoint me."

"If this doesn't work—"

"If it doesn't work, I'll know you tried—for me. I can't ask for more than that." His strong touch in the middle of her back urged her toward the shiny black limo.

The driver held the door open, patiently waiting for Kendall and Joseph to climb inside.

Joseph ducked into the plush leather interior after her. "This is like being in your living room." He pointed out the television, stereo, and bar.

"*Your* living room, maybe. Not mine." She laughed as she ran her hand across the butter-soft seat. Needing to be near Joseph, she moved closer, sinking into the comfort of the cozy car.

The driver lowered the divider window. "Where to, sir?"

"Union Street restaurant." He pulled Kendall into the

hollow of his arm. "And, driver, don't get us there any sooner than thirty minutes."

"Yes, sir. Thirty minutes." The divider closed.

Kendall couldn't contain her laughter. Joseph brought her much joy. He left no detail to chance, amazing her with his ability to plan the perfect evening while out of town. He wrapped his arms around her, touching her face as if trying to decide if she were real.

His eyes burned with passion, him taking in every inch of her. "I thought providing a distraction might make the ride easier for you."

"A distraction?" Kendall played along.

"A distraction of the best kind." Joseph's lashes closed atop his cheeks as he brought his lips to meet hers. His kiss was tender, longing, clinging for survival. That kiss said what neither could properly verbalize; they had missed each other terribly.

"Would you like a drink?" He remembered. "I had the driver stock the bar with plenty of juice."

Again, his attentiveness to her needs showed how much he cared. Kendall draped her arms around his neck and pulled him down to her. "I would rather have more of this."

"Kendall!" Joseph laughed, dipping to meet her demand. He pulled away, his breathing rough. "I didn't know you could be so . . ."

"What?" She dazzled him with her best smile.

"Brazen." A quick kiss. "Sexy, intelligent, *and* bold. I don't know how much more I can stand."

"I'm fighting to keep up with you, Captain Stewart."

Joseph's eyes flashed at her. "Did I tell you how beautiful you are?"

"You did."

"Thirty minutes is a long time. Would you like a snack?"

"No, I'm fine."

He lifted her legs into his lap, running his fingertips down her thigh over the sea of red sequins. "Sit back and relax." He lowered the straps on her shoes and gently pulled them off and away. He melted into the seat, bringing her feet across his lap. With lazy strokes, he caressed her feet.

"I'm so sorry I put you to so much trouble, Joseph."

"We decided—no more apologizing, remember?"

In the sudden quiet of the car, they could hear the soft jazz playing in the background. They settled into the comfort of each other's company.

Kendall spoke in a whisper, starting the conversation as if they were in the middle of it. "The frustration is enough to make me want to withdraw from the world. I've given up too much to name. I can't visit my friends. My family thinks I'm turning my back on them. They can't understand why I'm not happy to be alive—they think I'm being hysterical. What do you think, Joseph? Do you think this is all in my mind? Do you think I'm using it as an excuse to get sympathy?"

Joseph's strokes never faltered. He lowered his voice to match hers. "I think you're a dynamic young lady who had a major setback. The key is to fight to get your life back. I meant what I said at the opera house, I'll do anything I can to help you."

Relief washed over Kendall and she allowed her eyelids to drop. She felt Joseph's heat coming near and then he pressed his lips against her cheek before settling back in his seat.

"I'm proud of you for coming this far," Joseph said, resuming the hypnotizing work of his fingertips.

"Where do I go from here?"

"Where would you like to go?"

A broad smile filled her face. "After that spectacular

show you just took me to, I'd like to go back to my tango class."

"Then go."

Kendall's eyes flew open. She leaned forward to look Joseph in the eyes. "Just like that?"

"Why not? What's to stop you if you really want to do it?"

"I can't . . ."

"What?"

"Just start going to class again?"

"Yes, go back to class if that's what will make you happy."

Kendall watched him for a long moment. It *was* that simple. Greg had told her over and over again to resume her hobbies and return to work, but she wasn't ready. With Joseph's strength and confidence, she felt ready to take this step.

"One thing, Kendall." Joseph slipped on her shoes.

"What's that?"

"Choose a little gray-haired lady for your dance partner. Stay away from the muscular Latin playboy."

Kendall laughed. She hadn't laughed—been this carefree—in a year.

"Guess what, princess?"

Princess. A chill danced across her heart. "What?"

"We're at the restaurant." He smothered her with the power of his embrace. "Do you want to guess what your reward is for making it through this ride without getting sick?" Before she could answer he melted her with his kiss.

Chapter 16

They talked all through dinner and laughed all through dessert at Union Street. The cozy yuppie restaurant was dark, and Kendall's face was bathed in candlelight. Joseph watched her, all etiquette thrown out the window with her elbows on the tabletop, two tiny fists pressed against her chin. With her hair cut short and neat with yellow highlights, her soft facial structure and curvaceous body, Joseph wondered what he did to deserve her company. He listened intently, thrilled Kendall wanted to share her life, as she prattled on about restoring a shipment of jewelry at the gallery. The limo driver had broken the rules—at Joseph's insistence—and eaten dinner at the bar before returning to the limo.

"What?" Kendall smiled and Joseph wanted to climb across the table and forget etiquette himself.

Joseph placed his hand palm up on the table, his dark skin a stark contrast to the white tablecloth. Kendall dropped her hand into his, the smile never wavering.

"Does our age difference bother you?"

Kendall blinked rapidly several times.

"My question surprises you?"

"Yes. No." Her smile faded. "We've talked about this before. I thought we cleared everything up. Did I say something tonight to make you uncomfortable?"

"People were watching us at the opera house." He

held his breath. "It is important for me to know how it makes you feel when we're out together."

"It doesn't bother me, Joseph."

The way she said his name made him envision her naked body writhing beneath his, riding on a cloud of red satin.

"It doesn't bother you that people will mistake you for my daughter when we go out?"

"The Japanese restaurant—"

"You did hear it, but you chose to ignore the comment."

"He meant no harm."

Joseph cringed when he remembered the man assuming him to be her father. "He wanted to set you up with his son, Kendall."

She laughed but tried to cover her mouth to hide it.

Joseph placed his hand flat over the center of his chest. "I'm distressed and you're laughing."

Kendall sat forward so that she could place her hand on his cheek. "I'm sorry."

Joseph captured her hand as she pulled away. Gazing into her eyes, he placed a kiss on each finger before releasing her.

Kendall swallowed hard to gain her composure before changing the subject. "Tell me about your family."

"My father is a retired army officer. My mother was his secretary. Now she's his wife. There were four of us army brats—two boys and two girls. My sisters are younger so the boys ruled as we grew up. They didn't have an easy life with two big boys trying to scare their boyfriends off. Sadly, we grew apart when we each went to college or the military. I regret that I have a holiday family."

"Holiday family?"

"Yes. We send cards at major holidays and see each other only at Thanksgiving."

Kendall's eyes dropped to the table and Joseph realized he had tapped into her pain. "That is sad."

"You said you and your sister, Raven, were close."

A hint of a smile. She appreciated that he remembered Raven's name. "We were very, very close."

"What about your parents?"

Kendall exhaled a puff of air. "That's complicated."

Joseph was going to apologize for prying, but Kendall continued.

"The accident split my family down the middle. Some blamed me, others didn't. I couldn't handle the guilt of the accident and what it did to my family. I pushed everyone away. Especially those that supported me. I wanted them to have an excuse to turn on me and save their other family ties." She reached for Joseph's hand before continuing. "My dad supported me. My mom hated me for what I did."

"Are you sure it wasn't grief talking?"

"Oh, she never said it outright. It was in her eyes. I could feel it when she forced herself to touch me or kiss me when she visited."

Joseph gave her hand a squeeze. "Are you crying?"

"Just a little. This is hard."

"Go ahead."

"My parents separated once I was discharged. A year later they're still apart."

"Kendall, you know you can't take responsibility for your parents' marriage. Adults behave strangely under pressure, maybe they'll work it out."

Kendall blinked away the tears.

Joseph extended his lean arm across the table and cupped her cheek. "Does it help to talk about this? If not, say so and I'll leave it alone. Your eyes are too pretty to be filled with tears over something you can't—could never—control."

"It does help. I've never shared any of these feelings with anyone."

"And why did you choose me to be the first?"

"You make me feel safe, secure. You're nonjudgmental and let me say what I feel without telling me to stop. People try to help, but it doesn't make me feel any better when they tell me to dismiss my feelings and my guilt like turning off a kitchen appliance. I have these feelings—"

"And you need to work through them in your own time."

"Yes! You understand perfectly."

"Sir." The limo driver cleared his throat. "It's getting late."

Joseph did not take his eyes off Kendall. Was it possible she had grown more beautiful since they sat down? "We'll be out as soon as I pay the bill."

"Yes, sir." The driver disappeared.

Kendall fell back against her chair. Her scrutiny made him feel overdressed. His body stirred with forgotten need rekindled. "What is it, Kendall?"

Low and sultry, "I've had the best time tonight. Better than I can ever remember having on a date."

Joseph didn't remember the need for a woman being so strong that it became an intense longing with the fierceness of an addiction. "I'm glad that your date was with me." Levity didn't decrease his craving to caress her skin.

"What would you say if I told you I wasn't ready to go home?"

Joseph contained the urge to jump on top of the table and do a provocative dance. He answered with years of practiced coolness, "I'd invite you for an ice-cold glass of juice at my place."

Kendall offered a lopsided smile that made her look too coy, shattering his attempt to be cool. "Or we could go or do whatever in this world you want to do." He meant it. As sexy and desirable as Kendall looked wrapped in the red sequins, he'd move heaven and earth to give her what she wanted. Anything. She only needed to name it. "Name it and I'll make it happen."

"Is your place quiet?"

"And very comfortable."

"I'd like to see it."

The lights hidden in the lawn illuminated Joseph's house. Kendall stood outside the ranch home waiting for Joseph to open the door. Plump bushes surrounded the front porch and lined the walkway. The subtle eggshell coloring trimmed in pale green made the house blend into the trees and bushes surrounding the property. The fragrance of freshly mown lush green grass emanated from the picture-perfect lawn that wrapped around the house.

Kendall often dreamed of owning a home in this up-scale neighborhood. The country-cottage-style ranch home fit Joseph's personality. She could picture him sitting on the rail of the covered front porch. She guessed the multipaneled bay window on her left opened up his study to the bright morning sun.

"Is that your den?"

"Yes." Joseph smiled. "How'd you guess?" He pushed the front door open. "Here we are."

Kendall stepped into a huge foyer that opened up to a great room to the left and a formal dining room on the right. Skylights in the cathedral ceilings displayed a clear evening sky. The open floor plan allowed her gaze to follow Joseph as he moved through the house turning off bright lights and replacing them with the dim glow of recessed lighting.

"Come have a seat." Joseph returned to where she stood, removed her wrap, and escorted her into the sunken living room. "I'll get you something to drink."

Kendall wasn't thirsty but she needed the time alone to settle her nerves. Joseph remained cool and collected but she'd noticed the way he moved through the house attempting to make things perfect. She'd suggested this, she wanted this; she'd enjoy every minute.

Joseph soon returned with two iced glasses of lemonade. Within minutes, they were talking as comfortably as they had been at Union Street.

"Where was the best place you visited while in the military?" Kendall asked. She had removed her shoes and tucked her legs under her on the sofa.

"Italy, without a doubt."

"Have you returned since leaving the air force?"

"No. I'd like to someday." He trailed a finger down her thigh with an easiness that seemed second nature. "Maybe on my honeymoon."

"You'd like to get married?"

"Someday. Why do you sound so surprised?"

"Well . . ."

"I'm forty and have never been married. You're wondering why."

Kendall placed her hand atop his, stopping the easy stroke that ignited a riot inside her body. "I didn't mean to be rude."

Joseph sandwiched her dainty hand. "It's not rude to try to learn about me. I'm not married because I haven't found the woman I want to marry and start a family with. When I was younger all my attention went to learning to fly. Now that I'm older my focus is changing." Craving her touch, he pulled her into the shelter of his massive chest. "What about you?"

Kendall's hand came up to rest on his shoulder. She

snuggled into him, enjoying the security only a strong
black man can provide. "I've been close."

"Really?"

"Don't *you* sound so surprised. What? You don't think
anyone would want to marry me?"

"I'm surprised you haven't been snatched up long
ago."

"Good save."

His fingers combed through her short curls. "What
happened?"

"With Darren? I destroyed that relationship right
about the time I destroyed the one with my family."

Joseph tensed. "Are there lingering feelings?"

Kendall mulled over his question. "He'll always have
my respect. He is a good person who I treated unfairly
and I regret that, but no, those emotions are long gone."

They needed no more words after Joseph turned on
the stereo and easy-listening music filled the enormous
house. He cut off the speakers in the rest of the house,
trapping them in a cocoon of soft musical notes. Within
minutes, his jacket lay across the arm of the sofa and
Kendall's hands were pressed against the wall of his
muscled chest. She followed his lead as he kissed her
tenderly and then desperately. He kissed her with practiced expertise and amateur abandon. Soon, she knew
every sensitive corner of his mouth and he knew hers.
They kissed for hours and it still wasn't enough for
Kendall.

Kendall touched Joseph first. A casual cascade of
her hand down his rippled chest that ended at his belt
buckle. Her fingers curved around the cool leather
and held tight. He moaned when her fingers grazed
the sensitive skin of his abdomen.

Her thumb strayed next, fanning out as far as its
reach would allow. He shivered. She liked this newly

discovered power to make his body respond brazenly to her touch. Her fingers inched toward his navel. Crossing rocky terrain, without an inch of fat, Kendall compared the feeling to satin-covered granite. She slipped her fingers inside the space between the buttons of Joseph's shirt at the same time her lips wandered to his neck. She inhaled deeply, absorbing the manly aroma coating his skin.

Joseph's hand slipped slowly down Kendall's spine. Internally, static crackled beneath his fingers, making Kendall moan softly. He lifted her chin, breaking the suction of her lips against his neck, and kissed her. His tongue explored as her fingers stroked the exposed skin between the gaps of his shirt.

Breathing hard, Joseph pulled away. "It's getting late."

His eyes! His eyes locked on to Kendall and her skin caught afire. He blinked at her new level of intensity and broke the spell.

Reality set it in. "The thought of getting into your car scares me."

"We'll take the SUV."

Kendall gave a small shake of her head. "That's not what I meant. I mean, this evening has gone perfectly—everything was like a dream. I hate to ruin it by getting sick when you drive me home."

Dumbfounded, amazed, and a little nervous, Joseph kept quiet when Kendall stood and placed herself squarely in front of him.

"We've only been seeing each other a short time, but no one has ever made me feel this way. It's scary, but it's very good, too."

"Kendall—"

"The first time you kissed me, I wanted to melt. In my bedroom the other night, I wanted to make love to you." She hesitated, overcoming the embarrassment of her stark honesty. "I stopped because I thought you wouldn't find me—desirable."

Joseph looked at her with astonishment. "Sexy, smart, and sensitive—how could I not find you desirable?"

"I didn't tell you everything about the accident." She took two steps back. "I still have the scars."

"The scars?"

Kendall turned her back to him and said over her shoulder, "Would you help me with the zipper?"

Joseph's heat moved behind her and he slowly lowered her zipper. She pressed the sequin dress to her breasts. Joseph took a step back, taking his heat with him. Kendall inhaled deeply. She had shared her darkest fears and greatest mistakes with him tonight. If he could accept this one more thing, he would be the great man she believed him to be. She let the material fall from her left shoulder. She slipped the dress down her right shoulder and extended her arms, letting it pool on the floor at her feet. She squeezed her eyes together and awaited her fate.

"Does it hurt?" Joseph lifted his hand and gently touched her shoulder. His fingers examined the raised scar on her right shoulder and upper arm. Dark, raised scar tissue marred her otherwise perfect body.

"No." Kendall shook her head. "The nerve damage will probably never go away."

"This is why you have the hand spasms."

Kendall nodded.

He grasped her shoulders and turned her to face him. "Why are you showing me this?"

"I need to share the entire truth with you. I need to know if you still want to pursue a relationship with me now that you know everything." She raised her chin, her voice strong, eyes hopeful. "I want to know if you can hold me through the night with these scars on my body."

Obviously stunned by her blunt words, Joseph entered Kendall's body through her big, brown eyes. How much courage it must take to expose yourself, only asking to be accepted for who you are! The physical and emotional pain that plagued Kendall would crush the toughest man, but she had worked through her trials. His respect for her grew. His need to share himself with her mushroomed into uncontrollable need.

Kendall dropped her eyes and shoved the sleeves on her dress back into place. "You don't have to say anything. I put you on the spot. I'm ready to go home now."

Joseph transferred his heat with the touch of his hand on her cheek. "I was hoping you would stay."

Cautiously, Kendall met his smoldering gaze.

"I was hoping you would stay all night. Let me prove to you how unimportant those scars are to me."

Kendall's mouth opened, but there were no words.

"You want to know if I can hold you all through the night? Hell, yes. All night. Stay with me, because looking at you—all of you—I see the most beautiful, sexiest woman in the world and I don't want you to leave tonight."

Chapter 17

Kendall had never seen a man completely nude before.

Soft musical notes followed Kendall and Joseph into his bedroom. She sat at the foot of his bed, leaning back onto her palms, watching him. He stood a few feet away stripping off his clothes. Removing his tie drew her eyes to the speckled gray area at his temples. When he slipped the white dress shirt over his lean arms, her attention went to the mocha ripples of the chest that had comforted her during the evening. She held her breath as he undid his belt buckle. At forty, Captain Joseph Stewart had a nicer body than men twenty years his junior.

Kendall gasped when Joseph lowered the zipper over the bulge in his dress pants. He didn't glance her way until he stood before her wearing only his briefs. The stark-white garment did little to camouflage what lay underneath. White against mocha provided a vivid contrast.

And then he freed himself of the last restriction.

Kendall's heart fluttered at the sight.

Crazy thoughts assaulted her. For a brief moment, she panicked. Was it too soon? Would she be sending the wrong message? What about all her oaths and vows up to this point in her life? Did she know him well enough after two weeks? What would the atmosphere be between them in the morning?

Kendall flinched, thinking to bolt from the room. Fear of the unknown being the thing to jolt her into reality.

She started to run.

Until Joseph smothered her fears with smoldering brown eyes.

He reached out to her. Caramel went well with mocha. She stared at her skin against his for a long moment. Marveled at what they could create together.

"Kendall?" He wore a caring smile that said he would be gentle with her.

And all doubt melted away just as she had melted with their first kiss.

"Yes?"

"You're nervous." His mocha slashed her caramel when he grasped her wrists and pulled her closer.

"Yes."

"I'll take care of you." He pulled her into the embrace of his lean arms. She relied on the strength in those arms to keep her from falling the way her dress did. Joseph took her inside his mouth and when he released her, her dress surrounded her feet.

Kendall looked up at Joseph, amazed that she hadn't felt his fingers at work. Holding her gaze, he opened the snaps of her lacy red bra. With a polite hold on her waist, he turned her away from him. Inhaling deeply, he remarked on her abundance of his favorite part of a woman's body. His fingers traced the lacy red band of her panties. He hooked his fingers inside at her hips. "You are so sexy," he whispered beside her ear. His thumbs held on to her panties as his hands slid down her body. He nuzzled against her calf. "You are so beautiful."

Kendall placed a hand on his powerful shoulder to balance as she stepped out of the last article of her clothing.

Kendall had never been completely nude in front of a man before.

And Joseph's smile made her glad she had waited.

When Joseph pulled her into his arms for a kiss, she drowned in his mocha flesh. She closed her eyes, savoring the feel of the blunt part of him pressed into her belly button. He nipped near her ear and licked her neck. He pulled the tender skin of her neck between his teeth, cupping her bottom and dragging her deeper into the sea of mocha. He lifted her from the floor, at the same time pinching the skin of her neck between his lips. He marked her, the pain sharply erotic, and when he had finished, she lay on the bed on her back.

Joseph pulled back enough for Kendall to settle her nerves in his smoldering eyes. He grinned, which relaxed the intensity of his expression. She laughed, happy that she had stayed.

Joseph used his knee to push her thighs apart. He sank between her legs, glanced up when he sensed her tension. The expression on her face gave him cause to wonder. He extended an arm to the bedside table. Within seconds, the latex barrier was in place.

He placed his knees on either side of her thighs and leaned down for a kiss. His fingers danced across her body in rhythm to the sounds floating from the living room. He lifted the weight of her breasts in his hands, bringing them up to meet his waiting mouth. His heat engulfed her nipples and spread furiously through her like wildfire. His mouth remained behind as skillful hands explored other parts of her body.

Kendall moaned at the sparkle of his touch. He touched her everywhere. Scalp, face, neck, breasts, ribs, belly, thighs, calves, feet. Back up to the place he had missed. The part of her body that screamed for him. He continued to suckle her breasts as one and then more fingers caressed the dark thatch of tiny, tight curls between her legs. Kendall lifted her hips, lost in the pleasure of it. He gave her more, peeling back the layers of her and delving deep to find her core.

Kendall released her hold on the sheets and cradled Joseph's head to her breasts. One long stroke and she called out, "Joseph."

His head snapped up and fire blazed within his eyes. He moved her thighs apart with his knee and sank between her legs. He strained to remain gentle, his body quaking as he guided himself into a pool flanked by tiny ringlets.

Kendall gasped and grabbed his shoulders. "Be gentle with me."

Something in her phrasing made him aware. "What is it?"

Kendall didn't answer. She kissed him.

Another inch. She went stock-still.

Joseph stayed suspended above her. "Kendall, what is it?" Realization. "Are you a virgin?"

Kendall nodded.

Joseph rolled away.

"Joseph?"

He glanced her way. "Don't say my name that way."

"What way?" She rolled to face him. He was breathing hard.

"Stop being sexy. I'm upset with you."

"Why?"

"You should have told me."

She couldn't read his eyes. "Why? Does it make a difference?"

"Yes, Kendall, it makes a difference. A huge difference." He propped himself up on his elbow and looked down at her. "You're twenty-five, you were in a serious relationship, why did you wait?"

"I planned to wait until I was married."

Joseph fell back on the bed, mumbling something.

"Joseph?"

"Let's get dressed."

"Wait." She caught his arm as he tried to climb out of bed. "Why don't you want me anymore? Because I'm a virgin?"

"Kendall." He caressed her chin, the mark he left on her neck. "If you planned to wait, we should wait. You can't go twenty-five years—as hard as that must have been in our world—and then throw away your values and beliefs. This isn't right, we'll wait."

"Joseph." She returned the caress. "It *is* right. I know what I want, and I want you. I want you to be the first person I give my body to."

Joseph shook his head. "You don't understand the magnitude of this decision."

"I don't?"

Their eyes met.

"Joseph, I do understand." Her hand traced curlicues down his abdomen. "I know how much I'm willing to give to be with you. Are you telling me that I made a bad decision? That you don't care about me as much as I sense you do? Are you saying that what I feel with you is wrong? That it isn't strong enough to sustain having sex?" The back of her hand brushed his jutting manhood. "Or is it that making love will make what we're feeling stronger?"

"Kendall—"

"Tell me, Joseph. I can't be strong for much longer." And she couldn't. If her judgment had become impaired again, she couldn't handle it. She'd made one mistake with Raven she'd always regret. Watching Joseph fight his emotions, she knew Raven would understand her wanting to move on with her life. She'd put everything on the line tonight; being wrong wasn't an option she'd survive.

Joseph cupped her behind, kissed her lips, and laid her beneath him. He continued to kiss her as he found his place again. Slowly, he entered her. She desired more. He gave her more by inches.

He whispered, "Relax."

She clung to his shoulders to keep from drowning. Her heart fluttered; she'd seen the full size of him naked, unobstructed. If they didn't fit . . .

"One second of pain and then this will feel *so* good. I promise." He flexed his hips.

"Joseph!"

"Shh." His lips found the sensitive area of her neck and concentrated kisses there. "One second." He flexed again and the pain was gone. "Are you all right, Kendall?"

A breathy "Yes."

"Breathe, princess." A low rumble next to her ear. "Breathe and enjoy me."

Joseph gave her more kisses as he worked his hips in a slow push-pull. Kendall felt full. The intensity of the pain subsided with his rocking motion. She closed her eyes and fought sensory overload. Joseph inside her, filling her, stretching her to the point of breaking. Joseph's lips roaming her body. Joseph's hands touching her breasts and pinching her nipples. Joseph's sweet words confusing her thoughts. Every nerve in her body pulsated.

"Kendall, look at me."

She opened her eyes. He wore a grin that was both devilish and concerned.

"Relax. Breathe, princess."

She took a deep breath and he pressed deeper.

"No, don't close your eyes. Watch me make love to you."

Watching the flickering flame of his smoldering eyes changed the full sensation to something altogether different. The fullness became a sensuous glide that didn't go deep enough to touch that special spot. Like an itch she couldn't scratch, she needed him to reach that one place. Her thighs moved apart, willing him deeper. Still he did not give her relief from the itch. He would plunge, close—very, very close—and then pull back, teasing her. The frenzy built with each stroke. She found she could tighten her muscles and hold him inside her.

"Joseph."

He sucked in a shallow breath. His body shook.

"Joseph."

Joseph's eyes lost focus and Kendall felt he was peering into her soul. His hips plunged deeper, faster. He cupped her bottom and lifted her from the bed to meet his stroke. He withdrew too far and plunged too deep, touching the spot that set off sparks in Kendall's body.

Kendall lost control of her body, her mind. Visions flashed too quickly for her to discern. Her body writhed and quivered. She pressed her lids together, fighting for control. An array of colors shimmered in the darkness. She collapsed in a heap, panting to catch her breath. Above her, Joseph's hips jerked at a rapid pace, losing the well-timed rhythm he had seconds before. His hips dipped and he submerged himself firmly inside her. He threw his head back and groaned until it sounded like a growl. He wrapped her caramel in the mocha of him, consuming the pain of her past.

Chapter 18

Joseph was humble when educating Kendall in the sensitive subject of after-sex hygiene. He ignored her embarrassment as they shared the bathroom, teaching her the must-dos. He soothed her when he soaped her back in the shower. He reassured her when he changed the sheets, removing trace evidence of her inexperience. He whispered how lucky he had been for her to choose him as he tucked her into his bed.

Kendall fell asleep as soon as he cut the lights. Watching her, he knew he would do anything to help her overcome her fears and regain her life. This woman had touched him, a caress across his soul, as no woman had ever been able to do. This woman, fifteen years his junior, made him feel it was okay to break all the rules.

Joseph relived every minute of their night together. Until this moment, his greatest achievement had been his flying career. Kendall stepped into his life and changed his entire value system.

If he weren't strong and up to the challenges ahead, fear would have driven him away tonight. Their relationship progressed much too fast. The emotions swimming between them were too intense, dangerous. Kendall had issues. He had grown to believe he couldn't love a woman as much as he loved flying. When things became thick between them, Kendall had jumped right in, not fretting long-term consequences. How could he not jump in after her? Everything and everybody who would get in their way be damned—Kendall made him feel too good to let her go.

"I want you to be the first person I give my body to," Kendall had told him, her pretty eyes revealing the truth of it. A rush of emotions flooded the area around his heart. How special she made him feel. He had asked her if she understood the magnitude of what she was offering—did he? Truly? He stroked the possessive mark he left on her neck. Something primal chased the flowery emotions away and he vowed no other man would ever touch her body.

"Kendall?" His fingers fanned across her cheek until her eyes opened at half-mast.

"Yes, Joseph?"

The way she said his name! Her voice skipped across the nerves in his arms.

"Kendall, I was your first. I want to be your last."

She smiled, her eyes drifting closed. "Yes, Joseph."

Chapter 19

"You're doing so well today." Joseph turned around to check Kendall while waiting for the stoplight to change.

"This is a piece of cake."

Joseph chuckled and eased off the brake.

Kendall sat forward and wrapped her arms around the headrest. Joseph's heart lifted. She hadn't asked him to pull over once—and he had had to stop only one time this morning when driving her to work at the gallery.

"Can we make a stop before you take me home?" Kendall asked.

"Of course."

"Make a right at the next intersection."

Joseph did as instructed. "Where are we going?"

"A right at the next light." Kendall settled back in her seat. "We've talked about my parents, right?"

"Yes, but you haven't given me details."

"There's a good reason for that." She waited until Joseph completed the right turn. "Two blocks up and then make a left."

"Your parents?" he coaxed.

"We'll talk about it later. It's the corner house on the right."

Joseph pulled to a stop in front of a compact redbrick colonial. The yard was meticulously kept. The homes on the street were closely packed, each resembling the others—the epitome of the planned community. Every lawn was well manicured, many with colorful flowers or neatly trimmed bushes. Other than a barking dog, the street was quiet.

"Who lives here?" Joseph asked, ducking his head to check out the house.

"My dad. I'd like you to meet him."

"Are you sure?" For Joseph this meant Kendall wanted him in her life for a long time.

"I'm sure." She pulled her eyes away from the house. "I haven't seen him since immediately after the accident. This might be tense. I'd understand if you didn't want to go in."

"If you want me there, then I'm there. It's your call."

"I want you there." She paused. "It might be tense on another level, too."

Joseph turned toward her and waited.

"My mom and dad were very much in love when they got married, but they *had* to get married—if you know what I mean. My mom was pregnant with me. They were going to be married anyway—eventually, after college— so it's not like they were forced."

"It's happened to many couples."

"My mom was sixteen when she got pregnant with me. My dad was seventeen."

"Seventeen?" Joseph did the math. "Your father is forty-two years old? *My age?*"

"Don't get upset, Joseph. There won't be a problem. I just wanted to prepare you."

"Not a problem? What do you think your father will say when you waltz in the door, after disappearing for a year, with a man who is only two years younger than him? I'll be lucky if he only calls the cops. If it were my daughter, I'd shoot the son of a—"

"Joseph!"

"Oh, man." Joseph dropped his head back. "I'm old enough to be your father."

"Joseph, stop trippin'." Kendall poked fun at him.

"What does that mean?"

Kendall laughed outright. "It means stop worrying. And you don't know what that means because you're a nerd, not because of your age. My dad will be grateful to you for bringing me home after all this time. He's really cool. You'll have a lot in common."

"You aren't cute." Joseph jumped out of the SUV and hurried to open her door. "The least you could do is wait for me to open your door. I don't want your dad to think I'm a louse."

"What does that mean? A louse?"

"Not funny." Joseph took her hand and let her lead him up the walk.

Kendall's father pulled the door open and wrapped her in his embrace. The moment lasted a long time. Joseph turned away, offering them a measure of privacy, when they both became teary eyed.

"I'm so glad you're all right. I've missed you." He stepped back and took a good look at his daughter. "As pretty as ever." He acknowledged Joseph for the first time with a glance past Kendall's shoulder.

Kendall stepped aside. "Daddy, this is my friend Joseph."

His eyes flashed to Kendall, catching the hitch in her words. He took a cautious step toward Joseph with an outstretched hand. "Friend?"

Their hands met to shake as Kendall said, "We're dating."

Kendall's father stiffened and he worked hard at removing the disdain around his bearded lips. "I guess it would be silly for you to call me Mr. Masterson like Kendall's other boyfriends. Call me Frank."

And things went downhill from there.

Kendall didn't see it. She bounced through the house showing Joseph around while Frank's eyes burned a hole in his back. Reuniting with her father lifted her spirits. Another necessary step in her healing process and Joseph supported that. He'd drop her at her father's house every day if she wanted, but he wanted to get out as quickly as possible right now. A showdown brewed with every sip of beer the two men took and Joseph didn't have enough clout in Kendall's life to win the fight.

"Why don't you have dinner with me, Kendall?" Frank asked. The invitation did not include Joseph. "Your *young* man—" He overcorrected himself. "I mean, Joseph can come back for you. Or I can drive you home."

"No. Joseph can stay. We were going to dinner anyway." Kendall moved away from her father on the sofa and sat on the arm of Joseph's chair. His arm went around her waist by instinct, before Frank's scowl told him he made a grave error.

"Do you need help in the kitchen, Daddy?"

"No." He lifted himself from the sofa. "I can do it."

"We'll set the table," Kendall offered.

Joseph held a stack of plates and a bundle of silverware as he followed Kendall around the square glass dining room table that comfortably seated four. Although Joseph doubted that egos would barely allow room for three at this dinner.

"Kendall, I should go. Let you catch up with your father. You can call me when you're ready to leave."

"That's silly. You're here and you have to eat. I want you to get to know my father."

"He doesn't want to get to know me," Joseph mumbled. He didn't blame him.

Kendall turned to address his concerns, but Frank interrupted with a call for help from the kitchen. "Have a seat." She left him with a quick kiss on the lips.

Frank sat directly across from Joseph at dinner. Kendall sat between them to Joseph's left. They labored politely over gravy-soaked roast beef, baked potatoes, green beans, and Pillsbury biscuits. Polite compliments were paid to Frank. After that, the conversation became too strained for Joseph's participation.

Frank deliberately reminisced about Kendall's past—areas of her life that Joseph wouldn't have knowledge about. It bothered Joseph at first, but the way Kendall lit up and laughed was enough to soothe his anger. He planted his elbow on the table and gazed at Kendall's profile as she giggled about her childhood antics. Joseph smiled at her happiness over reuniting with her father. This wasn't Frank's plan and he switched to a more offensive topic when he observed Joseph's lingering gaze on his daughter.

"Darren stopped by last weekend."

"Daddy." Kendall's eyes darted in Joseph's direction and her body became tight.

Frank pushed the issue. "He asked about you. I told him to call you."

"Daddy." Kendall patted her hand with his. "Not appropriate." She paused briefly before trying to change the subject. "Joseph, did I tell you my dad was in the marines?"

"No, you didn't." Joseph remained cordial although Frank had hit his mark by mentioning Kendall's last boyfriend, Darren.

Kendall turned to her father. At the mention of his military past, his chest swelled. "You two have a lot in common. Daddy, Joseph was in the air force. You always said the air force bailed your troop out more times than you can count."

Frank's chest deflated. Kendall had served her father the ultimate insult. No military people wanted to be told that they had to be rescued by another branch of the service. He turned sharply to Joseph. "How old are you anyway?"

"Daddy!"

Joseph touched Kendall's hand, and remained calm. "Forty."

"Forty?" Frank turned to Kendall. "Forty! I'm forty-two, Kendall. What are you doing?"

Joseph tried to keep things under control. "I understand you might be worried—"

"Do you?" Frank pushed his plate away. "How many children do you have, Joseph?"

"None."

"Then you can't understand. Kendall has been through too much the past year. Almost more than she could handle and remain sane. I was afraid I had lost her and when I knew I hadn't, I didn't know what shape she'd be in. All this time after the accident, I still worry. Kendall has a great deal of emotional healing ahead of her."

"Daddy, I'm doing much better."

His icy stare went between Kendall and Joseph. "I'm not too sure of that. This man is old enough to be your— How serious is this? How far has this gone?"

Kendall answered in defiance. "You're being inappropriate."

"Stop telling me that, Kendall. I'm your father. It's impossible for me to be inappropriate when it comes to your well-being."

Kendall stood slowly. "Joseph, we should go."

Joseph followed her lead.

"I'll call you in a couple of days." Kendall kissed her father's cheek before leaving the house.

Joseph debated if he should try to make her father feel better about their relationship. Not knowing him well enough, he deferred to Kendall. She felt it best to leave: he left.

At the car, Joseph looked back to see Frank watching them.

Kendall giggled when they reached the car. "That went well."

"You call that going well?" Joseph asked, perplexed at her reaction.

"Yes. You should see what he usually does when I bring a man home."

"This may be different, Kendall." Joseph glanced back and decided he didn't want to know about Frank's normal reaction. He pressed the button on his key ring that released the locks and disarmed the security system.

"No," Kendall said when he opened the back door, "I'd like to ride up front with you this time."

Chapter 20

"Kendall," Joseph called, pacing in a rectangular pattern at the bottom of her stairs. The second he had pulled his SUV into her driveway, she jumped out and darted inside. By the time he cut the engine she had retreated upstairs.

The drive from her father's house had been hard on her. He pulled over to the curb five times, but she refused to give up and sit in the backseat. The last time he sat in the grass next to her, stroking her back as she suffered through dry heaves. Embarrassment, frustration, and pride pushed Kendall to angrily shun him. She had pushed his hand away, telling him not to "baby" her. Her words sliced his pride in two dimensions: the reference to their age difference and her rejection of his affection. Joseph had given her space by walking back to the SUV and leaning against the body of the vehicle until she stood from the grass, signaling she was ready to leave. She stepped up into the SUV muttering her apology.

Joseph stopped at the bottom of the stairs again. He checked his watch; twenty minutes had passed. "Kendall," he called, "are you all right up there?"

"Hi."

Joseph swung around. Standing underneath the archway was a man much smaller than he. The man remotely resembled Kendall, and Joseph assumed him to be a relative. He approached with an outstretched hand. "I'm Joseph Stewart."

"Captain Joseph Stewart," the man said, his eyes flashing in a way that confused Joseph. He had seen the expression before, but only on the faces of women that found him attractive. "I'm Max. The next-door neighbor."

"Kendall has mentioned you." She didn't mention the fact that her friend, confidant, and neighbor was a man.

"Is there a problem? I heard you calling for Kendall when I came in."

A second of debate before Joseph boldly asked, "How did you get in? I didn't leave the door open."

"I have a key." Max dangled the key in front of Joseph's face before returning it to his pocket.

Joseph's mission became to relieve Max of his key.

"What's going on?" Max asked again.

"Everything's fine." Joseph covered up the seriousness of the situation. He was worried about Kendall, but his pride wouldn't let another man resolve the problem. He sized up Max and his potential threat to what he was trying to build with Kendall. Max appeared to be much closer to Kendall's age—he couldn't do anything about that. He could wedge himself between them, placing himself in the position of being Kendall's friend and supporter.

"Thanks for stopping in." Joseph unceremoniously dismissed Max.

Max glanced toward the staircase. "Maybe I should go up and check on her."

"I really don't think that'll be necessary." Joseph slipped his hands into his pants pockets.

"I need to talk to Kendall about something."

Joseph didn't back down. "Kendall's had a hard day."

Max silently considered his options. Joseph burned his eyes into him, telepathically explaining that the matter had been decided—Max wouldn't be seeing Kendall this evening. She had forbade Joseph to come up; Max certainly wouldn't get past him.

"I guess I'll check on her in the morning." Max made a semiturn before delivering his last power play. "I know what Kendall needs me to do. I'll gather a few things and get going. If you would deliver a message? Tell her I'm running her errands in the morning and I'll see her after work."

"Errands?" Joseph took a quick step toward Max, startling him.

"She'll know what I mean," Max answered smugly.

"I'd like to know what you mean."

Max's eyes roamed his body.

"Let me be blunt," Joseph said, meeting the silent challenge of his authority. "I'm seeing Kendall now and I don't like other men hanging around interfering—"

"Interfering?" Max asked, indignant.

"Maybe that's too strong a word to describe your friendship. You're Kendall's neighbor and friend and I respect that. I want to be certain that you respect my relationship with her. We both need clarity on where we fit into her life. I appreciate everything you've been doing for Kendall, but I'll be here now and can handle what she needs."

"You're saying I no longer have a place in Kendall's life."

"Your role has been greatly reduced now that I'm here." Joseph had no intention on fighting this man over Kendall's affection. He wanted the ground rules established early and clearly. He would never be the victim of "It just happened" or "We were only friends but things got out of hand."

"You're speaking for Kendall?" Max questioned Joseph's possessive attitude. He knew this relationship had only begun and didn't understand why Joseph felt he had the right to step in and become ruler of Kendall's castle.

"I speak for myself." Joseph quickly added, "But I'll discuss it with Kendall tonight."

Max had no alternative but to walk away from this fight. He'd talk to Kendall alone and tell her how Joseph confronted him. Only Kendall could shift the boundaries of their friendship.

"I really care for Kendall," Max stated. "I'm sorry we aren't going to be able to be friends, Joseph."

Joseph shook off the sting of Max's words. He had made an unprovoked attack on the man. Later, when his relationship with Kendall was on solid footing, he'd make an attempt at mending the rift. Right now, he was fighting a battle to win her over and Max had unwittingly become a casualty of the war. Shaking Max from his mind, Joseph called for Kendall again. "Kendall, please come down and talk with me."

No response.

"Kendall Masterson, if you don't answer me, I'm coming up. I'm worried about you."

Kendall's bedroom door opened, adding a slice of light to the hallway. Joseph released a sigh of relief. He waited anxiously for her to appear. She took the stairs slowly. She had changed into a sweatshirt and jean shorts. Her face was free of makeup.

Kendall stopped on the last step directly in front of Joseph. "I didn't mean to worry you."

Joseph grasped her waist and lifted her into his arms. He held her against him as he consumed her mouth. He nibbled her bottom lip before sending his tongue probing inside her mouth. He crushed her in his arms, savoring the feel of her curves against his muscular mass.

After the dazzling kiss, he set her on the floor. "You have to stop running away from me."

Kendall moved around him.

Joseph followed her into the living room and they sat together. "What's the first step in making this better?"

"I don't know. I wish I did. The doctors said carsickness isn't caused by anything medical. They say it's related to the stress of the accident: post-traumatic stress disorder."

"Can I help? There has to be something I can do."

Kendall snuggled into the crook of his shoulder. "You've done enough."

"I don't feel like I've helped at all. Surely your father will have words with you because he doesn't approve of me. And now you're carsick."

"Today was good for me. I needed to make contact with my father again, and truthfully, I didn't want to see him alone. I'm not ready to hash everything out yet. I only wanted to extend the olive branch—let him know that I'm trying to correct my mistakes. The more I get into a car, the better the sickness gets. I know it doesn't look that way to you, but this episode wasn't as bad as I'm used to."

"That's where we'll start then. Every day I'll come over and we'll go for a drive. As your tolerance increases we'll drive farther and farther. Soon enough you'll be behind the wheel driving yourself around the city."

Kendall gazed up at him, unsure.

"We'll take it slow," Joseph reassured her. "You'll dictate the pace."

"Thank you."

"How does my proposition sound?"

"I'll try."

"That's all I ask." Joseph unpacked the bags containing their dinner.

Kendall went to the stereo and turned the radio on a jazz station. Her diversity delighted him.

Kendall returned and Joseph filled their plates with Chinese takeout. "What do we do about your father?"

"I'll handle my father." Her callous tone made him jerk his head. She waved away his concern. "My father and I have things we need to work out between us. His rudeness had nothing to do with you, believe me."

"I don't know, Kendall. If you were my daughter I would be upset too."

"Believe me, it'll be fine." Realizing the urgency in her voice, she smiled.

She lit the candles lining the mantel, then snuggled in Joseph's arms, listening to jazz swirl around them. He pulled her against the terrain of his chest, providing her with the quiet strength she needed.

"You know, it'll make you feel better to talk about your sister and the accident." He kissed the top of her head. "Holding it all inside will only eat you alive. Share your memories of your sister with me."

Kendall disclosed her guilt about her sister's death as the candlelight flickered across Joseph's dark skin. He listened patiently, offering silent reassurance by patting her hand. She felt revived after purging her soul. Joseph didn't judge her or try to offer pat solutions to her problem. He let her work through her issues, vowing to support her in whatever decisions she made.

Joseph's presence served as an aphrodisiac to Kendall. She wondered if he ever needed someone to lean on. Probably not, considering his work. She imagined he ruled his aircraft with quiet dominance. Not many would dare challenge him. She remembered how his temper flared when they went to the movies and wondered what had happened that day to make him react so uncharacteristically.

Joseph broke into her thoughts. "Your neighbor dropped by while you were upstairs."

"Max?"

"Yes. He said he'd talk with you later."

Kendall didn't respond.

"He's a friend?"

She nodded against his chest.

"He had a key," Joseph probed.

"I have a key to his place too. It's a long story." She didn't want to dwell in self-pity all evening. The episode with Greg and the police was a reminder of hitting bottom.

Joseph tabled that discussion and moved on to a more important topic. "My furlough ends this weekend."

Kendall sat up abruptly. "What does that mean?"

"I'll be back in the air on Monday."

"What does that mean?" She lifted her thumbs to the tiny twin pockets beneath his eyes, more proof of his distinction.

"It means we have very little uninterrupted time together left and I'd like to spend every second of it with you." He ran his hands down her arms and grasped her hands. "That's *all* it means."

"Once you go back to work, how often will I see you?"

"Depends on my flight schedule. I'm usually the go-to guy. The other pilots have family and commitments, so I'm asked to take extra flights quite a bit."

Kendall turned against his chest to look up into his fiery eyes. "We haven't been seeing each other very long, and I . . . I was rather forward the other night."

He smiled.

"I'm inexperienced but I'm not naive. I know how this can turn out. I'd always heard other women talk about how they could instinctively feel if they had the right guy to lose their virginity to, but I never really believed them.

With you, I learned they were right. I wanted it to happen and I'm glad it did—no matter what happens between us from here on."

"Kendall, princess, I'm going to work. I'm not leaving you. This—you and me—we're only getting started. I plan to be around for a long, long time." He wrapped his arms around her. "I think I'll start refusing the extra flights. If you don't mind me hanging out on your doorstep."

Kendall watched the movement of his lips with each word. She placed her palm against his cheek, comparing her caramel skin against his mocha complexion. Being this close she could smell the intoxicating scent of his aftershave. Her hand slipped to the smooth surface of his squared chin.

"Kendall," Joseph said in a husky hush, "why don't you just kiss me?"

Her eyes flickered. She placed her hands on his cheeks and moved over him. She pressed her chest against his for balance and received a shock of sexual electricity. She tilted her head and lowered to meet his lips. He remained still, allowing her to explore. She kissed the thin lines on each side of his mouth. She flicked her tongue against the fullness of his sweet brown lips. She snaked her tongue into his mouth, setting off an explosion in Joseph.

His arms went around her waist, pressing her tightly against him. His breathing rapid, he kissed her with a fervor that told her he had worried about their future too. In one sweep, Joseph switched their positions. He buried her body with his. His randomly placed kisses were distracting her from the deft movements of his fingers.

He cupped her breast and her nipple hardened immediately. He twisted and tugged until she found her hands on his shoulders, pulling him downward to apply the suction of his mouth. This new boldness came as the result of his passion-kisses. When his lips pressed against her mouth, a special place between her thighs responded to the caress.

Joseph's hands bunched the edge of her sweatshirt and pushed it above her head. His tongue left a wet trail down to her navel. Kendall's legs parted and Joseph immediately took refuge there. She liked the sensations shooting through her body. His bulge sank into her cavern and he rocked to demonstrate the perfect fit.

"Kendall," Joseph, breathless, whispered next to her ear, "we have to stop this."

"Why?" Kendall, breathless, whispered next to his ear.

"I don't have any protection."

As wonderful as Joseph's teasing made her feel, Kendall was not emotionally ready for the complications of bringing children into the relationship. She needed to date Joseph, get to know him better, if she expected longevity. Since meeting him, her life seemed to be speeding along and she didn't want to lose control. Returning to work, agreeing to go for a drive every day, dating, sharing her body for the first time—it overwhelmed her to think about it all.

Joseph pressed his forehead to hers. "Your silence tells me I should be heading home for the night."

"I—"

He pressed his lips to hers. "No explanation is needed."

Joseph helped to repair Kendall's clothes before coaxing her to walk him to the door. They stood in the foyer, his arms draped around her waist. "I'll see you in the morning." He had taken over Greg's job of driving her to and from work. "I'll be pretty busy getting ready for work, so I won't be able to take you out Sunday night. How about we see that movie I promised you tomorrow?"

"I'd like that."

"Me too." He transferred his desire in a kiss.

From the other side of the screen, Joseph turned and asked, "Would you like to spend my last night of vacation with me?"

Kendall smiled. "I would."

"I'll plan something special. You pack a bag and plan to spend the night at my house."

Chapter 21

Greg waddled into Kendall's work area. His puffy cheeks looked more pronounced, burying his sparkling eyes behind the excess flesh. "I'm about to call it a day. Do you need a ride home?"

Kendall placed the ruby necklace carefully on a beige cloth before she removed the magnification goggles from her eyes. "No. I asked Joseph to come at seven."

"Seven, hmmm." Greg rubbed the seams of his pants. "What is it? I know that sound."

"Will Joseph be driving you to work every morning?" Greg asked with an edge.

Kendall turned at the unprovoked hostility. "What's bothering you?"

"I'm worried about you, Kendall. Joseph seems to be controlling every aspect of your life these days."

Kendall wrapped the tarnished necklace in its cloth. "Controlling? Joseph helps me out a lot, yes. I don't like the undertones of what you're saying."

Greg waited for Kendall to pack the necklace in its box and lock it in the safe before he launched his argument. "You and I have always been brutally honest with each other. There's no need to change that policy now."

"No, there's not. Say what's on your mind." Kendall returned to her seat, fully prepared for Greg's harsh assessment.

"I'm worried about the dynamics between you and Joseph."

"You don't know what the dynamics are between Joseph and me."

"I know he drives you to and from the gallery every day. He runs all your errands while you're at work and spends the entire evening with you after work. He's even answering your phone! Do you know I called you last night and he had the nerve to tell me you were too busy to come to the phone?"

"Maybe I was."

"That's not the point. The point is he feels he has enough authority in your life to make that decision for you. He should have *asked* you if you could take my call."

Kendall tightened her arms in a pretzel across her chest. "So this is all about the fact that you couldn't reach me on my own time."

"You know better than that." Greg stalked up to where she sat. "How long have you been seeing Joseph? Two weeks? Two weeks, yet he's already taken over every corner of your life."

"C'mon, Greg. You're not being fair to Joseph. I don't understand you. You're the one always telling me to start living again. I really enjoy spending time with Joseph. He makes me feel special. I've told him everything— *everything*—and he supports me. Why don't you trust my judgment? Why aren't you supporting me on my choosing him?"

"I'm afraid that he's controlling you and you don't see it. Older men like to be in charge. They set boundaries early and if you don't put a stop to this . . . I don't know how far it'll go."

Kendall could see that he was genuinely worried about her. "Greg," she said and lowered her voice to diffuse the argument, "Joseph has been nothing but a gentleman. He's kind and supportive and gentle. He would never try to control me. We're at the beginning stage of our relationship and he's allowing me time to adjust. He doesn't pressure me in the least."

"My wife knows Joseph by association."

And now Kendall would learn the true source of Greg's worries. She waited for him to continue.

"She and Sara sit on the board of the museum together. Sara is Russ's wife. Russ is Joseph's best friend."

This sounded like the high school grapevine. The worried expression covering Greg's face made Kendall keep that thought to herself.

Greg went on. "Women love Captain Joseph Stewart."

"What are you saying, Greg? And be careful here. Don't make accusations you can't substantiate."

"All I'm saying is that he's one of the most eligible bachelors at the airline and women know it. They chase after him shamelessly."

Kendall came to Joseph's defense. "Why hold that against him?"

"I just want you to be careful. Know this man well before you let your emotions become involved. Consider the possibility that some of these advances by other women might not be shunned."

Kendall stood and draped her arm over his shoulder. Brutal honesty hurt every time. She knew Greg wanted only the best for her—he considered her his daughter. She would accept his warning with the good nature in which he intended, but he was wrong about Joseph. "I know you're coming to me about this because you're my friend, but don't worry."

"How can I not worry?"

Kendall climbed up on her stool again. "How can I prove Joseph's intentions are honorable?"

"I'm inviting you to dinner tonight with me and

Madge. The three of us haven't had dinner together in a long time."

Kendall's fingers went to the nape of her neck. "I already have plans tonight."

Greg shook his head. "With Joseph."

"Yes. His vacation will end soon and I want to spend as much time as possible with him."

"Okay." Greg looked defeated. "You're a grown woman and have to make your own decisions. I can only tell you when I'm worried. See you Monday morning."

Kendall called after him, "Don't be mad at me, Greg."

He kept walking. "I'm not mad. Brutally honest, remember? Don't you be mad at me."

"I'm not mad. Joseph is a good man," Kendall called as Greg pulled the door up behind him.

"I need to drop these off and pick these up." Joseph dumped the laundry bag on the countertop.

"Kendall Masterson," the man read from the dry-cleaning slip. "I miss her coming in. How come Max isn't getting her stuff? Is he okay?"

Joseph debated whether to answer the teenager behind the counter. "Max is fine."

The boy waited for more of an explanation, and when none came he turned and searched the rack for Kendall's clothing. "Here we go. Do you want to check the order?"

Joseph shook his head no.

"Okay, don't come back yelling at me if your daughter gets upset that something's missing."

Joseph froze, casting an evil scowl across the counter.

The young man stepped back. "Sorry, man."

Joseph paid the bill and hurried out the door. He had to stop letting innocent comments stress him out. The effects on his blood pressure were still a concern. The teenage boy had no way of knowing what kind of relationship he had with Kendall. Besides, who cared what others thought about him dating Kendall? She had assured him on two separate occasions that she had no problem with the fifteen-year age difference. Every time he thought of her warm smile and pretty brown eyes, long-forgotten emotions bathed him. Other people's opinions would not deter him in pursuing happiness with Kendall.

Joseph's next stop was the grocery store. He hated grocery stores. He muddled up and down the aisles— some twice because he couldn't find the things Kendall asked him to pick up. After soliciting the store manager's help, he completed her list. With that done, he searched for the things he needed for their day together. He had already stopped at the sporting goods store and by Russ's to borrow the tent. He quickly gathered what he needed, careful to watch the time because he didn't want to be late picking up Kendall from work. After completing his mission, he headed for the checkout.

Joseph couldn't believe his eyes. There were twenty-plus lanes in the superstore, but only four were open and two of those were for orders of fifteen items or less. He wheeled his basket into the shortest line and waited. The woman in front of him had a toddler that kept running away from her and returning with opened packages of goodies that he dropped at Joseph's feet. She also had a newborn that refused to stop screaming strapped in the car seat on the shopping cart.

Joseph's temple began to throb as his patience unraveled. He had finally reached the front of the line and was unloading his purchases when he remembered that he forgot to pick up the cosmetic items on Kendall's list. He discarded the idea of getting out of line, wheeling to the back of the store where the mini drugstore was, and having to get back in the long, twisting line.

"Don't grocery stores have bag boys?" Joseph asked as his food began to back up on the conveyor belt.

"They come in after they get out of school in the afternoon," the cashier answered.

Joseph checked his watch. It was well past the time he used to get out of school. "Where are they?"

"They come in after their after-school activities." The cashier continued to send his food down the conveyor belt only for it to join the growing mound. The bread was in danger of being smashed. A box of cereal toppled over, landing behind the counter, where the cashier stepped back onto it. A carton of fresh strawberries burst open under the pressure and berries rolled across the floor, where the mischievous toddler snatched them up and stuffed them into his mouth.

Joseph huffed as he pulled the plastic bags from the holder and started bagging his own groceries. He couldn't complain. Max had been doing this job. Joseph had insisted on taking on the added responsibility. Noting the tension mounting in his shoulders, he considered giving the tasks back to Max. Knowing Kendall would appreciate his efforts, he discarded that idea and hurried from the store.

Joseph remembered seeing a drugstore not too far from the gallery. He'd swing by there and get the rest of the things on Kendall's list before picking her up.

The pace at the drugstore was much less overwhelming than the superstore. Joseph took his time moving down the aisles, being careful to pick up everything on Kendall's list.

On the way to the checkout, Joseph passed a display rack of condoms. He scratched at his mustache, thinking of the night he had to walk away from Kendall's luscious body because he wasn't prepared. He wouldn't let that happen again. He stood in awe looking at all of the packages. There were too many choices—not like when he and his high school buddies came to the store in groups for moral support. Or they picked up whatever was available at the gas station.

He scanned the selections. Brand. Number contained in the box. Color. *Color?* Texture. Lubricated. Not lubricated. Reservoir tip or tipless. To spermicide or not to spermicide? It became confusing, as he stood there distracted by the anticipation of their use.

What is the proper etiquette regarding condom use these days? Joseph wondered. With him being Kendall's first lover came the responsibility to protect her in ways she might be naive about. It was his responsibility to purchase them. Luck had found him the night they ended up at his place—he hadn't planned on making love to Kendall this soon and was thankful his hand didn't come back empty when he rummaged through the bedside table. Exactly how long would he have to wear a condom with Kendall? Would she choose to use any other form of birth control? He already craved the ability to feel her tighten uninhibited against his instrument. Skin to skin without any barriers.

They should have had a serious discussion about it all by now. His head was clouded by her sensuality. The idea of having a baby had crossed his mind more and more often since meeting Kendall. He wanted to hold a baby in his arms that he had made before his age didn't allow him the opportunity. Like his parents, he wanted at *least* four children. He looked forward to playing sports with his sons. He would teach his daughters everything they needed to make it in the world when the odds were against them. He would love his kids and make a good home for them just as his parents had done for him. He smiled at the thought of Kendall's belly carrying his child.

"Slow down," Joseph scolded himself. He and Kendall had a long way to go before children entered the picture.

He called his attention back to the pressing issue. He had been standing in the aisle for a long time surveying the boxes. He scanned the rack again, still at a loss. He plucked four boxes off the display and went to the counter. He'd let Kendall choose. Maybe they would try them all and decide together.

Chapter 22

Joseph arrived at dawn, as excited as Kendall was about their special day together. He had stopped at his favorite Coney Island restaurant and picked up breakfast. They ate at her compact dining room table.

"Give me a hint."

"No. Stop asking," Joseph teased, lifting a glass of orange juice to his smiling lips.

"A little hint? I'll give you a kiss."

"Give me the kiss first." Joseph pushed his chair back from the table and helped Kendall into his lap.

She wrapped her arms around his neck and gave him a kiss that made his head swim. "Give me the hint now."

"You're going to have lots and lots of fun."

Kendall swatted at his arms. "You cheated."

"I gave you your hint." Joseph laughed, fighting her off.

After the breakfast dishes had been cleaned, Joseph went through Kendall's CDs and selected a few to take along on their outing. Dressed in a pale yellow blouse and golden shorts that made her skin glow, Kendall went to grab a light jacket while Joseph leafed through her music collection. The day promised to be eighty degrees and sunny, but the sun was only beginning to push away the moon and there was a chill in the air.

Kendall stepped out into the warm breeze of the early morning.

"Lock the door, princess." Joseph held the screen open while she did so.

"What's that?" Kendall asked as they descended the stairs together. A small trailer was hitched to the back of his gleaming red SUV.

"That's part of your surprise."

"Still no hint?"

"If you give me a kiss—"

"No way." Already, he had her face aching from too many smiles.

Joseph held the front passenger door open. Kendall looked up into his insightful gaze.

"You can do it." Strong conviction lay behind by his soft tone.

Kendall studied the lines of his face. She ingested the hope in his eyes.

"The other day was a fluke. You can do this." His firm touch pressed into the small of her back.

She could do this. With his support, she could do it. He had helped her accomplish so much already.

"Okay?"

"Okay." Kendall took a deep breath and climbed up into the SUV.

Joseph secured her seat belt before closing the door. He crossed behind the SUV and slid into the driver's seat. With a flip of the key, the engine purred. "Ready for your adventure?"

Kendall understood he was asking about more than the day ahead of them. "I'm ready." And she was, her confidence in Joseph boosting the confidence she had in herself. The incidents of carsickness were decreasing. She could get to work without making any stops. She wanted this special day with Joseph and she wouldn't let a car ride keep her from it.

The drive lasted forty-five minutes. There was one

shaky moment about halfway to their destination, but Kendall rolled down her window and drank up the cool air and it passed. Now she watched Joseph rounding the SUV to open her door. She stepped out into the blazing sun and warm temperature. She took in Joseph from head to toe from behind her sunglasses. Tall, darker than chocolate—sweeter, too—distinguishing gray specks at his temples, and lethally sexy eyes shielded from the public with dark glasses, Joseph kept her heart in a constant state of fluctuation.

Located in a suburb of Detroit, Kensington Park was made up of acres of sand and greenery. The water shimmered and the grass was a rich, dark green. There were plenty of picnic tables. Boating, walking trails, the beach, and the golf course were only some of the things that attracted a hearty summer crowd.

"I've never been in this part of Kensington before," Kendall remarked, following Joseph to the miniature trailer on the back of the Mercedes SUV.

"The coast guard doesn't open this section to the public." He fiddled with the lock.

"Then what are we doing here?"

The lock came free. "I have a friend in the coast guard." He worked at opening the trailer doors. "There's a beautiful stretch of land here that ends at a private beach area. We can stay as long as we want."

"Are you going to tell me what's in here now?"

"Yes." Joseph opened the twin doors and pulled down a ramp before climbing inside. After undoing some latches and cords, he rolled a motorcycle down the ramp.

Kendall knew absolutely nothing about motorcycles, but this one was superb. The luxuriously rich red bike was trimmed in shining chrome.

"This is my other baby." Joseph winked at her.

They spent time going over the features of the fully

restored Harley. Picking the Harley out of a junkyard after a crash that had left it totaled, Joseph spent a year putting it back into its original condition. Then he added a security system, sleek custom saddle, stereo, and twin saddlebags.

Kendall ran her fingers along the chrome. "This is great." She bent to examine the detail. "You did a wonderful job." Restoring art for a living, she appreciated fine work when she found it. "You never stop surprising me."

"I hope not. Are you ready?"

"For what?"

"I'm taking you for a ride on my hog."

"Oh, no. I've never ridden on a motorcycle before."

Joseph began to push the bike onto a deserted trail. "This will be great. Nothing makes you feel freer than riding on the open road on a motorcycle. And with this weather—it's the perfect day for your first ride." He threw his leg over the bike. The muscled thigh strained against his jeans. "C'mon, Kendall. I'll go slow."

Kendall watched a seductive smile spread over Joseph's face. He dipped his head and watched her over the top of his dark glasses. The smoldering eyes and gleaming smile posed a double threat that Kendall couldn't resist. She threw caution to the wind and hopped onto the back of the bike.

"Ready?" Joseph asked Kendall after helping her secure her helmet.

"Ready as I'll ever be."

"Hold on around my waist. Lean your weight into me."

Kendall placed a vise grip around his tapered waist. "Don't go too fast."

They drove across the private footpaths, then down near the lapping waves. The ride was exhilarating! Soon Kendall was screaming for Joseph to go faster and faster.

The wind gave way, bouncing off their bodies as they moved through time and space. Crystallized rays emanated from the river. Joseph's body heat teased Kendall's senses. The charge of the Harley's power rippled over her skin.

That ride on Joseph's Harley released something in Kendall she didn't realize she still possessed—joy.

After their ride, Kendall helped Joseph wipe the dirt away from his Harley. Then they locked it in the trailer and Joseph surprised her again. He produced two bathing suits and towels. They changed inside the coast guard station and went for a swim. The matching suits were conservative, blue and white, Kendall's not revealing excessive female flesh. Joseph's trunks were conservatively cut also, but his sinewy legs were muscularly obscene.

Joseph wrapped his arm around Kendall's waist and pulled her against him when the men on duty at the coast guard station gawked at her. He bristled with jealousy. Knowing that the brave, suave Captain Joseph Stewart didn't want other men commenting on her visual assets gave Kendall a new power she enjoyed. He led her to the water, where she confessed she wasn't the best swimmer. But Joseph had learned in the air force and was an excellent swimmer.

"Am I ever going to have the chance to teach you anything?" Kendall asked as they swam together, Joseph very close to her in the water.

"You've taught me more than you'll ever know," was his serious reply.

A man who possessed knowledge and freely shared it was the sexiest man of all. Kendall liked to learn new things, had a hidden sense of adventure. Joseph openly gave to her from his world and she rewarded him with a kiss. Each time she met the tenderness of his lips, the dominance of his tongue, Kendall's emotions imploded and rocked her foundation. Joseph's touch screamed experience; his touch announced he worshipped her. Kendall didn't know if she would be able to endure the heat of their relationship, but she knew she'd never survive being without him.

"Wow. What was that for?"

"Complaining?" Kendall swam away, chasing the horizon.

"No, ma'am."

By early afternoon the sun perched directly over them. Joseph kept the surprises coming when he returned to the trailer for a picnic basket, cooler, hibachi, and tent.

"I borrowed this from my friend Russ. You know his wife, Sara. She introduced us at the museum."

A member of the high school grapevine. Kendall nodded and put up a mental block against Greg's words of concern.

"Russ and Sara are big campers. They've traveled all over the country, camped everywhere. He said this one is a snap to put up." Joseph fumbled for a minute before finding the button that made the tent pop into its intended dome shape, the dark material sure to block the heat of the sun. Kendall spread a blanket inside, covering the canvas flooring while Joseph fired up the hibachi.

Kendall explored the contents of the cooler, offering Joseph a bottle of cold water. She wiped his glistening forehead with a napkin. "Do you want some help with that?"

He smiled up at her and she wished she could see his eyes behind the dark glasses. "I can handle this, princess. Why don't you drape yourself across that blanket and give me motivation to get these steaks just right?"

"Oh, Captain Joseph Stewart! That was the most sexist thing you've ever said to me."

Joseph ducked the swat of her hand, laughing at the emergence of Kendall's true grit.

Kendall uncovered the delights inside the picnic basket while Joseph finished the steaks. When he was done, she served them both at the "table" set on the blanket outside the tent. The blazing sun didn't bother her as she feasted on the food that was second only to Joseph's smile. Crisp garden salad, fresh fruit dripping cool juices. Grilled steak and buttery corn on the cob. Cold pasta and scrumptious oatmeal raisin cookies. Kendall could only wallow in delight once she consumed it all.

"Joseph, you are going to make me fat if you keep feeding me like this. Did you cook all of this? The pasta? Cookies?"

"All of it—last night."

"Well, everything was wonderful."

"I'm not much of a cook so most of my first attempt went into the trash. But I had a cookbook and motivation to try, try again." He leaned over and gave her a quick kiss on the lips. "I'm glad you enjoyed it."

"I've enjoyed every second of this day. Thank you."

Joseph dipped his head; his eyes boldly roamed her body over the sunglasses, uncensored possession heating her skin. From deep in his throat, "It's hot and I can't afford too much more of a tan. Do you want to go inside?" He indicated the tent.

Inside, Joseph shed his shirt. Having thought of everything, he tied down the door of the tent and directed a battery-operated portable fan on them. He lay down on his back, one arm slung behind his head for support. "I'm stuffed."

Kendall joined him, using his shoulder for her pillow. She splayed her fingers across his abdomen, just below his rib cage. She marveled over the contrast of his mocha and her caramel. Smooth mocha that looked like cappuccino, felt as luxurious as silk, and smelled as rich as leather. Ripples of muscle across his chest, absences of fat at his tapered waist, and thighs cast from iron. All this bound in mocha.

The urge to taste the mocha overcame Kendall before she could control her actions. She propped herself on one elbow and looked down into Joseph's face. She carefully lifted his sunglasses up and away. His eyes were closed, his breathing even. Her hand left his abdomen and touched his eyebrow. Lazily, he opened his eyes, giving her what she longed for—a glimpse of his smoldering eyes—in careful measures tapered by the length of his silky lashes. Too soon, his eyes closed, but a slight smile appeared.

Kendall moved her fingers down the bridge of his nose and captured his smile. She tested the strength of his chin as she tilted his head up for her kiss.

Exploring suited Kendall. Her fingers trickled downward over broad shoulders, the cut chest, and rippled abdomen. She pressed her caramel palm against the mocha skin beneath Joseph's navel. He had an outie. A new yearning hit her. More than anything, she wanted to caress his navel with her tongue. Taste him intimately. She backed away from the thought, still a virgin to many things.

A line of cottony-soft hair captured her attention. Between his navel and the snap of his jeans was a perfectly laid road of black hair. She swirled her fingers in it. Curled, tugged, and teased it, becoming lost in the seclusion of their private beach, the sounds of the waves, and the birds overhead.

Joseph yanked her out of the daydream, focusing her attention on his body again. He opened the obstructive snap and lowered the zipper. He lifted his hips and shoved his jeans down his thighs.

Kendall glanced up to read his expression, to find an indication of what he expected her to do next. His eyes were closed, his mouth set with cruel seduction.

Kendall glanced down. The jeans and briefs were gathered at his knees. She laid her head on his chest and guided her hand downward into a forest of cottony-soft hair. She watched as he rose to meet her approach. Magnificent and odd, the jerky movements. She thought to ask what he felt, but astonishment over the swelling action silenced her. Watching, she remembered the feel of him inside her, the delicious tightness of being full.

"Have you ever seen a man before?" Joseph's voice startled her. She pulled her hand away, but Joseph put it back.

"No." There had been close calls, rubbing and bumping, but no, she had not seen a man—not had the opportunity and inclination to explore a man's body.

"You can touch me."

She glanced back at him. He was watching her, fighting to give her this time to know all of him—it was a struggle; the heat of his eyes said so.

"Don't spend too much time there or we'll be doing things on the beach that could get us arrested."

Kendall started at the bottom and worked her way to the top. She stopped along the trip and checked out the sites. She observed Joseph's reactions—fluttering eyelids, rapid breathing, heaving chest, squirming legs—she memorized the hot buttons. She wanted to learn more, see if she could push him over the edge. But Joseph was right—they might be arrested. When he groaned his plea for her to stop the torture, she helped correct his pants and returned to her place on his shoulder.

Kendall's eyes flew open with the first spasm of her fingers. Within seconds, her hand jerked, sending shock waves up her arm. Joseph bolted upright, grabbing her and stopping her from running away from him. She didn't know where she was going, only away so that he wouldn't witness her weakness.

"Relax," Joseph whispered, taking her jerky hand in his. "I learned this while in the air force."

Joseph began with gentle strokes to her wrist. He moved into the palm of her hand, relaxing her muscles with a rub-press-pull motion. His words persuaded her to fall back on the blanket and let him work magic. The pain subsided. He positioned her hand on his thigh and continued his manipulations.

"At my house, I have candles and incense that would help you to relax," Joseph said apologetically.

Kendall closed her eyes and concentrated on relaxing her muscles. "How do you do that? Work out the pain?" The spasms diminished to jerks that soon disappeared.

"I can't tell you all of my secrets or there wouldn't be any reason for you to keep me around."

"Is there anything you can't do?" Kendall asked, regaining control of her body.

"I hope you never find out." He brought her into his arms, held her tight, both falling asleep with the cool breeze of the fan washing over them.

Chapter 23

Kendall awoke first and when Joseph opened his eyes she was there to feed him cold fruit. The sun passed over them and the heat became more tolerable. They walked along the nature trail and sat on the beach, their feet in the water, talking about nothing and everything.

Joseph pulled more surprises from the trailer and they played horseshoes and badminton through the afternoon.

Before packing up the tent, Joseph produced a portable stereo and he asked Kendall to show him more of the tango.

"You're getting better." Kendall was amazed by his progress and his determination to learn something that meant much to her.

"Am I?" Joseph asked, watching his feet, counting his steps as they danced. "I don't feel like I'm getting better."

"You are. You're a big man. You have to learn to relax and let the music lead you." She lifted his chin. "Pay attention to me, not your feet."

They danced until Joseph could maneuver the basic steps. Early evening was before them so they loaded the trailer and got ready to head back to the city.

Joseph appeared at Kendall's window. "One more thing." He opened her door and helped her from the SUV.

"What?" Kendall asked, curious about his serious tone.

Joseph led her around the front of the Mercedes. "I unhitched the trailer. I want you to try to drive."

"Me?" Instant panic. "I can't drive. I haven't driven since the accident."

"Not on the street." Joseph continued leading her to the driver's side. "Just a little stretch here. This road is blocked off from traffic. The coast guard is out on patrol—we haven't seen a military car or truck in hours."

"Joseph, I can't." Kendall felt tears coming. Her chest tightened, her breathing became rapid.

He pulled her into the protection of his arms. "I'm going to be right beside you. Relax." He stroked her temples. "Just a little stretch. You've come so far. There's only this one hurdle left. You can do this. You're not a quitter. You're strong."

Kendall melted in his eyes. She absorbed all his words, leaned away to check out the stretch of road he referred to.

"I'll be right next to you."

"I don't know."

"I do. You can do this. If it's too much, I'll never ask it of you again, but you have to try."

Kendall considered the consequences. The worst that could happen on the deserted road was that she would run off into a grass embankment. The best, that she would overcome the fear that kept her paralyzed—a prisoner in her home. "You'll be right here?"

"I won't leave you."

Kendall surveyed the road again.

"Well?"

She met his blazing gaze. His eyebrows shot up in question, his expression cautious but hopeful.

"I'll try."

Joseph kissed her forehead and helped her inside the

SUV. He secured her seat belt and jogged around to the other side of the car. He slipped across the seat and placed his arm behind her.

"No," Kendall demanded, "put on your seat belt."

He did. "Start the engine," he coaxed.

Kendall took several deep breaths and willed her shaky hand to the dangling key. She turned it quickly—if she couldn't start the truck, she couldn't drive it. The finely crafted Mercedes SUV purred to life with only a flick of her wrist. She glanced at Joseph and silently cursed him for having the financial means to afford such a nice ride.

"What?" he asked.

"Nothing." She adjusted the seat and the mirrors, anything to buy some time.

"Let's go, Kendall. Put the car in gear."

"Don't rush me," she snapped.

"Don't stall. You can do this."

"Sorry," she mumbled.

"Put the car in gear and ease up off the brake."

Car in gear, Kendall froze.

Joseph's hand found her knee. "Ease up off the brake. Relax."

She squeezed her eyes closed.

"Open your eyes, Kendall, please." There was humor in Joseph's plea. "Please don't drive my Mercedes with your eyes closed."

Kendall couldn't help laughing. The tension of the moment gone, she eased off the brake and the SUV inched forward.

"Okay, this is great," Joseph said after a few minutes, "but you won't get anywhere unless you give it some gas."

Kendall smiled, his easy humor with the situation comforting her.

"Doesn't take much to make this car go. Go easy on the gas."

Kendall let her foot hover over the gas pedal. Visions she'd thought she'd forgotten tried to block her reemergence into life. She pushed them away and pressed down on the accelerator.

"Lead foot, I see," Joseph remarked.

"Are you going to be like this about your car?" Kendall teased, braver now. "You've surprised me twice today with sexist comments."

"Keep your eyes on the road and don't even *think* about touching up your lipstick right now."

Kendall laughed from deep in her belly. She didn't feel confident enough to take to the roads and highways, but weeks ago she hadn't been able to sit in the front seat. Look at her now. She was driving. "I'm driving!" she yelled out the window, both hands gripping the steering wheel for dear life. "I'm driving! Thank you, Joseph!"

Chapter 24

Joseph drove home, reaching his house as night cloaked the city. Kendall warmed with erotic memories as soon as the country cottage came into view. She carried the picnic basket inside while Joseph unhitched the trailer.

"Princess, put that cooler down," Joseph scolded from behind the SUV. "I'll carry that stuff inside. You go in and make yourself comfortable." He stopped tinkering with the trailer long enough to carry her overnight bag inside. He returned to securing the motorcycle, leaving her inside.

Kendall stepped into the elaborate bathroom of bronze and black tile. Matching towels hung neatly on the rack. She checked her appearance in the reflection of the mirrored wall. Sun-kissed skin framed a bright smile. Simple but elaborate, Joseph's picnic had been the most fun she'd ever had on a date. No one had ever gone to such trouble—all to make her happy. Her smile widened, stretching her cheeks. She had driven today! "Yes!" She pumped her fist. Now that Joseph had arrived, her life was turning around.

Kendall removed her clothes and stepped into a hot shower. She lathered up with Joseph's designer-name liquid soap. She shampooed her hair with his designer-name shampoo. She had brought her own toiletries in her overnight bag, but she wanted to carry his essence in every pore of her body. Stepping from the shower, she found evidence that Joseph had come in, but not disturbed her, in the form of a raised toilet seat. After applying baby oil to soften her skin and moisturizer to her hair, she slipped a hot-red nightgown over her head.

"Wow." Joseph froze at his dresser when she stepped into the bedroom. "You know how much I like red."

"You like?" Kendall held her arms out, not concerned with the scars on her right shoulder, and twirled in a circle for him. Red lace hugged her breasts; red satin flamed near her ankles.

"Very much." Lust burned in his eyes. "I'll be right out. Make yourself at home."

Adrenaline pumped through Kendall's veins as she flipped through seventy cable channels. Her eyes were glued on the bathroom doorway, anticipating the thrill Joseph would give her body. Her day couldn't get any better.

"Wow," Joseph said, stepping from the bathroom. "I seem to say that a lot when I'm with you."

Kendall smiled at his adornment. Tall, dark, and handsome, Joseph wore black satin pajama bottoms with a matching V-neck top. Kendall calculated how long it would take her to open the buttons. She had enjoyed her exploration earlier—it was time to pick up where she left off.

Joseph kneeled on the bed and Kendall went to him like a magnet for a kiss. Reluctantly, he pulled away. "Do you want anything?"

"Nope. Only you."

Conversation became a joyful distraction. Then came Joseph's challenge at Perquackey. They truly enjoyed each other's company and felt no pressing need to rush the joining of their bodies. Fatigue found Kendall dur-

ing the tiebreaker game and she nodded off as Joseph
shook up the letter cubes.

Joseph brushed his knuckles along Kendall's cheek.
This is what life should be about. He couldn't believe what
he had been missing. To know he could have flown a
regular schedule and used his days off, not to take extra
flights, but to cuddle with Kendall, made him reevaluate
his life choices. No, he would not doubt himself. He
would rejoice in his successes and thank his stars for
bringing Kendall to him at this point in his life. Any
sooner, she would have been too young and he would
have been too absorbed in launching his career to value
a good thing.

He dipped to place a kiss above the arch of her brow.
He hesitated, inhaled deeply. She smelled of him, her
hair washed with his shampoo. Funny how something as
trivial as her choice of shampoo could constrict his
throat with emotions. This woman, tender and ener-
getic, willing to learn from his years of wisdom and share
her untainted vision of the future, this woman had done
something no woman had ever been able to do to Captain Joseph Stewart. This woman had made him love her.

Joseph turned off the television and burrowed underneath the sheets with Kendall. He cut the lights and
took her into his arms. "Good night, princess."

Kendall wanted this night to go on forever. That's why
she didn't wake Joseph when her eyes flew open and
chased sleep away, her body finding it difficult to sleep
in a strange bed with another occupant. She slipped
from beneath the sheets and used the wall as her guide
to the hallway. Closing the bedroom door behind her,
she flipped a switch on the wall that turned on the recessed lighting. She padded across the shiny hardwood

floors into the kitchen. Minutes later, she sat in the huge kitchen drinking warm milk and watching a comedy skit show on a thirteen-inch television.

"Is everything okay, princess?"

Kendall jumped, sloshing her milk over the sides of the glass.

"I didn't mean to scare you. What are you doing up so late?"

"I couldn't sleep."

Joseph joined her with a glass of milk. "Want some cocoa?"

"The caffeine will keep us up."

"Good." He gave her a smile full of mischief and intent before grabbing the powdered cocoa from the cupboard. He pulled a spoon from the drawer and returned to the table.

"I had a good time today," Kendall said, handing Joseph the spoon, "thank you."

Joseph stirred cocoa into his drink.

"What you did—"

His head snapped up in question.

"Getting me back behind the wheel—I don't know how to thank you." She shook her head, the glass of cocoa at her lips. "Many have tried, but no one succeeded."

"What was different today?"

"You. You were there to catch me if I fell. And I knew you wouldn't judge or lecture if I didn't meet your expectations."

"It's not about my expectations. It's about having what you need to be happy. You weren't happy with not being able to get around on your own. I understand you have a ways to go before you'll be tooling down the highway, but you took a giant step today and I am very, very proud that you had the courage to do it."

"Your kindness means a lot to me." Kendall conveyed her sincerity by looking deep into his heart by way of his dark, heated eyes.

They drank in silence, laughing at the silly actors on television.

"Where did you come from?" Kendall asked, Joseph's expression saying she caught him off guard. She explained, "One day I was muddling through life, scared and unhappy. I run into you at the museum and everything's changed." She sipped her drink. "I can't remember the last time I laughed before meeting you, but today I couldn't stop."

"Why are you saying all these things, Kendall?"

"Because they're true and you're going back to work soon and you should know how I feel."

"Tell me how you feel, but don't thank me for doing what a man should do for the woman in his life."

"Okay. When you look at me with those dark eyes, I melt. When you touch me, I see mocha chocolate mixing with caramel and I think it's so good it should be sold as a candy bar at the grocery store."

"Stop." Joseph laughed, finishing his drink.

"Really. Captain Bar or something—I'm still working on the name."

"All right, princess."

"Why do you become embarrassed when I compliment you?"

He turned off the television. "Drink up."

"Why?" Kendall drank.

"I don't want you to be grateful to me. I worry about our ages being a factor in this relationship. I don't want you to see me as a teacher or disciplinarian. I want you to see me as a man who adores you and wants you to be his equal. I want you, princess, to take your place on the throne."

Kendall's insides quivered. Being adored felt good. "So, if I tell you that I'm glad I waited for you to come along before I gave my body to a man, that would make you feel good?"

"Yes." He stood and cleared away their cups.

"And if I told you how sexy I think you are in those black, silk pajamas, that would make you happy?"

"Yes." He turned to her, all smiles.

"I wonder what would happen if I said that every time we're together, I want to be intimate with you again."

"I'd do this." Joseph crossed the room and gave her a boiling-hot kiss.

"And if I said," breathless, "make love to me, Joseph, what would happen?"

Joseph lifted her, kissing her as he carried her to his bedroom. He placed her in the center of his bed. He rummaged through the bedside table before turning on the lamp. He lifted a brown paper bag and poured four boxes of condoms down on Kendall.

"What are these?" More laughter. Kendall thought her face would ache for a week.

"I couldn't decide which one."

"Like I know?"

Joseph laughed. "I see your point. Choose one now and we'll test them all. Find what works for us."

"Test them all? Tonight? Is that possible?"

Joseph laughed at her innocence. "Not in one night, but we'll get to it."

Kendall closed her eyes and selected a box at random. Joseph ripped it open and tucked it under the pillow before replacing the other boxes in the nightstand.

"What are you doing?" Kendall asked, pointing to where he'd put the condom of her choice.

"I'm not ready to use it and I don't want to lose it. You don't have to uncover all the secrets to sex, Ms.

Curiosity. There are some things a man likes to keep to himself."

The room went dark, extinguishing Kendall's next question.

Joseph found Kendall in the dark, pressing their lips together. Joseph's cocoa tasted different from her cocoa. She marinated in the extra sweetness his tongue provided with every swirl. She liked the steady pressure he placed on her lips, deepening when his hand went to her breast.

Kendall touched his torso, the indentation of his waist. Placed her hand underneath his shirt and caressed his taut nipples. His hand slid down the length of her leg, cascading across the red silk. He pulled away and placed kisses on her face, neck, the aroma of cocoa enticing.

Joseph's hand came back up, lingering on her thigh. Kendall began to work at his buttons. As his shirt fell open, his hand moved to her hip. Kendall pushed the shirt away. He bunched her gown in his fist, working it slowly up her body.

Remembering the temptation on the beach, Kendall found the hollow of his neck. The desire to taste the mocha overwhelming, she flicked her tongue along his collarbone. His moans told her he liked what she was doing. His moans made her want to do more. Her tongue went to his nipple. She pulled it inside her mouth, nibbled.

Joseph held her gown bunched in both hands, moved her body so that he could pull it over her head.

Kendall placed her hand in the middle of his chest and pushed. He fell back on the bed and let her continue her explorations uncensored. She moved to the other nipple, sampling. She kissed a trail down his abdomen, breaking the pattern to lick each of his ribs, the experience becoming almost biblical.

Kendall straddled his thighs, his moans spurring her on. His response to her touch made her heated and anxious for him to explore her. She raked her blunt nails down his body from broad shoulders, over rippled abdominal muscles, and across strong thighs, leaving Joseph trembling. Tentatively, her fingers inched toward his dark forest. Finding the cottony curls, she searched for more in the darkness. The tremble running through Joseph's legs told her when she found the base. One hand chased the other up and then down, marveling in the size and hardness—long, thick, steel cocooned in mocha-colored felt.

Several strokes and Joseph grabbed her waist, tossed her to the bed. Skylights in the cathedral ceiling displayed a clear night sky. She hadn't noticed the view the last time. Kendall welcomed his weight pinning her body. Luxuriated in the feel of his fingers massaging her scalp. Inhaled deeply his designer cologne. Licked her lips after his kiss, tasting the cocoa. Relished in the sounds of desire emanating from down deep inside Joseph's chest. Closed her eyes and pictured his mocha slashing her caramel as he took her breast inside his mouth.

Joseph seemed lost, in another world, worshipping her body as if the first or last time he'd have the pleasure. He worked meticulously, touching and caressing every inch of her. Gentle hands stroked, anxious fingers pinched, hungry mouth devoured.

Joseph's knees pushed Kendall's thighs apart. His hand slipped between them and he cupped her, holding her captive to whatever he wanted to do. One long finger swirled through her tight curls. She sucked in a breath that arched her back. The finger strayed, found an opening, and probed its origin. Joseph slipped inside easily, her body well prepared for his exploration. She sighed at the shattering rhythm of his finger, her body becoming pliant, ready for bigger things.

His mouth was on her belly when his other hand trampled through the tight curls. Her mind splintered, trying to analyze, learn, and enjoy. His lips were kissing her thighs when she felt his finger withdraw, cool air washing over her juices like the waves crashing on the sand.

Kendall's heart fluttered when Joseph's shadow dipped from view. She cried out at the first flick of his tongue. She flinched as pleasure pulsated through her body. *Too much.* Joseph continued to taste, ignoring the possibility that he could ever give her too much pleasure. Steady strokes while his hands held her thighs apart. She felt flush, pleasure so intense she couldn't separate it from pain. He ignited the incessant itch that burned at her core, needing to be scratched. Teasing, teasing, teasing. Very close to satisfying the itch, but not quite reaching it. Joseph upped the stakes and one, two lean fingers slipped inside. Caught between his tongue and his fingers was the itch that begged to be scratched. Needing relief, Kendall moved her hips and found a rhythm that seesawed Joseph's tongue across the itch. And then he found the place that provided her relief and gave it to her freely until she collapsed in a heap, fighting to breathe.

Kendall closed her eyes and let joy wash over her, through her. She heard Joseph rip the paper, felt him shift on the bed.

"Kendall." Joseph's lips were next to her ear, his body moving over hers.

Kendall took him into her embrace, decided he needed to wear her mark, and set about her work. His hands were on her hips, steadying her for his entrance. He released her with his right hand. She tensed. She had seen how much there was of him, remembered the intense pain of the last time. His blunt tip stroked her down and up. She remembered the fullness, the stretching.

"Relax, Kendall." Joseph's voice sliced the darkness. "Don't you want me? Don't you want this closeness with me?"

Kendall remembered the bliss after the tearing pain, the fullness, and the stretching.

"For a little while," Joseph confessed, "we can be one person and I want that more than anything."

"I want it, too." She gripped his wrist that held her hip. "Joseph."

He immersed himself in one stroke. The pain gave way to fullness to stretching in quick seconds. "Joseph," Kendall moaned, riding each stroke.

Joseph stroked, matching each movement with a carefully placed kiss. He rekindled her itch and extinguished it without ceremony. His fever built, and the rush of heat burned Kendall. He worked her with a loving touch and with tenacity. He oscillated his hips, dipped, and surged. "No man," Joseph growled his oath between thrusts. "No other man will ever touch you this way."

"I don't want any other man to touch me. Only you, Joseph."

Joseph threw his head back and dove into the wet heat. He exploded, his body jerking with every drop of liquid heat he released. He collapsed, covered in sweat and breathing hard, pulling Kendall to rest on his chest.

"Promise me, Kendall. No other man."

"I promise you, Joseph. Only you."

Chapter 25

"Captain Stewart, sorry for the wait." The nurse in crisp military whites swung the door open, inviting him into the exam area. "You're our last patient of the day." She smiled over her shoulder. "We get to go home after we're done with you."

Joseph checked his watch. He still needed to do a few things to get ready for work in the morning. He had hoped that he could be done with this appointment, prepare his uniform, pack a travel bag, and have time left to spend with Kendall. He didn't know how he would stand being away from her.

"Have a seat," the nurse instructed.

Having had no luck in the chair on his last visit, Joseph opted for the gurney. He dropped down on the stiff white sheets and watched the nurse wheel the electronic blood pressure machine over to him.

"Let's get started." She applied the cuff, hit the button that inflated it around his upper arm, and started asking her usual questions. He answered no to every symptom she described—except the headaches. Stress often triggered the throbbing of his temples. She added a new twist by asking about his compliance to the medical regimen Dr. Bennis had prescribed. He sputtered for an answer but was put out of his misery when the long beep came from the machine.

Joseph held his breath.

The nurse jotted down a series of numbers. To his horror, she grabbed her stethoscope from the counter. "Let me check this manually."

Joseph's head pulsated. Two readings later, the nurse began to question him about the symptoms again. This would be worse than the previous visits.

"I'll get Dr. Bennis." She left, taking his chart.

Joseph tried to mentally prepare himself for Dr. Bennis's assessment. He would explain to the doctor about his whirlwind week. Tell him man-to-man that he found himself profoundly attracted to a woman and had to stretch himself a little thinner than usual to win her over. He'd confess that he'd never been a man who believed in taking unnatural things into his body—medicines included. He'd promise to get his act together—if he could have just one more chance.

Dr. Bennis came in and plopped down on the stool. He rolled over to the desk and opened Joseph's chart. In a no-nonsense tone he questioned him, "Have you been exercising?"

"As much as time allows."

Dr. Bennis threw him a look. "What about the diet the nurse went over on your last visit? Have you been following it?"

"Well, I met this woman and we eat out quite a bit—"

The doctor gave Joseph a you've-got-to-be-kidding-me glance before going on. "Does this woman see to it that you take your medications every day?"

"I meant to get the prescription filled, but time just rolled by and—"

"You're going to have plenty of time to get those prescriptions filled now, Joseph." Dr. Bennis rose from the stool and faced him. "I'm grounding you."

"Grounding me? You can't—"

"Yes, I can. You sat in this very room two weeks ago and promised to do what was necessary to bring your blood pressure down. You didn't do one thing I prescribed. I told you at that time I would ground you if I had to."

"But, Dr. Bennis—"

"Joseph, this is about much more than flying. High blood pressure can lead to heart attack, stroke, and kidney damage. We're talking about your life here."

"Flying is my life. If you ground me, I have no life."

"What about the woman you just mentioned? Your family and friends? Aren't they motivation enough to live?"

Joseph sank back on the gurney, reality hurled in his face. The thought of losing Kendall sobered him quickly. He couldn't storm into her life and then fade away. She hadn't fully recovered from the loss of her sister. He couldn't inflict any more pain on her.

Dr. Bennis recognized Joseph's hurt and softened his tone. "How can I—in good conscience—let you fly when a sudden onset of symptoms might cause you to make a grave error? Hundreds of people place their lives in your hands every day. If I gave you the choice, would you endanger your passengers' lives?"

"No." No, but he needed one more chance.

Dr. Bennis blew out a long breath. "This doesn't have to be permanent. You have the opportunity to be reinstated. But the only way you're going to do that is to follow my instructions to the letter, bring your blood pressure down, and prove to me you can keep it down."

Admitting his own responsibility in his demise, Joseph nodded. "I understand."

"I'll have the nurse come in and go over everything again. I'll see you in one month. If you have any problems before then, call my office right away."

"One month?"

"One month." Dr. Bennis rested his hand on Joseph's shoulder before leaving the exam room.

Joseph dropped his head into the cradle of his hands. For at least one month he couldn't fly.

One month to get his act together or everything he had worked for—all his life—would be lost.

How could he survive one month away from the open skies?

One month that might become permanent.

"Knock, knock. Can I come in?"

"Max, what are you doing here? Come on in." Kendall ushered him inside her office.

He appeared tired. Lines of concern marred his forehead. His bright, happy eyes remained diverted to the floor. "I wanted to talk with you. You haven't been around the entire weekend. I figured I'd find you working on a Sunday."

"I fell a little behind." Spending time with Joseph had been worth it. "Joseph's a little late so I'm cleaning up for the day and then I'm heading home. What's wrong?" She found two folding chairs. They opened the chairs and took a seat.

"I hope I'm not out of place coming to your job," Max apologized.

"Of course not. Tell me what's so wrong that it couldn't wait until I came home."

"I'm worried about you."

"Me?" Kendall hiked her thumb into her chest. "I'm doing the best I have in over a year. Why would you be worried about me?"

Max's eyes touched every object in the room in an attempt to avoid the intimate act of looking directly at

Kendall. He took a deep breath and blew out his answer, "Joseph."

Kendall went on alert. "What about Joseph?"

"Did he tell you I came by the other night?"

"He did. I've been really busy and haven't gotten the chance to stop by and talk. I'm sorry."

"I'm surprised he told you. Did he tell you about the animosity he showed me when all I tried to do is be cordial to him?"

Kendall's face registered her disbelief. She knew Max and he was not the type of person to find trouble where there wasn't any. Greg's warning crashed down on her.

She encouraged Max to vent his feelings. "Tell me everything."

As Kendall listened, she weighed her assessment of Joseph against that of her only remaining friends. Could she be completely wrong about Joseph? Were her friends overreacting? There had to be a huge misunderstanding. Joseph treated her like his "princess." But her friends were true friends and wouldn't do anything to hurt her. She could see that balancing herself between Joseph and her friends would be rough and if not handled properly, disastrous.

Max stood, his face showing a measure of relief. "I just wanted you to know."

"Max, I'll talk to him and straighten everything out."

He nodded in agreement, but she couldn't read his expression.

"For the first time in a long time I'm really happy and I want to keep my friends in my life. I know I haven't been around much, but Joseph was on vacation and I wanted to spend time getting to know him before he's jumping from city to city. You understand that, don't you?"

Max softened. "I do."

Kendall smiled, relieved. She quickly changed the subject. "Can I share some news with you?"

"Of course, spill." Max was always ready to share good gossip.

"Let me call Joseph first. I don't know where he could be. He's never late." Kendall tried Joseph's home and then his cell. He didn't answer either.

"C'mon and tell me the news," Max encouraged her. "He'll be here by the time you finish."

"I'm going to start tango class again. I called and my instructor has a spot in the advanced class. I can start tomorrow."

"Get out. Are you rejoining the living?"

"There's more." Kendall grabbed her jacket.

"What?"

"I drove Saturday."

"Drove what?"

"A car, silly. Don't mess with me."

"Just teasing. Good for you."

"I'll tell you all about it if you offer me a ride home." She followed Max out the door, securing her office for the night. "I wonder what happened to Joseph."

Kendall recognized her father's beat-up car parked behind the new Honda Accord. The tail end of the awkwardly big car spilled over onto the sidewalk causing joggers to veer around it in the street.

"Is that your dad?" Max asked.

"I'm afraid so." Kendall was glad to see her father, but they hadn't talked since she introduced him to Joseph and that meant there was unfinished, unpleasant business to be resolved. She checked her watch; still no Joseph—she was anxious to call him.

Max pulled into his driveway and Kendall crossed the lawn, greeting her father with a hug. "Daddy, what are you doing here?"

Frank greeted her with a kiss. "I don't know why you're surprised. You were the one that cut off all communication. I thought since you showed up at my house you were ready to be a family again."

"I am, Daddy. Come in and sit down." Kendall noticed how deftly he steered her up onto the porch, blocking her view. "Who's that sitting in your car?"

"A lady friend of mine," Frank answered casually as he found a seat on her sofa.

Remembering her manners, Kendall asked, "Does she want to come in?"

"I'm not ready for that yet."

Kendall silently acknowledged that blessing. Her father would never allow her to question his actions, but she wanted to know who this woman could be. She wanted to ask if they were more than friends, and if he said that they were, she wanted to remind him that he was still married to her mother.

"I have something I want to discuss with you." Frank waved her away from the door.

Kendall took a seat next to her father and waited for him to start.

Frank unleashed his frustration in a long string of sentences. "I don't like you seeing that Joseph character. He's too old for you—my age. I don't like the way he looks at you. A man that old who has seen the world could only want one thing from dating a young girl. I know his type and I don't want it to be my daughter that he's messing around with."

"Daddy, you don't like any guy I bring home."

"That's not true. I thought Darren would make you a good husband. He's respectful, loves you to death, and is going somewhere in life."

Kendall dropped her head. She didn't have time for this timeless, endless argument that started anew with every man she introduced her father to. "Daddy, we do this every time. Could we not do it this time? There are things about Joseph that are special to me. I really want to see how far we can go, and to be honest I've never felt like this about any man."

"What about Darren?"

Kendall stood and crossed the room. "You didn't like Darren when I brought him home to meet you and Mom—look at you now, singing his praises. Give it time and you'll feel the same way about Joseph."

"Never. I'll never agree to my baby girl dating a man old enough to be her father."

Kendall could venture down the road that pointed out the obvious, but chose not to. He forgot that he had fathered her at seventeen. Their family dynamics were different.

"Kendall." Frank pushed himself up from the sofa and joined her across the room. "I want you to tell me why you've latched on to Joseph. Are you using him as a father figure because you think I wasn't there for you during your recovery from the accident?"

Kendall watched him with unbridled horror. "How could you say that?" Her voice began to quiver as she fought to hold back the tears. "How could you take something good in my life and try to associate it with something so horrible? Why can't you be happy for me and help me get over the accident?"

At the threat of tears, Frank backed down. He always backed down when one of his girls began to cry. "My friend and I were talking—I shouldn't have said that to you."

"Your friend?" Kendall became angry at the thought that a strange woman knew her personal business and had the audacity to offer advice. "Who is this woman?

She doesn't know anything about me. Why is she trying to analyze me?"

"It's not like that. I was upset after you left the house and I asked her advice."

"She doesn't know me, Daddy. She can't offer you advice about me. I'm your daughter, why do you need a stranger to help you figure me out?"

"Just a minute." His words were firm, but not angry. "Yes, you're my daughter, but I don't know you anymore. Not since the accident. You and I were always very close—and then you shut me out. You turned me away like I was a gawking reporter hunting for a story."

"I needed to work things out alone."

"Alone? We were all hurting—you, me, your mother. We needed to work things out *together*—as a family. Look at how our lives are torn apart. Your mother is I don't know where. We live in the same town and you won't let me visit."

"I'm trying to make things better." Kendall felt herself being drawn into an emotional argument that she couldn't handle. Just when she felt she was regaining control, her father made her feel she wasn't strong enough. This was why she shut her family out—she wasn't ready to deal with them.

Frank took her hands in his. "I know you're working real hard to get back to normal. From what you told me at dinner, you're making great strides." His voice softened but carried that fatherly tone. "This is why I'm worried about you and Joseph. You're trying to go back to the way things were overnight. Joseph came along and you jumped at the chance to have a relationship again."

"You're wrong about Joseph."

"Maybe I am. But if I am, how will you ever be able to have a real relationship with Joseph if you haven't closed the door on Darren? You know he still loves you. He has it in the back of his mind that when you do get back to your old self, you'll call for him."

Kendall didn't want to hurt Darren any more than she already had. "I never made any promises to Darren."

"Since when do you have to make a promise to a man for him to keep loving you? To keep hoping things will go back to the way they were?"

"We don't have any contact."

"He calls me every Sunday."

Shock found Kendall. She assumed Darren had moved on with his life and found someone worthy of him.

"Darren and I talk like father and son. I know what's in his mind. He's keeping the connection, giving you space, but not letting you get too far away. After everything, are you going to let him flounder like that? Are you going to try to start something with Joseph when you haven't put your past to rest?"

Renewed guilt over her sister's death, hurting her family, and learning about Darren's lingering hopes threatened to pummel her into withdrawing from life again. She allowed her father to pull her into the safety of his embrace.

"Kendall, all I'm saying is to take things slow. I don't want to see you to get hurt. Before you can move to the future you have to clean up the past or else it'll come back to haunt you when you least expect it."

Chapter 26

When Kendall called Joseph a fourth time and got no answer, she stepped into the shower to wash the work-day's dirt and emotion-soaked dirty laundry away. They had one night of his vacation left and she didn't want to spend it using him as her personal shrink. She wanted laughter and smiles, hugs and kisses.

The double beep on her phone line signaled she had missed a call. She dialed in her code and listened to Joseph's weary voice tell her he couldn't see her tonight. "I'm really tired and have a lot to do. I'm not going to be able to go out tonight. I'll call you later."

Kendall's hopes plummeted. Her mind played nasty tricks, whispered in her ear that maybe Greg and Max and her father had been right. Joseph had had his vacation fling and now he was dumping her.

She refused to give in to the doubt. She had looked into Joseph's eyes and she knew the truth. Still wet with a towel wrapped around her, Kendall called Joseph.

"We're not on for tonight?" she asked. After the long day and emotional roller-coaster ride her father had dragged her on, she needed to see him. He would be leaving soon, flying here and there, not coming home in between. She needed him to hold her again before he left her.

"Uh, I have to cancel. I'll make it up to you this weekend." Joseph didn't sound the same. He was distracted, edgy.

"I'd really like to see you before you go back to work. I'll wear red." She planned to ask him about his schedule. What cities would he be in and when? She never got the chance.

"I'm sorry, I'm just too tired. The drive." He used her handicap against her.

"I understand." A touch of hurt left her heart and escaped past her lips.

"Listen, Kendall, I'll call you back in a little while."

"Okay." But it wasn't.

Joseph considered calling Kendall back and trying to explain his mood, but found he didn't have the strength. He could hear the hurt he inflicted. He would make it right but he had to make it right with himself first. Only another pilot—or someone in the business—would understand what it meant to be grounded in the prime of your career.

Being alone in the big house with nothing but his regrets would make him sadder. He drove to the airport, jazz from his stereo drowning his thoughts. He checked the roster and found that Russ was in town for a day. He headed to the pilots' lounge to find his friend.

"Joseph—I mean, Captain Stewart."

Joseph knew who owned the tender voice before he turned around.

Gabrielle ran to join him at the bank of private elevators.

"What do you want, Gabrielle?"

"I saw you walking through the airport." She paused to catch her breath. "I wanted to apologize for what I said on the plane."

The proposition. Joseph softened, startled by his nasty reaction to her presence. "Apology accepted. Let's not have anything like that happen again."

In her native language, "I hope you'll reconsider the things you said. I assure you I can remain professional during our flights. It would be devastating to my career to have to explain why I've been banned from your plane."

"Don't worry yourself about that," Joseph answered in Italian. If his health didn't improve dramatically in the next month, she wouldn't have to worry about flying with him ever again.

"Then you won't ban me from your flights?"

He shook his head no.

"You look like something is bothering you." Gabrielle switched to English.

Joseph followed the switch in languages without missing a beat. "I won't be flying for a while." He might as well get used to telling people about his sudden absence from the air.

"Why not?" Gabrielle bolted to his side, wrapping her arm around his.

Joseph looked down into her crystal-clear green eyes. She pressed the figure eight of her body against his stress-stiffened muscles. Her dark flight attendant's uniform fit snugly over her breasts, pushing them up in the perfect position for worshipping.

Gabrielle caressed his chest. "Joseph, you can talk to me. Why won't you be flying?"

No longer being a part of this world would paralyze him. He studied Gabrielle's eagerness to please him. With her, things came easily. No issues. He could drive his two-seater Benz convertible along the beach with her at his side. Her beauty was undeniable; men would envy him wherever they went. And thank goodness, her father was tucked away in Italy somewhere. There was no pressure to prove himself or his intentions. Gabrielle had made it clear on several occasions she was attracted to him and willing to accept as much or as little as he wanted to give. As her perfume floated up to him, her golden hair cascading over his shoulder, he remembered that Gabrielle's body came with seasoned skills.

"Gabrielle, would you like to have a drink?"

Chapter 27

"Joseph?" Kendall questioned with a degree of alarm.

His voice, groggy, pushed through the phone line. "Hi, Kendall."

"I want you to come pick me up."

"Do you need something?"

"I need to be with you. I want to see you tonight."

"Kendall, I'm sorry. I don't feel like going out tonight, but like I promised earlier I'll make it up to you."

"I don't want to go out either. I want to be with you. I can tell something's wrong. Why don't I come over there for a little while?"

Silence.

"Joseph, you've always been a gentleman. Are you going to deny me the one thing I'm asking from you? I feel like I need to be there with you."

A long silence told Kendall Joseph's answer. "Kendall, I really want to be alone. I'll call you."

"Joseph—" The line went dead before she could finish.

Kendall stood at a mental crossroad that would determine the direction of her relationship with Joseph. Obviously, something was bothering him. She couldn't figure out why he chose to shut her out when he had been more than supportive of all of the problems plaguing her life. The way she figured it, if she turned her

back on him when he needed someone, their relationship would never grow into the pillar of understanding
and companionship she wanted.

"That's it. Joseph needs me." She didn't remember
how to get to his house. Her mind raced. She bolted up
the stairs and rummaged through the clothing hanging
from the rack. Joseph had put her laundry there when
he picked it up from the cleaner's a few days ago. She'd
been too busy fighting carsickness to pay attention. Finding the suits covered in plastic, Kendall ripped the
payment slip from the bag. She scanned the bill and
found Joseph's address scrawled along the top.

Kendall tilted her head in question. "Is Captain Stewart here?"

Tall, green-eyed, golden hair flowing, the woman nodded with a smile. "Joseph is here," she answered in a
thick Italian accent.

Kendall took a long step backward; the woman's
breath smelled heavily of alcohol. The way the woman
swayed and held on to the door for balance confirmed
Kendall's suspicions. She waited for the woman to call
for Joseph. When she didn't, Kendall asked to see him.
"I'd like to see Joseph." She went for the screen.

"One minute." The woman shut the door in her face.

Kendall turned to Max and waved. She thought about
having Max wait until she saw the condition of Joseph,
but knowing him to be the proper gentleman, she realized that wasn't necessary. Max blew his horn and pulled
away from the curb.

She took in a deep breath and blew out all the emotional baggage dropped by her father. He didn't
understand what she was feeling for Joseph—she
couldn't explain it to herself. The level of emotional at-

tachment associated with the newness of their relationship surprised her. The only thing she could think of when her father had driven off with the strange woman was getting to Joseph—offering him support to overcome whatever the problem could be.

Realizing how long she had been waiting, Kendall pressed the doorbell again.

The door swung open and a perplexed Joseph appeared. "Kendall, what are you doing here?"

Kendall couldn't decipher the origin of his surprise. "Didn't your friend tell you I was at the door?"

Joseph glanced over his shoulder. "No."

After a moment of silence, Kendall asked, "Aren't you going to invite me in?"

He snapped out of his trance. "I'm sorry, come in. How did you get here?"

"Max drove me." Kendall stepped into the huge foyer. The open floor plan allowed her to see the Italian woman draped across Joseph's living room sofa.

"I thought you wanted to be alone." Kendall let her eyes drag from Joseph to the shapely woman on his sofa.

"Joseph, come back," the woman called with an alcohol-induced slur.

Kendall turned to him with questioning eyes.

He secured her arm and led her into his study. He closed the door before turning to her with an explanation. "She's a coworker."

His vagueness made her fear the worst. "A coworker? She doesn't look like a pilot."

"She's a flight attendant."

"Joseph, what's going on here?"

He took a long breath and released it slowly before answering. "I've had a trying day—I received bad news that threw me for a loop. I ran into Gabrielle at the airport and we decided to come back here for drinks." He paused. "Looking back on it, it was a stupid thing to do."

Kendall watched him in disbelief. Joseph stood before her openly admitting to bringing a gorgeous woman back to his place for drinks. He didn't bother to lie, because he and Kendall didn't have a solid relationship—they'd only been dating a few weeks. Kendall felt foolish. She should have known that if a man said not to come over, he meant he had plans with another woman. Her father had been right—a worldly man like Joseph could never see her as his intellectual equal, he had only one thing on his mind when it came to her. All the pretty words were worthless— the tools of his seduction. If she doubted his insincerity, all she had to do was look at the beautiful Italian woman on his sofa.

"I should get going." Kendall started for the door.

"Wait." Joseph used the towering height of his body to block her path. "You just got here."

"And that may have been a mistake on my part."

"You mean Gabrielle?" He rested his hands on her shoulders. "The mistake was mine and it was bringing Gabrielle to my home instead of picking you up when you asked me to." Noticing her stiff posture, Joseph pulled her against him in a bear hug and tried to correct his wrong. "I'll send Gabrielle home."

Smelling rich, heady alcohol on his breath, Kendall pulled away and crossed the room. The comfort of his hard chest and the warmth of his touch clouded her judgment. "She's drunk, Joseph."

He slipped his hands inside the pockets of his khakis. "I should drive her."

"Joseph!"

"What?" he asked, dumbfounded.

"You're going to abandon me to take a woman who is obviously attracted to you and drunk back to her place?"

"It's not like that. I have to see her home safely. You come with us."

Kendall's eyes dropped to the hardwood floors. "You know I can't do that." She had come to trust Joseph enough to ride in a car with him, but she could still get carsick. She refused to let a stranger see her like that—especially the competition. Besides, she didn't like the idea of Joseph driving the woman home at all.

Joseph came to her. "I forgot." He paused, considering the options. "You could wait here until I return."

"I think I should go home." Kendall moved around him.

"Kendall, wait." Joseph caught her hand before she made it to the door. "How are you going to get home?" He paused. "I'll call Gabrielle a cab."

That was a solution she could live with.

Kendall turned. "Okay, call her a cab."

Joseph made the call.

"Joseph, why did you invite her here? I knew something was bothering you and I wanted to be with you. Instead, you go to the airport and bring Gabrielle home?"

"I didn't plan it that way. I went to the airport to clear my head. I ran into Gabrielle while looking for Russ, we talked and ended up here. After a few drinks, I planned to drive her home. That's the whole of it."

Kendall crossed her arms over her chest. "I wonder if you would believe the same story coming from me."

"What?"

"Think about the way you practically put Max out of my house when he stopped by—and Max is gay."

Confusion and then enlightenment covered Joseph's face. "I did do that, didn't I?" He pulled Kendall into his chest again.

"Yes, you did and now you want me to believe that Gabrielle being here is completely innocent."

"I messed up. I'll make it right with Max." He tilted her head up to him. "You know that I'm telling the truth, don't you? Nothing happened here between Gabrielle and me and nothing would ever happen between us. I know better when I'm trying to win your heart. Do you believe me?"

Kendall studied his face. His eyes couldn't lie. As much as she wanted to be mad at him, she couldn't. "I do believe you."

Joseph descended with puckered lips.

Kendall pressed her palm to his mouth, stopping him. "Just because I'm being understanding this time doesn't mean I'll have the ability to do it again."

"Understood." Joseph removed her palm and leaned in for a kiss.

"Joseph!" Gabrielle's slurred voice interrupted their private moment.

Joseph took Kendall's hand in his and led her into the living room.

Kendall stopped short at what she saw. Gabrielle lay draped over the sofa, the skirt of her flight attendant's uniform too high on her thigh for it to be regulation. Her wild thick hair gave her an air of mystery. She looked like the fantasy flight attendant men dreamed would welcome them at the door of the aircraft. Kendall held her tongue and remembered the calm, understanding front she had displayed moments ago for Joseph's benefit.

"Gabrielle, this is my girlfriend, Kendall."

Kendall glanced up at him. At least he had made the attempt to give her clout in the situation.

Gabrielle's hazed eyes went to Kendall. She struggled to sit upright on the sofa and pointed at Kendall. "You're the girlfriend?" She broke out in hysterical laughter. She laughed so hard she fell forward.

Kendall held Joseph's hand tight, reluctant to release

him when he lunged to catch Gabrielle before she fell to the hardwood floor. Gabrielle collapsed in his arms.

Joseph looked up at Kendall and pleaded, "I can't put her in a cab like this."

Kendall watched Gabrielle's arms come up around Joseph's neck and she felt a stabbing pain pierce her heart. Gabrielle mashed her hourglass figure into his chest and pressed her face against his. Her lips moved next to Joseph's ear, speaking in Italian. The blush of Joseph's mocha cheeks said he recognized the words.

"How well do you know Italian?" Kendall asked for clarification. She remembered it was one of the four languages he'd learned in the air force.

He cleared his throat while trying to manage Gabrielle's slinky body. "I did a tour there."

Gabrielle said something else in Italian that made her laugh hysterically. She brought her nose to rest against Joseph's. The laughter stopped abruptly. She said more words in a low, seductive tone.

Joseph stiffened. "Let's get you off the floor."

He lifted Gabrielle to the sofa. Her words kept flowing. Kendall didn't know what the words were, but the seductive tone rang clear. Gabrielle's hands began to grope at Joseph's shirt. Kendall watched in stunned disbelief, shocked that this woman would blatantly hit on Joseph with her standing there.

Joseph politely removed Gabrielle's hands from his chest and stood to face Kendall. He repeated, "I can't put her in a cab in this condition. I am responsible. I should have cut her off a long time ago."

Kendall wanted to tell him he should never have brought her there. He should never have invited her for a drink. She refused to think about what might have happened if she hadn't shown up at his door unexpectedly. Joseph might believe having a drink with

Gabrielle was innocent, but Gabrielle obviously had an entirely different idea.

Kendall moved past her jealousy and let Joseph off the hook. "I'll wait here," she said through clenched teeth.

Joseph thanked her with a kiss. "I'll be right back."

Kendall watched as he gathered Gabrielle's pliable body against his solid strength. He wrapped his arms around her to keep her from falling. Gabrielle threw her arms around his neck and let him drag her toward the attached garage.

Kendall felt the jealous twinge stir in the pit of her stomach. The thought of them being alone again made her afraid she might lose Joseph, but her fear of riding in a car—who knew how far?—kept her feet glued to the floor as they walked away.

Chapter 28

The house was dark and quiet when Joseph returned. He checked the living room and study first. He moved to the kitchen as regret roped in one bad scenario after another and made his temples pound. Noting the late hour, he hurried to his bedroom.

He had asked himself a million times on the drive home, "What were you thinking about?" He had actually let the bleakness of his work situation rule his rational thought. He remembered the satisfaction that spread across Gabrielle's face when he told her he needed to talk. The space in his two-seater, even with the top down, didn't allow enough room between their bodies. As his mind sought refuge in a place that would help him forget that his career hung by a string, Gabrielle opened her compact and painted her lips. He couldn't believe it had been his suggestion to bring Gabrielle back to his house for a drink. But it had been and now he had to take responsibility for it.

Joseph should have stopped Gabrielle after the second glass, but he liked her uninhibited nature. Reliving wild flight tales temporarily eased his blues. When the stories came to an end it was Gabrielle's forwardness that distracted him. She had just thrown her arms around him and smothered him in a kiss when Kendall rang his doorbell.

Joseph gyrated his shoulders, shaking away the memory,

as he opened the door to his bedroom. Cuddled against his pillow, Kendall lay on his bed. He kissed her cheek very softly so as not to wake her before lowering himself down on the corner of the bed. His stupidity and self-pity had almost cost him what he was trying to build with her. Their new relationship was tender and as fragile as a house of cards—bringing Gabrielle back to his place had almost demolished that house of cards.

Joseph straightened the sheets and covered Kendall. He stood observing the peaceful sleep encompassing her. He hoped she'd be in the same peaceful frame of mind when she woke up. He fully expected her to rant and rave, accuse him of all sorts of things for which he'd rightfully have to account.

Joseph pulled his shirt from his pants and stepped into the adjoining bathroom. After brushing his teeth and dressing for bed, he returned to his bedroom.

"How long have you been back?" Kendall asked.

"An hour maybe." He sat next to her, his bare feet pressing into the thickness of the only carpeted room.

"Did Gabrielle get home safely?"

He turned to her, bringing his knee up on the bed. "I owe you an apology."

"Do you?"

Houses had been burnt to the ground over less than what he had done. Manhoods had been clipped and tossed onto the freeway. The fact that Kendall hadn't smacked him or called him every vile name ever conceived of spoke a lot of her character and self-confidence.

"Yes," Joseph answered. "I'm trying to build something between us, and I—well, I shouldn't have had another woman in my house. Especially when you asked to be here and I told you no."

"Was she here when I called?"

"She was."

His honesty would either dig his grave or endear him to her. He waited nervously to see which. No matter what the outcome, he knew that a relationship did not mean anything if it was built from lies and hammered together with broken promises.

Kendall sat up, shedding the quilt, looking sexy as hell in his crisp white T-shirt. "Something is bothering you. Why won't you talk to me about it?"

Joseph opened his heart a little wider to Kendall. Any other woman would have stomped, cursed, and flung ultimatums around the room like a Frisbee. Instead, Kendall focused on what was bothering him. She wanted to comfort him rather than crucify him.

"You are a special woman," he acknowledged with a stroke of his hand on her thigh.

Kendall smiled. "Why?"

"You're putting my problems above your feelings." He searched her face while he reeled in his emotions. "I feel bad that I might have disappointed you tonight. I don't ever want you to see me in a negative light."

"No chance of that. You've understood my crazy behavior, you've run my errands without complaint. I think this is what people do for each other when they're in a relationship—they support each other's weaknesses."

Joseph cupped her hands in his, pulling them to rest on his thigh.

"I admit that I was jealous—and a little angry—when I saw Gabrielle in your home, but I don't really know if I had the right to find my way over here without an invitation."

"That we can resolve right now. You're welcome here any time you want—with or without a formal invitation."

"An invitation is always nice."

"Consider this a standing invite." He leaned forward and pressed a kiss into her lips.

"I won't do this," she said earnestly.

"What?"

"Share you or be made to feel that I'm sharing you. If I think there's competition, I'll walk away. If you find I don't fill your world completely, without the need for other women, we don't need to be together. I deserve more than a piece of you."

"Understood." Joseph kissed away the harsh set of her jaw.

After Kendall recovered from the heat of his lips, she returned to the matter at hand. "Tell me what's bothering you."

Joseph didn't want to burden Kendall with his problem. He worried he might further disappoint her. She should see him as tall and strong—her savior, not easily tempted by another woman or unemployed because of bad health.

Kendall took in a deep breath before she spoke. "These past few weeks have been very special for me. I don't know where this is going between us, but if this is all I ever have, I will cherish every minute. But if you're going to run, I want you to leave now before I invest any more feelings into you. Before the heartache would be too much to bear."

Joseph began to say something, but Kendall continued. "Tell me what's going on. I know it's something awful, because in this short time I've learned that you would never place another woman in a position to interfere with our relationship unless you were distraught and not thinking clearly."

Could he be more of a screwup? Joseph moved next to Kendall on the bed, his back against the headboard, and prepared to expose himself. "I've been grounded for another month."

She searched his face, trying to understand his disparity. "Why? What does this mean?"

"My health isn't what it should be."

Fear ricocheted across the planes of Kendall's face.

Joseph hurried to put her mind at ease. "My blood pressure is very high—too high to fly. My doctor worries that it could effect my performance."

Kendall rested her hand on his iron thigh. "How serious is this?"

"I need to take medication, follow a diet, exercise. My doctor thinks if I do those things my blood pressure will come down and be manageable. I should be able to fly again."

"Why couldn't he put you on medications and still let you fly?"

Joseph had to take responsibility for his mistakes. "The doctor has given me many chances—I wasn't compliant to treatment. He had no other choice but to take this drastic step." He crossed the room, keeping his back to her.

"I don't understand. Why didn't you follow the doctor's orders? You love flying, why would you jeopardize everything you've worked for?"

"That's the million-dollar question," he grumbled before facing her. "Pigheaded, stupid—there's no good reason behind my actions. And now I'll have to pay for being pigheaded and stupid."

"How does this affect your career?"

"If I can beat this, everything should be fine. If not, I'll be forced to retire early." He rubbed a hand over his smooth face. "Can you imagine being forced to retire at forty years old? I've worked all my life to build my flying career. It's all I've ever wanted to do. I don't even have a wife or kids because I put my career goals first. Now it might all end." He paced the carpet. "I've always avoided trouble, stayed away from any behaviors that might put my name in the rumor mill, studied hard, and gone the extra mile—now it could all be for nothing. My career might end because my blood pressure is too high."

Kendall sprang from the bed and went to him. "I don't know a lot about high blood pressure, but I know it's a serious disease and you fit the profile: black man, forty, with a high-stress job. If you're not careful, you could have serious medical problems."

Joseph wrapped her up in his arms. "I know my mistake now."

"You can beat this. The doctor told you so. I'll help."

Thrilled with her concern and her commitment to him, Joseph pulled Kendall closer. "How will you do that?"

"I can cook for you; I'll make sure you're eating right. We'll cut out dinner at fancy restaurants. We could jog together every morning."

"Why would you want to do that?"

"There's something about you that wants me to have you around for a long, long time."

"Really?" His voice dropped to a seductive tone. "With an offer like that, I think I want to be around for a long, long time."

His hands went to the hollow of her back. His fingers splayed wide, caressing. He captured her bottom lip between his teeth. Hungry for his kiss, Kendall parted her lips in encouragement. Their kiss grew feverish. The sensation of their bodies touching fueled their fire.

Kendall pulled away, breathless. "I want to be with you tonight."

"You will." His voice had grown husky. "I want you more than possible. My body is feeling things right now I thought I could no longer feel." He nibbled her neck. "The only good thing to come of this is that we'll have plenty of time to be together."

* * *

Things could not have been going any better . . . until that vamp disguised as Little Red Riding Hood showed up at Joseph's door.

Gabrielle held her head as she sat upright in her bed. The pounding reminded her that she didn't handle her liquor well. She glanced down—still fully clothed. She had hoped her nightmare had not been true. She hoped Joseph did not help her to bed and leave without making love to her. No sneak peak at her breasts. No undressing her for bed while trying to feel her up.

Gabrielle took getting out of bed by slow measures, holding her head all the time. Too much liquor the night before. She crawled into her bedroom and checked her appearance in the mirror. Awful. She twisted the knob that started the shower, letting the water heat as she disrobed.

As the water pummeled her shoulders, Gabrielle asked herself what to do about Captain Joseph Stewart. The most logical thing to do was walk away. Obviously, Joseph desired the cute, helpless type. A strong, sensuous woman like her must be intimidating. The word amongst her coworkers was woefully wrong; if given a choice, a black man did not choose a white woman over a black woman every time. And her accent did nothing for Joseph. Even when she let Italian words of seduction roll off her tongue, Joseph only smiled politely and told her she didn't really mean what she was saying.

Gabrielle let the warm water move over her head as she asked herself again, *What should I do?* Giving up didn't sit well with her. She'd seen the competition, and she said aloud, "Joseph, she is not the right woman for you."

"Your little girl is in trouble and she needs her mother."

Helen removed the nighttime eye patch she wore to

blacken the room and allow her a good night's sleep. "My daughter is a grown woman." She pushed herself up and against the headboard, reading the early morning hour on the bedside clock. "Frank, why are you calling me, after all this time, at this hour?"

"Didn't you hear me? Your little—your daughter is in trouble."

"What kind of trouble?"

Frank spent fifteen minutes relating every detail of his meeting Captain Joseph Stewart and his subsequent talk with Kendall. As he listened to himself rationalize his fears, he knew that deep down he needed to hear his estranged wife's voice and that was why he had called her at dawn overreacting to Kendall's new boyfriend.

"I didn't hear the part about her being in trouble, Frank."

"This man is our age."

"So?"

"So, that doesn't bother you? Don't you think she might be compensating?"

"For what?" Helen asked, venom dripping from her tongue. "You not being a good father?"

"I was an excellent father to my girls. I'm offended that you would even suggest—I'm here, dealing with the problem, where are you? Who ran away when their child needed them the most?"

Helen's voice lost the soft corners and sharpened into a defensive edge. "I tried to be there for Kendall. I went to that hospital every day with a smile plastered on my face, telling her that I didn't blame her for Raven's death. And what did she do? She cursed me, told me to get out, said she never wanted to see me again."

"You know what state of mind she was in. They were giving her too many drugs. The girl couldn't walk. She couldn't use her hand." Frank swallowed hard before muttering the next words. "Raven was dead."

"Don't spew facts at me like I didn't live through that nightmare. Raven was my daughter too. I shared your bed every night. I held you in the front pew of the church at the funeral when you couldn't stop wailing. I stayed up all night waiting for you to come home and help me deal with the grief."

"It was hard on the entire family." Frank offered an apology for his cowardly withdrawal from his wife during the hardest part of their marriage.

With a brief silence, Helen accepted his attempt to mend his wrongs. "Did Kendall ask for me?"

Knowing the answer would bring pain, Frank hesitated. He had never lied to his wife and he never would. "I told her I didn't know where you were."

Disbelief silenced Helen.

"I couldn't tell her that you ran away from her because you blamed her for Raven's death. It would have killed her. I told her that we were having problems dealing with the situation and grew apart."

Helen called up her hard exterior. The grit that had helped her to survive the death of her youngest daughter—her favorite daughter—for the past year. "Then why are you calling me now, Frank? I'm out of her life. You deal with her problems."

Frank held the receiver to his ear as it buzzed and hummed. He told the disconnection, "Because *I* need you."

Chapter 29

Kendall pulled off her rubber gloves and jumped down from the step stool. She surveyed the mess in the kitchen. She had removed everything from the cabinets and spent the day changing the lining paper to a bright yellow. With her new mood, she wanted to change the color of her kitchen to a festive tangerine and yellow.

Redecorating the kitchen was only the beginning. Kendall called that morning and rejoined her tango class. Max had sat in the front seat while she drove her new Accord into the garage. She'd had lunch with her father two days this week. They were discussing old hurts and slowly mending the wounds. Greg was tickled with her work on the jewelry exhibit and was already planning her next assignment. Her hand spasms were more controllable, hardly a twitch. Even the guilt about Raven's death didn't plague her every minute of the day. She still had a ways to go, but she was making progress by leaps and bounds.

Joseph had been a dear and picked up everything on Kendall's redecorating list while she was at work. After dropping off the materials he went home to prepare for their drive to the beach tomorrow, where they would walk, breaking the monotony of his exercise routine. That's why the doorbell ringing surprised her.

Kendall ran her fingers through her short curls and

smoothed the edges of Joseph's oversize shirt. She had gotten into the habit of carrying a little piece of him with her wherever she went. She hurried across the kitchen floor, her socks sliding over the freshly waxed floor. She opened the door with a huge smile in anticipation of Joseph's handsome face, surprising her maybe with dinner. He would be thrilled to see her wearing his shirt. Small things that showed she cared pleased him.

"Darren."

"Hi, Kendall." Standing on her stoop, looking as good as the day she had met him in the superstore supermarket, was Darren. His large, rough hands pressed a small box into his stomach. The nature of his work kept his body in prime condition. A dark blue tank strained against his chest, designer jeans with a sharp crease defined his legs.

Kendall's eyes moved up from the designer gym shoes that matched his casual outfit. He hadn't changed much. Skin very light, hair very dark. The light from her foyer made the gold chain bracelet—the one she gave him on his birthday—glisten. Her eyes moved to it, and her heart slipped down a slope of warm memories. Darren's fingers drummed the box. Thick, old packing tape hung from the sides of the brown shipping box. The top was battered, but Kendall could not see inside from her angle.

Breaking the silence, Darren said, "You look good. I heard you running for the door."

Kendall's heart plunged into a pit of regret. Her mind reeled. Her physical therapy schedule roved through her brain. In an instant, with one sentence, Darren took her back to a place Joseph had helped her forget ever existed. As she watched the intensity in Darren's eyes, she wondered if she should forget or confront.

"I know this is a surprise." He shifted the box into the crook of his left arm. "But can I come in?"

Left-handed, Kendall remembered. She had held him close the night he told her the stories of how his teachers used to punish him for writing with his left hand. They tried to force him to use his right hand with dexterity. When he couldn't, they called him defiant. He broke down in tears one day after a verbal lashing from his favorite teacher. That's when they called his parents to the school. The teachers explained that a left-handed child was the equivalent of a retarded child. The next day he was sent to special education classes. Those teachers would never know the damage they had caused; Darren abandoned his dreams of a college education and accepted hard labor as his future.

"I'll leave if you still don't want to see me," Darren said, breaking Kendall's long silence.

For a flash in a moment of time, Kendall felt desperate he should stay. She felt as frantic as the day she made him so mad he grabbed his jacket and ran out of her place without a sweet good-bye or a soft kiss to her cheek.

Kendall unlocked the screen security door, opened the gate around her heart that guarded against memories of what could have been, and let Darren walk in. As he passed, brushing her shoulder, she recalled a line from an old vampire movie, "He can't come in unless you invite him."

"Russ, tell him to bring Kendall over for dinner," Sara called from the kitchen.

"I will," Joseph answered.

"Do it when the doctor releases you. We'll celebrate your return to the skies."

"Sounds good." But Joseph still had doubts that his blood pressure would be under control with four short weeks of therapy.

Russ slipped on his shoes and walked Joseph outside. "Are you feeling okay? How you holding up, buddy?"

"It's not as bad as I thought it would be. Which probably has a great deal to do with the time Kendall and I have been spending together. If she wasn't around for me to be with, concentrate on, I'd lose my mind."

They veered to the left, toward Russ's garage. Joseph didn't ask why they didn't go through the kitchen to the garage as always. He could have kissed Sara hello and good-bye.

"You're noticing that there is life outside that airport. Kendall's cooking for you, huh?"

"Keeping me healthy. Fussing like only an angry black woman can if I miss taking my medications. If she has time before work, we work out together. If not, she makes sure I do."

"I bet," Russ said with a grin. He grabbed the garage door handle and shoved it above their heads.

"It's not like that."

"I bet. Be careful of these young girls, buddy. Don't get too comfortable."

Joseph didn't want to know what that meant.

They went to Russ's workbench and began sorting through the tools.

"Why don't you clean this place up?" Joseph asked.

"I will. I haven't had time. I've been picking up extra flights."

Joseph shifted a heavy wrench from one hand to the other. "I noticed we didn't come through the kitchen to the garage. Now the extra flights. Anything you want to talk about?"

"Maybe I'll stop over for a beer while I'm home. We could catch the game. I'll get tickets."

The fact that Russ was springing for baseball tickets to see the losing Detroit Tigers meant the trouble ran deep.

"There's a game tonight." Joseph grabbed a power tool. "Can you make that? Tomorrow I have plans with Kendall."

"Tonight's no good, but soon."

They walked to the end of the driveway where Joseph had left his two-seater Benz.

"I'll talk to Kendall about dinner."

Russ nodded, his mood gloomy. "Let me know."

"You let me know about the game."

Russ gave a listless wave as Joseph backed away.

"How is it that you have my favorite cake waiting for me?" Darren asked in that low, appreciative tone he used after a good meal. "Did your father tell you to expect me?"

Kendall placed a thick slab of black forest cake before him. Reminiscing had made her forget the time she had watched him leave her town house brokenhearted. She placed a tub of vanilla ice cream in front of him with the spoon sticking out like the broken needle of a compass. So many signs warned of danger ahead.

Kendall slipped into the chair at the kitchen table that faced him directly. He had released his grip on the box long enough to eat dinner and now dessert. "Maybe in the back of my mind I knew that if Daddy showed up you weren't far behind."

Darren sliced into the cake with the edge of his spoon. "Your dad and I did bond."

"Not at first." Kendall laughed.

"Not until I promised him I wouldn't touch you until we were married."

This warning sign thumped Kendall in the middle of her chest. They were moving down a one-way street that could only bring two results. They would reach their end. Or they would turn around and retrace their path.

"I kept that promise." Darren watched her with unrelenting eyes as he slid the shiny spoon between his pink lips.

Kendall filled her mouth with ice cream. She didn't need to answer. She didn't know what to say. She hoped the silence would derail Darren's runaway train.

"I kept that promise for almost a year. I never tried to take it to that level. All my buddies knew—after your dad announced it at that barbecue, remember? I didn't care. I lived with the ribbing because I knew you were worth the wait." He pulled the spoon from the ice cream where Kendall had replaced it and let it slide between his lips. "You remember that?"

"I remember." Her dad had challenged Darren's manhood in front of her family and his; all his buddies and coworkers were at her parents' anniversary celebration.

"I kept that promise until you came home from the hospital. You asked me. Remember? You asked me to make love to you. I said no, I had made you and your father a promise."

Kendall tried to move away from the harshness of those times by placing distance between them. Unlike most men, Darren had always wanted to discuss every glitch in their relationship. He'd keep her up all night to solve a disagreement. He forced her to acknowledge their problems, talk them out. Kendall kept her back to Darren until he insisted she turn and face him.

His voice softened to that just-ate-a-good-meal level. "You were vulnerable that night. You needed to know that I still loved you. Said we'd do it only once. Told me that after we did I should go get the ring and make our engagement official. I told you that you would regret it if we did. You told me over and over that you needed me, remember?"

Kendall's body quivered with hard emotions. Things

she wanted to avoid, never address or deal with were being hurled at her at rocket-fast speed. Tiny explosions in her mind opened doors welded shut. She wanted Darren to leave, but needed him to stay. Now that he had taken her into the desert, she needed a drink of water.

"Do you remember that, Kendall?" Darren waited for an answer.

"I remember."

"Remember what happened when I gave in?" He popped another spoonful of ice cream in his mouth while he waited for his answer.

Unable to speak and take credit for the hard time she'd given him, she nodded.

"Do you understand why I did that?"

She went to the sink, putting distance between them. "I don't understand why you're doing *this.*"

"Sit down."

Kendall didn't move. Strolling over to the kitchen table and sitting down because he demanded it put a new spin on his visit. Him issuing commands and her docilely following changed the dynamics of their meeting. This was the perfect time to inject Joseph into the conversation. His presence, if only through words, would slow down Darren's confidant stride back into her life.

Darren stood and tucked the brown box under his arm. He moved to Kendall, slipping his arm around her waist. She tried to resist, but relaxed at the familiarity of his touch.

"Let's go into the living room."

Kendall let him lead her. They sat on the sofa with him balancing the brown box on his knees.

"What's in that box?" Kendall asked.

Darren removed his arm from around her shoulders and stroked the box. "Us."

Warmth splashed her face and moved through all corners of her body like hot water.

Darren carefully opened the lid of the box as if it were a treasure wrapped in expensive foil paper instead of a worn packing box with old tape. He pulled out a stack of old cards and letters and dropped them in her lap. While she sifted through her words of devotion and love, he removed another stack of cards—his promises of undying love and commitment. Those fell into her lap, and his hand dipped back into the box. He sprinkled her with old trinkets: a necklace, a bracelet, and a tiny stuffed animal.

As Kendall let the past rain down on her, Darren jiggled his bracelet in front of her. "Never took this off." He fingered the diamond stud in his left ear. "Never took this off. Never will."

Joseph popped into Kendall's head with such clarity she had to blink to be certain he wasn't standing in front of her.

"Darren, I don't know why you came. If you talked to my dad he should have told you that—"

"I came because I still love you. I didn't give up on us. I want to fix us—tonight."

"Darren, I—" Kendall scooped up the symbols of their relationship and put them back in the box. Before she could stand, Darren had her hand, pulling her back down.

"I should never have walked away. I should have used my key and forced my way back into this house and made you talk it out. Everyone ran away—I should have been stronger than that." He pushed the box onto the sofa and shifted his body, grabbing her hands and pulling them to his face. "We both made mistakes. Hell, maybe I needed to leave so that you could get better. I don't know. All I know is that you're the one that got away. I'm sure of that because I wake up every morning wondering what it would be like to have you lying next to me in my bed."

"Whoa." Kendall pulled her hands away and bolted across the room. "Darren, I'm seeing someone."

He did his king-of-the-jungle impersonation. "Is that supposed to mean something to me?"

"It means I'm seeing someone."

"Are you sleeping with him?"

"Is your ego getting in the way of why you came?"

Darren's chest deflated and the softness of his voice returned. "No. I just want to know."

"I'd never share that with you. It's irrelevant." Kendall softened her own tone. "I don't want to keep hurting you. I take responsibility for what happened between us. But you have to realize it did happen."

"Say you don't love me. Say you don't have any feelings for me and I'll walk out that door."

Kendall eased back to the sofa. "I can't say that, because it's not true and I won't hurt you just to make a bad situation easier. I will say that the time wasn't right for us. My memories of you are wrapped inside the memories of the worst time in my life and I can't separate them. I've tried, but I can't. It would never work between us because it would always be tainted."

"It can work if we make it work. Kendall, I'm not about walking away from this. I'm about taking it day by day until the past is so far behind us it doesn't matter."

"I'm seeing someone. A good someone. Be happy for me." Kendall give an apologetic touch to his cheek. "Find someone that deserves a good brother like you."

Chapter 30

Joseph carried the last of the grocery bags into Kendall's kitchen. Her tolerance of the rides home from work had increased by the day. He didn't pull over once during today's trip. Instead of rejoicing, Kendall seemed preoccupied and solemn. Joseph began to unpack the groceries while Kendall started dinner.

"Would you like to go out tonight?" Joseph asked while stacking canned goods in the cabinet.

Kendall pulled her attention away from the stove. "I have plans tonight."

"Plans? You didn't mention having any plans this morning. I assumed we would spend the night together."

"I'd like you to stay for dinner."

"I'd like that." Joseph studied her. Something was different. Since when did she make plans without telling him? When asked, she gave no indication what these "plans" were. At once he felt possessive, jealous of anyone diverting her attention away from him. She had never done anything to make him question her intentions—she had long ago earned his trust—but something wasn't right. "Did I do something wrong?"

"No," Kendall answered, her back to him while cooking. "There are things I need to do."

"Do you need me to drive you?" Joseph asked with

caution. She said he hadn't done anything wrong, but he got the feeling he had.

"No." She didn't elaborate.

Joseph watched her. Something was bothering her, but she didn't want to share it with him. This offended him. He felt shunned, unimportant in her life. He wanted to be her strength. He wanted to help her in any way he could. If something bothered her, he wanted her to come to him for comfort.

He decided to back off for now, as pushing might alienate her further. "Should I plan on driving you to work tomorrow?"

Kendall smiled over her shoulder. "That would be nice."

"Saturday night is date night. Would you like to have a date with me?" Joseph approached her from behind, wrapping his arms around her middle.

"Boy, would I like to have a date with you!" Kendall giggled, her mood dramatically lightening.

Joseph nibbled her neck. "You're sure I didn't upset you?"

"I'm sure."

"You seem out of sorts."

Kendall turned in the circle of his arms to face him. She traced the pocket under his left eye with the blunt tip of her manicured nail. She had no idea how good it felt when she did that. He could never describe vividly enough the way a current shimmied down his spine when she touched him in her private way. She outlined the tiny pouch of skin that had initially caused him to believe she wouldn't be attracted to him. A sign of aging that would make her politely refuse his offer for dinner or a movie. But Kendall embraced the flaw as part of what made him who he was and it made Joseph want to have her even more.

Kendall broke his trance. "Joseph, things are moving a little too fast between us. I need a day to myself."

"Are you saying I'm smothering you?" A pain shot through his skull, making his temples throb.

"I'm saying I want to take this slow. I want to move at a pace that's right for both of us."

"I never meant to pressure you. My time at home is limited. I wanted to spend as much of it getting to know you as possible."

Kendall's hand caressed his cheek. "This feels right between us . . . I need to be sure. I'm trying to rebuild my life, find my direction again. You're a major distraction."

"Is that good or bad?"

"Good."

"But?"

"But I have to stay focused. I'm making progress—thanks to your help."

"Do you want me to back off until you tell me it's okay?" Joseph's temples pounded with the fear that she might say yes.

"No! I'm looking forward to Saturday date night."

Before any more doubt could creep into Kendall's mind, Joseph seized her lips in a kiss that made her knees shake.

"Time for an old friend?" Kendall stood on Max's back porch with a pan of fresh-baked brownies.

Max's round face widened with a smile. "What do you have in there, neighbor?"

"Fudge brownies with walnuts, slathered with chocolate icing."

"My personal favorite."

"Do you have any ice cream?"

A brief silence stood between them where an apology was given and accepted.

Max flung the screen door open. "I rented movies."

After dinner, Kendall had sent Joseph home but not before sharing a string of kisses in her foyer. Kissing Joseph made her loosen up and calm down. His kisses weren't rushed. He didn't spare only enough time to make her horny so that they could jump into bed together. There was purpose behind every stroke of his tongue. Mostly, the purpose was to communicate how special she had become to him. Sometimes, it was to show her that he wanted to take their relationship to the next level.

"What are you in a daze about?" Max asked from his end of the sofa.

"I don't understand what went on between you and Joseph, but I'm sorry."

"You can't apologize for him, Kendall."

She mindlessly watched another scene from the movie before she continued. "It must have been a misunderstanding. Joseph is such a kind person, I can't believe he has an ulterior motive behind the time we've been spending together."

Max used the knife to slice another chunk of brownies from the pan. "He came on mighty strong. But I'm willing to see the other side of things. Let's talk this out."

"Okay." Kendall tucked her leg underneath her and turned to him.

"Does he order you around? Tell you what's best for you all the time?"

Kendall shook her head, relieved Joseph had passed one area of the test.

Max dropped a corner of the brownie into his mouth while he contemplated his next question. "Has he been isolating you from your friends?"

Max never realized the depth of mental devastation left behind from the accident. He knew she didn't drive anymore and that her relationship with her former boyfriend had ended, but that was all. He didn't know that she had isolated her family when in the beginning stages of rehabilitation. Instead of ruining the mood by explaining all of this, Kendall simply shook her head. "No."

"Then I guess he just has a problem with me. Maybe I did read our conversation wrong."

"It was a bad night for me," Kendall said, remembering the way she had barricaded herself in her bedroom.

"He sounded worried," Max conceded. "Tell me how you feel about him."

"I like him a lot. I'm really hoping this develops into something serious. But your warning. And Greg's. And my father. And then Darren showing up out of the blue. And getting pieces of my life back. I'm not sure of anything right now. Maybe I'm not seeing the complete picture."

"I don't want to come between you and Joseph, but I didn't think I would be a good friend if I didn't tell you how I felt. I couldn't keep what happened from you—it affects our relationship. Maybe my feelings were hurt—he did dismiss me and basically tell me I'm not important in your life now that you have him."

Kendall scurried across the sofa and pulled him into her arms. "That's not true. You've saved me more times than I can count. No matter what happens between Joseph and me, you'll always be my friend."

"Get off of me before I start crying." Max playfully pushed her away. "What are you going to do about Joseph?"

Kendall hesitated a moment. "Nothing. Things are good between us. I'll relax and see where it goes."

"A piece of advice: take it slow."

Kendall nodded. She'd heard that enough times.

"Not like Dan and me," Max added with a mysterious lift in his voice.

"What does that mean? Are you holding out on me, Max?"

He tossed the last of the brownie in his mouth, chewing with an exaggerated grin.

"Max! Tell me what happened!"

He made her suffer through his chewing and a long swallow of milk. He wiped his mouth free of crumbs and tossed the napkin on the coffee table before answering. "We made love."

"Get out of here!" Kendall exclaimed, happy that her friend's life was heading in the direction he wanted it to go.

Max whispered in a conspiratorial tone, "Do you want to hear about it?"

Kendall matched his tone. "Every detail."

At two in the morning, Max walked Kendall back to her side of the duplex. Both were as giddy as teenagers having spent the night comparing their new boyfriends. After every detail of their new relationships had been dissected, they moved on to life issues. Kendall described her carsickness. Max confessed the hurt still ringing in his heart over his family's refusal to embrace him as one of their own. By the end of their evening, both made vows to end their silent suffering.

Kendall climbed into bed with Joseph on her mind. Greg and Max cared about her and had only her best interest in mind, but they were wrong. She decided that they both let stereotypes guide their opinion of her relationship with Joseph. Only she and Joseph knew the sensations that bloomed when they were together.

Kendall smiled in the darkness. Judging by the four boxes of condoms he'd brought from the drugstore, Joseph felt those sensations the strongest. Knowing that he wanted her in that way gave her a boost of power. To purchase condoms must have been embarrassing for him. She suspected his generation wasn't as open about the business side of making love.

Kendall checked the clock as her eyes began to droop with sleep. In a few hours he'd ring her bell with a smile. She would invite him in for breakfast. He would become all flustered and apologetic, saying he'd be happy to take her out for breakfast. He'd sputter about allowing a woman to do too much for him. That argument had led her to let him purchase her week's groceries. When he started down that path in the morning, she'd kiss him and pull him into the kitchen by his sleeve. She would ask him to have a seat and then she'd climb into his lap and feed him every bite.

Joseph saw it all over Kendall's face when she opened the door. His excitement deflated with each word. "Good morning. Are you ready to go?"

"I'm running a little late." She hurried to the stairs without giving him his usual welcome kiss. "I made you breakfast. Eat. I'll be right down."

Joseph closed the front door and stood bewildered at the bottom of her stairs. "Is everything all right?" he called after her.

"Just running late."

She could play the denial game with him, but she couldn't hide the red, puffy eyes that glanced at him full of sorrow. Many tears had been shed last night. He wondered what had triggered her sadness.

"Joseph," Kendall called from the top of the stairs, "drink orange juice. Not coffee."

"You're nagging me already?"

"Get used to it."

The telephone rang three times while Joseph ate breakfast alone in Kendall's kitchen. Curiosity made him slow down his chewing so as not to impede his hearing— as if he could hear her talking on the phone upstairs.

The fourth time the phone rang Joseph placed his empty dishes in the sink and moved to the bottom of the stairs. "Kendall, is everything all right up there?"

A minute later, Kendall called back, "It's fine. I'll be right down, sorry."

Joseph saw the box of Kleenex tissue before he noticed the cards and photos spread across the living room sofa. Before he read the first card he had a mental picture of Kendall sitting on the sofa crying over her last boyfriend.

"It's not like it appears."

"That sounds like guilt since I didn't give you any idea of how it looks to me." Joseph dropped a photo of his heartthrob in a loving embrace with a tall, light brother that reminded him of the pretty boys making slow-grind R & B records.

Kendall appeared small, like a child, when she crossed one foot over the other and locked her hands behind her back.

"Maybe we should set up Gabrielle and Darren." He lifted his chin for confirmation of what he already knew.

Kendall's lashes dropped. "Darren."

"Maybe we should set them up on a blind date. Kill two birds with one stone."

The expression on Kendall's face said she didn't think Gabrielle was good enough for Darren.

"Why do you have these out?" Joseph picked up another card and began to read the inside.

"I wish you wouldn't do that."

Joseph glanced at her, seething. He continued to read.

"Please, don't do that."

"Why not? Secrets?"

"There are no secrets between us."

"What is in this card that I can't know?" His anger was coming to a boil. Jealousy spurred him on.

"If you ever want to know something about me, all you have to do is ask." Kendall held her hand out for the cards.

Joseph glared at her, his grip tightening until the cards began to fold over. "I'm not sure I believe you."

Kendall approached, prying the cards from his fingers. "I don't lie to you."

"Then let's have some truth. Is this something I should be worried about? Are you starting to come back into yourself and beginning to feel like you might have left something valuable behind?"

"I don't like to see my past and my future occupying the same place at the same time." Kendall pulled the cards away from him. She scooped up the memorabilia scattered on the sofa and locked it away in a beat-up brown box.

Joseph watched Kendall hide the box in the étagère decorating the corner of her dining room. He wanted her to go through the kitchen, to the back porch, and dump the box in the garbage. It didn't happen. He noticed the rise of her shoulders before she turned to him with a fake smile. "Are you ready?" She joined him in the middle of the living room.

"Call me shallow," Joseph declared, "but I have a problem with whatever you're hiding from me. I know I should take it with the same maturity as you did finding Gabrielle at my place, but somehow this seems more intimate."

"Are you accusing me of something?"

"I'm asking you straight out—what's with the trip down memory lane?"

The phone rang. Kendall's eyes sprang toward the cordless resting on the end table.

Joseph didn't like what he saw.

"Excuse me."

Joseph used his full girth to block her path. "The

phone's right there." He pointed to it in case she forgot where she kept her telephone.

Indecision rang louder than the telephone. Kendall dropped to the sofa and picked up the receiver. "Hello? I can't talk now. I will. I will."

Joseph crossed his arms over his chest and fixed his sight on every movement of her lips, not missing a word.

"I remember." Her eyelids flipped up at him and back to her lap. "I remember." She hung up.

Joseph asked a hundred questions with the jut of his chin.

"My father has called up the troops to save me from the wrath of you." An attempt at humor.

Joseph waited.

"Darren came by the other night."

"With a box of memories—in case you forgot yours."

Kendall didn't respond.

The other night. "And he's been calling ever since." Joseph dropped beside her on the sofa. "What happened between you?"

Kendall moved across the room and posed in front of the fireplace. "Darren is a good guy."

"I never attacked his character. Why do you feel the need to defend him to me?"

Kendall ignored the barb. "We fell apart. The accident happened and I pushed him away."

Joseph scratched his temple, taking time to search for calm words to express his emotions. "Sounds like he didn't want to go and you're kicking yourself for sending him on his way."

"I'm kicking myself for hurting the people that love me. I did a lot of that back then. I still haven't mended all of the wounds I caused."

"Vague," Joseph mumbled. Jealousy had a grip on his stomach and was twisting it counterclockwise.

"Not vague," Kendall snapped.

"Very vague," Joseph retorted. "Do you still care for this guy or what?"

Kendall took too long to answer. "It's hard to explain."

"Do you think I've suddenly been struck stupid? You tell me the truth; I'll be able to understand."

Sadness cloaked Kendall's beautiful brown eyes. "We're fighting over this?"

Joseph nodded. "We will be if you don't tell me something quick."

She struggled to maintain eye contact with him. "I care about Darren as a friend. I have a lot of regrets."

"Is this the reason you suddenly need time away from me? To see if maybe you made a mistake?"

"No." Alarmed, Kendall bolted across the room so that they were standing together. "No, I'm in a totally different place than I was when I was seeing Darren. I'm where I want to be—with you. I told him that."

"But the phone has been ringing off the hook."

"Joseph." His name rolled off her tongue in a warm whisper.

"What?" He didn't mean to sound so sharp. "If I wasn't here, would you be talking to him now?"

"If you weren't here I'd be asleep."

"Don't be flippant, Kendall."

He didn't like the twisting in his gut and the throbbing in his temple. Darren would be another problem in their relationship. He thought of Max, Greg, and her father. He saw Gabrielle draped on his sofa. His career swirling down the toilet. Kendall couldn't drive. She couldn't ride in a car from point A to point B without puking on the side of the road. So many obstacles; where was the payoff?

"Do you need time for closure?"

"Joseph, you're taking this all wrong. There is no

question in my mind about us. Darren showing up again—it opened some doors I wished would have stay closed. I've told you everything about the accident. But I did things during my recovery, things I wish I could take back but can't. The time has come for me to correct my mistakes—I have to apologize to the people I hurt and try to make it right."

Joseph scratched at his mustache to keep from pulling Kendall into his arms and telling her to forget the other people in her life—he was all she needed. Selfish, jealous thoughts ricocheted between his temples, intensifying the throbbing. Kendall was on a mission to put her life back in order. How could he interfere with that? If he cared about her and trusted her, he had to let her resolve the problems of her past. The payoff would be great—he'd have her, unscarred, in his life. The thought of her rehashing the past with her old boyfriend was unbearable. But he knew the right thing to do.

Joseph grasped Kendall's arms with an affectionate squeeze. "I'll pick you up from work today, but we should cancel our plans for tonight."

"Why? Are you upset about this? It's nothing. Believe me."

"I do."

"Then why are you canceling our plans for tonight?"

Joseph glanced to where the beat-up box had been stowed away. "You have things you need to take care of and I can't be around to watch."

"I don't understand."

"I'm giving you space."

"But—"

He kissed her lips, stopping the protest. He quickly changed the subject before he lost the courage to do the right thing. "Listen, Russ and Sara want us to come by for dinner before I go back to work." *If I ever go back to work.* "Would you like to go?"

"I'd like that."

"Okay. I'll call her and tell her it's a go."

"Joseph—"

"We need to go or you'll be late for work."

Joseph heard the phone ringing when he slid his key in the door. He hurried across his living room and dove on the sofa, snatching up the receiver.

Kendall said, "You keep running away when things don't go the way you want them to go."

"Sometimes I need to be alone—to think."

"I need to know that I can count on you. I can't count on you if you keep running away."

Joseph scrubbed his chin. "You're right."

"It hurts me when you shut me out."

"I never, ever meant to hurt you. Sometimes you need to be alone—to think."

After a pause, Kendall spoke. "I turned Darren away because—although he's a good guy—he never made me feel the way I feel when I'm with you."

After a pause, Joseph said, "You have unfinished business with Darren."

"True."

"Finish it."

"I will, but I don't want to lose you."

"Finish it and then call me."

"Joseph—" A whisper.

"I'll be waiting."

"Joseph." His name sounded like a soft caress.

"No other man will ever touch you. Don't forget your promise."

Chapter 31

It was Joseph's doing. He pushed Kendall away so that they could grow closer, willing to accept all her issues, but not willing to accept her lingering feelings for another man. She honored his wishes, as he had honored hers about Gabrielle.

Joseph's request forced Kendall to make tough decisions. It also allowed her time to grow and find herself. The first thing she did was talk to Greg. He heartily agreed to her returning to work full-time. She grew comfortable enough to ride along with Max as he ran errands. She rejoined her tango classes, becoming a dancing diva. She was even considering entering a tango contest in Montreal.

Thinking of Joseph, Kendall dressed to reluctantly go clubbing with Max. He was determined to cheer her up. Although her life was going well, she missed Joseph. She knew how to fix things with him, but fearing her resolve wouldn't hold against Darren's armor of memories, she hesitated to do what had to be done.

"Oh, no, girlfriend." Max's mouth dropped when Kendall descended the stairs. "You're not going out dressed like that, are you?"

"What's wrong with how I'm dressed?"

Max grabbed her hand and led her back up the stairs. "Nothing if you're going to work in an office. Take off that business suit. Show a little skin."

Kendall dropped on the bed while Max rummaged through her closet. Her heart wasn't into hitting the trendy club, but he wanted her to meet his treasured Dan. She wanted to spend the evening cuddled with Joseph but he had been clear. Their relationship remained on hold until she talked with Darren.

"Am I going to be the only straight person in this club?"

Max smacked his lips. "No. It's mostly straight. Straight and tolerant."

Kendall knew that downtown Royal Oak on a Saturday night was the equivalent to a New York freak party. Leather shops with window mannequins depicting acts of S & M lined the avenue. On every corner were bars where the amount of fun you had was gauged by your inability to walk straight. The alternative lifestyle players called the tiny city of Royal Oak their capital. Prior to tonight, the only hot spot Kendall visited anywhere near downtown Royal Oak was the Detroit Zoo.

"Get undressed," Max ordered as he pulled a midnight-blue camisole out of her closet. "And lose the loafers."

With a wary heart Kendall complied. "I can sit in the backseat, right?"

"Yes." Max scrounged around on the floor for a pair of high heels.

"And Dan will stop if I need him to pull over?"

"I covered the rules with him. Don't worry. You've been doing well. We drove all the way to the mall this morning and I didn't stop once." Max joined her near the bed. "You have a gorgeous body. Why are you covering it up? Put this on."

Kendall slipped into the silky camisole before stepping into the hipster jeans. "These are really low cut."

Max ignored her.

"I need something." She shrugged her right shoulder, discreetly reminding Max of her scars.

"You need to stop fretting. With a killer body like that, no man is going to pay a lick of attention to your shoulder."

"The only man I care about seeing my body is Joseph."

"Whoa." Max laughed.

Kendall tugged at the top of her jeans. They were so low cut that she almost needed a bikini wax. She wandered into the bathroom while Max searched for a cover-up top. She twisted and stretched to see how far the dip went in the back. This pair of pants had been purchased while she and Raven raced through the mall feeling confident and sexy. After the accident, with the scars, she hardly felt that way anymore. Except the times Joseph kissed and massaged her body until she trembled shamelessly.

Max appeared in the mirror beside her. "You really do look good." He helped her slip her arms into a matching top. "Try to ease up and have fun tonight. I want you to like Dan and I want Dan to like you."

"I will."

"Listen, I know I've been down on Joseph, but if he makes you happy I want things to work out for you. Tonight you're claiming more of your independence—getting back to living and having fun. It'll help you clear your mind and then you can work things out with your pilot."

Kendall smiled. "My pilot's cute, isn't he?"

"I looked twice."

Laughing, Kendall opened her arms for an embrace. "You're a good friend."

"Step into the heels and let's go pick up my man."

"Mommy, your trunk is full of ka-pow!"

Kendall turned with her alcoholic-free drink in hand. She stared down the young man. "Who are you talking to like that?"

"You, Mommy. Wanna dance with a lonely brother?" He splayed his diamond-heavy fingers across his chest.

"No." Kendall turned away from him, her eyes searching the dance floor for Max and Dan.

The man's hands snaked around her waist. "C'mon. What you come here for if you don't want to dance?"

Kendall asked herself that same question once she saw the six gold teeth of his upper plate.

The DJ said something about booties shaking and the people flooded the dance floor.

The man smiled. "Dance with me, pleazzz."

Max returned to the table in time to save her.

"This your man?"

"Yes." Kendall wrapped herself around Max's arm. He glared down at her, perplexed.

"That's all you had to say." The man finger-popped to the next table.

"I'm going to leave," Kendall announced.

"Why? It's too early."

"I'm not having a good time and I don't want to ruin it for you and Dan. I'll grab a taxi."

"No way. Dan and I will drive you."

"No." Kendall slipped her purse onto her shoulder. "Stay. I see the way Dan is watching you. You need time alone."

Max's face broke into a wide, hopeful grin.

"Drop by tomorrow and give me the juicy details."

"If you're sure . . ."

"I am." Kendall leaned in for a kiss before disappearing into the crowd.

Clean, cool air rushed into Kendall's lungs when she exited the club. Outside, the valet parkers were hopping in and out of cars trying to keep up with the steady stream of partiers that lined the avenue. They arrived in boy-girl, boy-boy, and girl-girl couples. Some were dressed to the nines in designer suits and mink stoles. Others were dressed in jeans and colorful gym shoes. Kendall watched the diverse crowd while clearing her lungs of cigarette and cigar smoke.

After people-watching for a few minutes, Kendall hailed a taxi.

"Where to?"

A sudden impulse came over Kendall. She leaned close to the Plexiglas separating her and the cabbie. "What time is it?"

"Almost one."

Kendall hesitated. Coming to a rash decision, she leafed through her address book. She gave the cabbie the address she had long ago forced out of her mind and sat back contemplating what she would say when she arrived.

"Kendall." Darren pulled his robe tight around his waist. "What are you doing here at this hour? Is something wrong?"

"No." Looking at the fine hairs of his chest made her doubt her reasoning. "Can I talk to you?"

"At this hour?"

Kendall waited.

Darren shook his head. "Come in." He opened the screen door and pulled her inside. Kendall heard his breath catch when he helped her remove her jacket.

"I don't know why, but I needed to talk to you tonight."

"Sit down." Darren turned on the living room lights. "Can I get you something to drink?"

"No, thanks."

"I'm having juice. I'll bring you one too." Darren always believed he knew what she needed. Even if she told him otherwise.

A picture frame on top of the thirty-five-inch television

caught Kendall's eye. She wandered over. Raven had snapped this picture on the Fourth of July at Metropolitan Beach. Darren sat bare-chested in the sand with Kendall between his legs. A satisfied smile covered her lips; Darren wore an expression full of love. He couldn't have been happier if he owned a million gas stations. Seeing this picture flooded Kendall with happy memories that would make her visit harder to complete.

"That's my favorite picture of you."

Kendall turned to find Darren inches behind her. She took a glass from him and found a seat on the sofa.

Darren settled next to her. "I miss Raven."

Kendall sipped from her juice.

"I miss you, too."

Kendall let the emotions dissipate before she spoke. "Darren, I don't know what to say to make this easy. I have to say it outright."

"What?" Darren placed his glass on the coffee table and reached for hers. He took her hand in his.

"As much as I cared for you—"

"Loved. You loved me."

Kendall refused to make it easier for herself by denying what they had. "I did love you."

"Past tense?" Darren whispered.

"Past tense. I'm sorry."

Darren sank into the sofa.

"I couldn't let you keep pursuing me, thinking that we might get together. It's not going to happen. If I didn't still care for you, I wouldn't be this blunt. I don't want to hurt you unnecessarily. I want to be honest. I owe you that much."

"Why?"

"I don't know." And she didn't. "Everything happened and I changed. I'm not the same woman you loved a year ago. It would only be a matter of time before you realized that. Things would end badly—I don't want that. I want us to be friends, but you have to understand we're only friends."

Darren looked crushed. Kendall hated what she had to do, but it would be better in the end. Darren wouldn't hold out hope. He could go on with his life.

"You said you were seeing someone."

"I am."

"If he wasn't in the picture?"

Kendall shrugged. "He is."

Darren crossed the room. "What if I don't want to accept this?"

"What are you going to do? Keep me prisoner? Force me to love you back?"

Darren acknowledged her logic with a nod.

"Now that you know, you can find the woman you deserve."

"Do you think I'm just going to run out and replace you? I can't do that."

Kendall stood and watched pain drain the color from Darren's face. "Darren, you're such a good man: handsome, strong, honorable, and loving. You deserve someone that returns those sentiments with as much energy as you give."

She moved to the door before he could stop her. There was no rationale in drawing it out. It was over between them and the sooner Darren accepted that, the sooner he could go on with his life. "I wish you the best."

Kendall hurried out the door to the waiting taxi. She managed to give the cabbie directions to her town house before she broke down into uncontrollable sobs. She cried for love lost, for hurting a man who didn't deserve it, and for fear of placing her heart on the line for Joseph.

Chapter 32

Greg's ruddy cheeks were drawn tight as he stomped up to Kendall. "You're forty minutes late, Kendall. Where have you been? The men from the dig came by unexpectedly. They're in my office right now—waiting to meet you." He stopped in his tracks. "What the hell? Kendall, what's wrong with you?" He snatched her up by the arm before she sank to the ground, bearing all her body weight. "Somebody get me a chair!"

"No." Kendall panted to catch her breath. "Not here. Take me to my office."

Greg did as she asked, passing curious workers on the way to her office. He helped her to a chair before getting a cool cloth to press to her clammy brow. "You're so pale. What happened?"

Kendall smiled, throwing Greg off guard. "I drove myself to work today."

"What?" Disbelief and then pride crossed Greg's chubby face. "What do you mean you drove to work?"

"I woke up this morning and I was tired of being a burden on other people. I marched out to my garage, started the Honda, and drove to work. I couldn't do the freeways and I had to pull over several times but I made it."

"Is Joseph with you?"

"I did it alone. I made it to work on my own."

"You made it," Greg repeated, his voice quivering. "Why now? After all this time, what was different about today?"

"Joseph gave me the push I needed. He took me to the beach at Kensington last week and put me behind the wheel again. Once he showed me the way, I took the ball and ran with it."

"I'll be."

"I did it, Greg."

"Yes, Kendall, you did it."

Joseph missed Kendall. Foolish pride. He told her to go, take care of her finished business with the ex—Darren— and then come back to him. Did his pride ever consider she might enjoy being with Darren again?

He surveyed the refrigerator, searching for something to fix for dinner. Kendall had stocked his refrigerator with the things recommended on Dr. Bennis's diet plan. Going to the crazy superstore hadn't been so stressful with Kendall by Joseph's side. Nothing seemed insurmountable with Kendall supporting him. The diet was doable. Their walks broke the monotony of his exercise routine. Running her errands, driving her to and from work made long days shorter. Cuddling her in his arms filled his once empty nights.

Joseph seasoned fish—Kendall had dumped the salt in the trash—and placed it on the grill. He had checked his blood pressure earlier that day at the drugstore while picking up shaving supplies. The high numbers disappointed him. A week into his treatment plan hadn't made much difference. He planned to step up his exercise regimen in the morning.

Joseph removed the fish from the grill and sat down to dinner for one, craving the ability to reach out and touch Kendall, drawing out her serenity to soothe his mind. The aura of calmness surrounding her did wonders for his temper. Maybe he would pick up the phone and invite her to dinner tomorrow.

He couldn't.

Kendall had to come to him in her own time, on her own terms. He had to remember their age difference, their different levels of life experience. Kendall might discover that she wasn't ready for a long-term relationship and he'd have to respect that.

A month ago, no woman could have claimed his heart. Kendall traipsed into his life and had him daydreaming about a wife, kids, settling down, and enjoying life. Maybe one call wouldn't hurt. He hurried through dinner, rushing to the phone in his bedroom. He hung up before the seventh digit was punched. If he truly cared for Kendall he had to allow her time. He had to loosen his hold and hope that she felt as strongly about him as he felt for her.

Chapter 33

Kendall peeked out through the curtains to see the shiny red SUV parked in her driveway. The dome light illuminated Joseph's delicious mocha skin as he stepped out carrying an oblong box. Ruggedly handsome in the faded jeans and a pullover sweater, he stepped up to the porch with the stern look of determination.

Ecstatic at the surprise visit, Kendall opened the door before he could ring the bell. She tried to contain her joy, not look anxious. "Hi, Joseph."

"Going out?" Joseph scanned her body, as if searching for another man's fingerprints.

"Coming in from tango class." Kendall smoothed the flaring skirt, distracting his attention from her exposed waist.

"I wanted to talk to you." Still stoic, he lifted his chin, making it a question.

Kendall stepped aside, allowing him entry into her home. "Would you like something to eat?" She tipped barefoot across the scattered rugs toward the kitchen.

"No." Remembering his manners, "Thank you. Dance class lasts this late?"

Kendall turned to him in the darkened hallway. The gray of his temples sparkled against his mocha skin. No sign of mistrust, only worry. "We're practicing a difficult routine. I stayed late for help."

Joseph watched her, eyes burning with desire. "You didn't ask what I needed to talk to you about."

"You'll tell me when you're ready."

Joseph's smoldering gaze coupled with the intense silence unnerved Kendall. She knew what he waited to hear and she didn't withhold the information. "I closed a painful chapter of my life."

"You seem sad about it."

"In order to move on I had to hurt someone I deeply care about."

Joseph held her eyes. The hum of the refrigerator provided the backdrop for their thoughts. "You hurt this person because of me?"

"I really want you in my life."

"I feel like I shouldn't be happy about it. Like it's wrong that I want to celebrate that you chose me and not him. I can't seem to muster up the guilt. Plain and simple, you're mine. I wouldn't let you go without one hell of a fight."

Kendall looked away in order to gather her thoughts. "It had to happen. Despite you asking, I would have had to face my history." She looked up into the portals to his soul. "I don't want you to have any doubts about us."

Joseph's chin jutted upward. "Are you okay?"

"Outside of feeling like a jerk, I'm fine. Darren is a good man." She paused to study his reaction. "He's just not the man for me."

"And am I?"

"I think so."

"Despite what Max, Greg, and your father say?"

"Despite what anyone thinks, yes, you are the man for me."

Joseph shifted his weight.

"What made you come by?" Kendall asked.

"After two weeks, I was afraid you weren't going to erase Darren from your life—you would erase me."

"Never."

Relief washed over Joseph, softening the stoic set of his brow. He held out the oblong box. "I thought we should create memories of our own."

Kendall took the box, ripped it open. "Joseph! I can't accept this." She let the box slip to the floor, running her fingers over the smooth wood grain of the fertility statue. It still held an air of mystique. Intricate cornrows, thick lips, and exaggerated breasts, the statue was a true tribute to the ancestors. This had been the start of it all. Overcome with memories of how she had lived then— scared, sad, and hopeless—compared to where life—and Joseph—had taken her, Kendall turned her back to Joseph.

With the fluid movement rivaling a sleek panther, Joseph locked Kendall up in his arms, resting his chin on her shoulder from behind. "This statue was never mine. I'm simply returning it to where it belongs." He turned her to face him, kissed her eyelids before capturing her lips. After a heated kiss that left them both breathless, he set her away from him.

Still fighting tears, Kendall asked, "Are we okay?"

"Never in danger, you and me." His chin shot upward. "Where will you put it?"

"I don't know. In my bedroom until I find the perfect place." Avoiding the heat of his eyes, Kendall changed to a benign subject. "Did I ever tell you the myth behind this idol?"

"No, you didn't."

"Are you sure I can't fix you something to eat?"

"I'm not hungry for food."

"Yeah, we're okay." Kendall laughed. "I'm starving—"

"I can take care of that."

"For food, Joseph." *And you,* she didn't say. "And I need a shower." Dance class had been particularly gru-

eling; sweat pouring from her body, leaving her in need
of a long, hot shower.

"Why don't you take a bath?" Before she could answer,
he added, "I could help."

"Kendall, it's me," Max shouted from the kitchen. "I
wanted to check on you and I need—" He stopped
suddenly upon seeing Joseph.

"I'm fine. Joseph is here."

Joseph's lips went to Kendall's neck, heating her to
the core before backing away and leaving her body
cold enough to shiver. He stepped up to Max, hand extended. "I owe you an apology."

Max glanced between Kendall and Joseph before reluctantly shaking his hand.

"I shouldn't have tried to exclude you from Kendall's
life. I'm sorry."

"It's forgotten." Max looked to Kendall as he said it.

Kendall watched as Joseph backed up to the stairs.
"I'm going on up. Don't be long." The blatant seduction
of his eyes stayed behind as he turned and took the stairs
two at a time.

Max cleared his throat. "Who was that and what was
that about? Definitely not the same brute I met before."

"I told you Joseph isn't a bad guy. He apologized. Now
you do your part and try to get along with him."

"Don't worry about me. Listen, Dan is here and I'm
out of wine."

"You know I don't drink."

"I stowed a bottle in your washroom the last time I ran
your errands."

"Why did you do that?" Kendall asked but her attention was focused on the shadow moving at the top of the
stairs.

"So I would have it at a time like this." He paused.
"You know how I get when I'm down."

She did. If life kicked Max in the butt he would polish off an entire bottle of wine alone in one night. She could hear running water in her bathroom.

"Kendall?" Max asked.

"Yeah, take the wine."

She followed Max to the washroom, both in a hurry to get back to their dates. Max broke the seriousness of the hunt with a nervous chuckle. "Look at us."

Kendall joined him in laughter. "I guess we're both anxious to get back to what we were doing." The robust fragrance of lilacs floated down the stairs. The hairs on the back of her neck stood straight in anticipation of what Joseph was doing. She tossed dirty clothes about in search of Max's wine. "I can't find it."

"Here it is!" Max pulled the bottle from behind the bleach on an upper shelf. "I knew I put it in here. Hid it from myself." He clutched the bottle to his chest. Their eyes locked. "Big night."

"For me too. Good luck."

Max made his way to the back door. He stopped on the porch and turned to Kendall. "Did I tell you, you're gorgeous? Very sexy. If I wasn't gay, I'd hit on you."

Kendall smiled. "Dan's waiting."

Max gazed in the direction of his door. "Yes, he is."

Kendall watched Max until the darkness consumed him. She remained in the doorway, taking the opportunity to calm down. Imagining what waited at the top of the stairs made her giddy with adventurous delight. She let the early evening breeze wash over her, inhaled it deeply. Laughing, hoping—she never thought she'd get back to this place again. She looked upward at the stars dotting the sky, certain one belonged to Raven and that she was looking down at her big sister, proud for fighting her way back.

"Kendall?" asked Joseph. "What are you doing out there? Is everything all right?"

Kendall closed the door on the stars and turned to her future.

"Kendall?"

"I'm not so hungry—for food—anymore. And I think the bath can wait."

Joseph stepped forward and locked the back door. Taking her into his arms, he asked, "You okay? You're a little misty eyed, princess."

Always princess when he sensed she needed pampering. "I'm fine. Very, very happy and I didn't think I'd ever be happy again." She wrapped her arms around his neck. "Thank you."

Joseph answered with a kiss that showed two weeks apart was too long. He used his solid frame to dance her around the kitchen, stopping when they were near the counter. He hoisted her up. Keeping their lips meshed, Joseph bunched her flaring skirt in his hands and eased it above her knees. Kendall used deft hands to open his leather belt. She drowned in emotion and when she emerged Joseph held her body captive, riding her through crashing waves of pleasure. She locked her legs around his waist, sliding across the cold tile with every thrust of Joseph's hips. They exploded together, exhausted, sated, ready for more. With her legs still wrapped around his middle, Joseph carried her up the stairs to a waiting bath.

"That was the best bath I've ever taken." Joseph climbed between Kendall's sheets completely nude.

Kendall darted from the room.

"Come to bed, princess," Joseph called after her.

"I'm coming." Her voice sounded farther away.

She returned carrying the fertility statue. Joseph watched the shift of her behind as she paced the room. Kendall had a mysterious magnetism that made him crave the sensation of her skin next to his. Her hair glistened with droplets of water from their bath. "Are you doing something different with your hair?"

Kendall set the statue on top of the television and stepped back to observe. "Letting it grow out a little. What do you think?"

"I think you're beautiful no matter how you choose to wear your hair."

Kendall turned to him. "What do you think about putting the statue here?"

"Good, now come to bed."

"Be patient." Not happy with where the statue was, she looked around the room.

"And lose the robe."

"Joseph," Kendall said, exasperated, but smiling. "I've got it." She placed the idol on the antique trunk at the foot of the bed before crawling in next to him. "What do you think?"

"Perfect." Distracted, Joseph reached for her. "Lose the robe."

"Did I ever tell you the myth behind this statue?"

"No, you didn't."

"It's really interesting. See, there was this boy—"

"Kendall, you can tell me the story if you lose the robe."

"One-track mind." Kendall let the robe slip from her shoulders, revealing creamy caramel skin and firm breasts. She shielded her right shoulder from view.

"Don't do that." Joseph reached for her. "You're a beautiful woman. Especially completely naked."

She snuggled against his chest, eyes glued on the statue staring back at them.

"Show-and-tell. Tell me your story so that I can show you something."

Kendall threw her head back in laugher, pushing at his chest. "Be serious, Joseph."

"Okay, share your story, princess."

"There is a legend about the first young boy in a pre-historic African village to be wed. At fourteen, he was considered an adult and he chose to marry the pretty daughter of the tribal chief. Because his family was not of royal standing, the chief refused. But the elders reminded the chief that the boy could choose whomever he pleased. To break that sacred rule meant to anger the gods. The rains would come and flood the village. The crops would die. Wars would start with the other tribes in the region."

Mesmerized by the tempo of Kendall's velvety voice, Joseph was drawn into the story. He relished in the sensation of their naked bodies molded together. He gave her a squeeze, encouraging her to finish the story.

"The chief reluctantly agreed to the marriage, but only if the boy could complete a task. The boy had to give his daughter a wedding gift that proved his worth. Short version, the boy spent eight days alone in the forest searching for the perfect tree. He chopped it down and used some of the wood and made this idol.

"Knowing an idol wouldn't be enough to please the chief, the boy spent three additional days in the forest summoning the gods. They came to him in a clearing, and by moonlight he asked the gods to bless the statue so that he might give his father-in-law many heirs.

"The chief accepted the gift. The boy was married and fathered sixteen children. He passed the idol on to his eldest son, who fathered sixteen children. And so on and so on. Legend has it that the power of the idol has faded with the passing of time, but when given as a gift from a man to his wife, the woman will bear many children."

"So you're saying I just impregnated you."

"Get out of here." Kendall beat at his massive chest with her tiny fists.

"Hey." Joseph easily wrestled her to the mattress, using his body to pin her beneath him.

Their eyes met.

The giggles faded.

"That wouldn't be a terrible thing," Joseph said.

Kendall's lashes fluttered.

Joseph slipped his hands between them and caressed her belly. "It would be nice to know my child is growing inside you."

Kendall didn't look away. Her chest heaved with the depth of her breathing.

"I want at least four kids."

Kendall licked her lips.

"I'm forty years old."

She tried to laugh. "I know how old you are, Joseph."

"With you."

Kendall's eyes grew into giant brown saucers.

"I'd like to have at least four kids with you. What do you think about that?"

"I—I—"

"What?"

"We've never talked about kids—"

"And marriage."

"And marriage."

Joseph's fingers massaged her scalp. "I want to get married and have kids. Lots and lots of kids. What do you picture when you think about your future?"

"I want those things too."

Joseph kissed her forehead, eyelids, chin. "Then why did you become pale when I brought up the subject?"

"Because while we were apart the past two weeks I realized I want those things with you."

Joy burst free inside Joseph's heart. Holding the intensity of the moment, he captured Kendall's mouth and demonstrated how much he wanted those things with her. He imprisoned her heart with the gentle caress of his tongue. He held her tight, flipping over so that she covered his body. With skill, he maneuvered their bodies without breaking the seal of their lips. He sat with his back against the headboard, Kendall straddling his lap, facing him. He released his hold only to retrieve the foil package from under the pillow and apply it to the throbbing steel beating against Kendall's behind.

Kendall feasted on his neck, lifting her hips to allow him entry. Joseph glided into the narrow tunnel with one stroke. He grabbed her hips, encouraging her to endure because the pleasure would come quickly.

Kendall's head dropped, perspiration dripping onto Joseph's chest. She found a bouncing rhythm that pleased her.

Joseph's fingers sank into the satin of her hips. "Kendall, take what you need." He fell back against the headboard, allowing her to control all movement.

Kendall panted; perspiration coated her body. With a glazed expression she found Joseph's eyes and would not let him look away. Her lips were slightly parted. The sight hardened Joseph's body to painful proportions. He slipped his thumb between her lips. "Taste me."

Kendall slipped her lips around Joseph's finger. She bounced mercilessly on his lap, now moaning with every stroke. Her head fell back and she screamed his name, sending Joseph to heaven. He pushed his thumb deeper inside the heat of her mouth while pushing to relieve the throbbing pain. Kendall suckled. Joseph steadied her hips. He bent his knees and pursued maximum depth. Soon, he screamed her name.

Breathing hard, "Joseph?"

"Yes, princess?"

"You should think about leaving a change of clothes here. Pajamas. Maybe a uniform."

He cradled her head to his chest. "Yes, princess."

Chapter 34

Having missed Kendall the day before, Frank showed up bright and early at her town house. He rang the bell, bracing himself for the talk that was long overdue between him and his oldest daughter. He stumbled backward when Joseph answered his daughter's door barefooted and bare-chested.

"Frank."

His gut twisted. "Where's my daughter?"

Joseph looked uneasy, but Frank refused to let him off the hook. "Where's Kendall?"

"She's sleeping."

"Tell her that her father is here." He grabbed the door handle and yanked on the screen. He couldn't have been more insulted to find the door locked. His daughter's house and he was locked out while a half-naked man old enough to be her father pranced around inside. He had a mind to take Joseph out back and give him a good marine butt-kicking. They'd see who had to save who then. "Open this damn door."

Holding his tongue, Joseph opened the door. Frank marched past him to the living room. Joseph disappeared on the second level. Five minutes later Frank stood at the bottom of the stairs yelling. "Kendall Masterson, you get down here right now. I know what's going on. Get down here!"

Only a second passed before Kendall bounded down the stairs, but Frank was so angry even that was too long.

"Is this how I raised you, Kendall? To let a man take advantage of you?" He dipped near her face, gritting his teeth. "How many times did I tell you not to sleep with a man until after you're married? And don't try to deny it. Joseph answering your door before eight in the morning—naked. I know what's going on here."

"Daddy, calm down."

Frank stomped away from her. First Raven died, his wife ran away with another man, and now his daughter—who just came back into his life—was slipping away. "Oh, this is calm. I started to grab that man and—"

"Daddy! That's enough."

Thank God she was dressed. Frank would have lost his mind if—he couldn't think about it, picture anyone stealing his baby's innocence. "Kendall, baby, what were you thinking? I warned you about men like him."

"Daddy, sit down. Please."

They sat together on her sofa, Frank waiting for his daughter to tell him he had the wrong idea.

"I'm twenty-five years old. You have to let me live my life. I care about Joseph. He's good to me and he's good for me. You have to accept him in my life."

"This why you told Darren you couldn't see him anymore?"

"I haven't been seeing Darren in over a year. It's not going to work out between us. You have to realize that and stop feeding him things that make him think there's a chance. He has to go on like I've gone on."

Frank took Kendall's hand. "You're confused right now."

"No, I'm not. For the first time in a long time I know just what I want and Joseph is a big part of that. Try to get along with him."

"Never."

"Don't make me choose."

"What's that mean?" He dropped Kendall's hand.

"It means I have to live my life and concentrate on what will make me happy. I'm not giving Joseph up, Daddy."

"Kendall." Frank's heart ached. He couldn't lose her again.

"Just try. That's all I ask. Be polite to him. You'll see in time what kind of man he is."

Frank dropped his head. He wouldn't give his daughter over to this man. He'd do as she asked and be there prepared to pick up the pieces when Joseph showed his true colors. This would be one lesson Kendall would have to learn on her own.

"Daddy, why did you come by?" She ran her hand down his arm and squeezed his hand.

He sobered, remembering his mission. "I'm having a dinner in two weeks. I want you to come by the house."

"Why?"

"I talked to your mother. She'll be there."

A myriad of emotions crossed his daughter's face, the most painful yet to come.

"You found Mom?"

He glanced away from her probing eyes. "She was never lost."

"I don't understand."

The hardest part, but they'd never heal as a family with lies between them. "I didn't tell you the truth about your mother. Things were strained between us when Raven died. We argued. She found comfort with another man. That's where she's been—living her life with this man."

"Strained because of me?"

Frank moved away from her palpable pain. "Strained.

I want you to come to dinner and talk things out with your mother."

Kendall shook her head. "I can't do it. She still blames me for Raven's death."

"You won't know what your mother thinks until you talk to her. This has gone on long enough. We need to deal with this as a family, put it behind us, and try to salvage what we had. I'm your father and I'm your mother's husband. Both of you will be at my house for dinner in two weeks and we're going to work everything out."

"I can't do it alone, Joseph." Kendall took two steps to match one of Joseph's long strides. The walking trail in the park near his house was deserted at the early hour.

"I don't know. Your father won't want me there."

"I want you there. I need your support." Kendall stopped abruptly.

Joseph turned and walked back. "I don't want to make things worse."

"How could it be any worse? My mother hates me because I killed her favorite daughter."

Joseph stroked her cheek. "Kendall, I'm sure you're wrong."

Kendall's eyes glistened with tears, the pain of it all overwhelming.

"If you want me there, I'll be there."

She buried her face in his chest.

"C'mon, princess. We better head back so that you can get to work."

They had fallen into a comfortable routine. Spending most nights together, Joseph driving Kendall to work every morning. He worried about her being behind the wheel alone, but he held his tongue and encouraged her to soar. He missed the time when she was totally dependent upon him. It gave him sure footing in her life and he never questioned his worth. With newfound independence, Kendall might question her reasons for being with a man her father's age and move on to better prospects. Although she had ended her relationship with Darren, Joseph knew that he lurked in the shadows waiting for one mistake that might allow him in.

Joseph sat in his kitchen drinking juice and waiting for Kendall to dress for work. She had taken ownership of his meals and monitored his exercise routine.

"Joseph," she sang, rushing around the kitchen. "We have to go." Grabbing an apple from the refrigerator she dangled a package of ham cold cuts. "This is not healthy. What is it doing in here?"

"I'll throw it out."

She left the cold cuts on the counter and moved to the cupboard.

Joseph cleared his plate from the table. "Are you ready?"

"Uh-huh." She scurried around the kitchen, returning to him with a glass of water and a bottle of pills. "Don't forget."

"I won't."

"Right now."

Joseph took the water and pill bottle. "Nurse Ratched?"

"If I have to be. I'm not going to lose you because you forgot to take a pill." She waited for him to swallow the medication. "I care about you too much for that."

Joseph bent and stuck out his tongue for her inspection. "Happy?"

"Yep." Kendall laughed, kissing his lips and sending a heady current through his body. "When is your doctor's appointment?"

Joseph followed her to the garage. "Two weeks, Friday."

"The same day of dinner with my parents."

Joseph didn't respond.

"I'm taking off that day. I want to go with you."

"That's not necessary."

"Joseph, I want to be there to support you."

"Okay." He wanted her with him every step of the way.

Scarlet surrounded the brilliant greens of Gabrielle's eyes. Dragging herself from the bathroom, she downed a glass of Alka Seltzer. Again, she had spent her night off drinking too much and crying over Joseph. He seemed to drop out of sight. And worse, Russ kept showing up at her apartment, apologizing, riddled with guilt. He was only part of the master plan, insignificant in her life.

Time to step up her actions. The first thing she needed to know was where Joseph was hiding and how she could contact him. She dialed Russ's cell phone, whispered Italian, and waited for him to ditch his wife and show up at her place.

Kendall pressed the collar of Joseph's crisp sky-blue button-down shirt to her nose and inhaled deeply. As Joseph's scent filled her nose, visions of him standing before her bare-chested wearing checkered pajama pants filled her head. His shirt fit her as comfortably as his caring personality made her feel. She added ground coffee to the coffeemaker before opening the tall steel door of the refrigerator.

She froze to listen; Joseph hadn't stirred. She imagined he would sleep late, what with the incessant ringing of the phone all through the night. He had finally taken it off the hook, but not before Kendall heard him utter words of Italian into the receiver. She hadn't questioned him last night, but she questioned herself this morning.

Ignoring the fact that Joseph had a woman calling his home all night was not healthy. She placed a hand over the wounded area of her chest. Maybe Greg, Max, and her dad were right—Joseph had one thing on his mind and getting it from her or anyone else willing would do just fine.

"Good morning." Joseph's voice sounded sleep-husky.

Startled, Kendall jerked around to face him.

Joseph pulled his head back. Her eyes reflected the disappointment she had not yet voiced. "You look hurt and confused."

Kendall rested her back against the refrigerator. "Doubt slipped into my head last night."

"We can't have that." He placed a palm down on the counter. "I don't want that."

"Everyone has expressed their feelings about us."

"Everyone?" Joseph asked with a lift of his proud chin.

"Max, Greg, and my Dad."

"Hmmm. You thinking they may be right?"

"When February rolls around, will you be playing with a more age-appropriate toy?"

"I don't like what your advisers are telling you."

"Gabrielle could be a Barbie doll."

Joseph shifted his weight onto the hand resting on the countertop. "Last night we made love. This morning you have doubts about us. What did you dream about?"

Kendall laughed despite of the seriousness of the conversation.

Joseph lifted his chin again. "I don't like what happened last night." He paused. "I promise you nothing has ever happened between Gabrielle and me and nothing ever will."

Kendall nodded.

"I don't like the look you had on your face when I walked into the room. I don't ever want to see it again."

Kendall followed a strong aroma to the coffeemaker.

Joseph followed, his bare feet slapping the Formica. "I have to make sure I never do anything that places doubt in your mind."

"Gabrielle?"

Joseph reached over Kendall's shoulder and opened the cupboard door. He grabbed a large coffee mug decorated with the airline's logo. "It was Gabrielle."

"None for me." Kendall stopped him when he went for the second matching cup. "I'll drink orange juice."

"I'm not sure if I have any." The heat from Joseph's bare chest consumed the distance between them, making the innocent words take on a seductive meaning.

"I checked." Kendall's breath caught in her chest. "You didn't, but you had oranges. I made fresh squeezed. What did Gabrielle want?" Kendall lifted the coffeepot and filled Joseph's cup. "What do you take?"

Joseph's chest grazed her back as he settled into a comfortable stance behind her. "Black. No cream, no sugar. She wanted to talk. See if there is a way in."

Kendall heard him blow softly into the cup before taking a sip. The warm steam tickled the back of her neck and she remembered his aggressive lovemaking the night before, the way he pinned her to the bed, his chest pressing against her back. "Who is this woman?"

"Gabrielle has tried and tried and I've always said no. How can you not drink coffee? Maybe you should try adding sugar."

Kendall turned to him. "Except the night you invited her over for drinks. People could get the wrong idea."

Joseph extended his arm and placed his coffee cup on the counter. He grabbed the edge of the counter with both hands, trapping her inside his intimate circle. "You or Gabrielle?"

"Both."

"I only care about what you think." He studied the erotic excitement pinging and ponging between her eyes.

Kendall traced the definition of his chest muscles. Joseph's head dipped, watching her fingers flow over him, leaving a line of pimpled skin in their wake. Kendall's blunt nails stopped below his navel at the tie of his pajama bottoms. Her eyelids held a long blink before lifting to meet his wanting eyes. Neither took a breath as they held silent negotiations about the state of their relationship. Joseph's mouth dropped in surprise when Kendall gripped the waistband of his pajamas.

Joseph closed his eyes and tried to calm the raucousness upsetting his groin before descending on her lips. Kendall accepted the warm, bitter richness of his coffee kiss with an open mouth. Her tongue swirled and gathered the remnants of coffee coating Joseph's mouth. He pulled away, shifting his weight into her, onto the palms of his hands. "I took care of Gabrielle. I don't know how she got my number, but I told her not to use it again."

Silence surrounded them.

"Kendall?"

"You made me promise."

"And I promise right back. I keep my promises." He backed away, crossing his arms over his chest. "Because if you believe you have competition—"

"We better get dressed if we're going to walk before I go to work."

"You have no competition, Kendall."

Kendall's eyes moved away from him. "It's getting late."

"I'll get dressed." He stopped in the doorway; the sunshine from the tall windows framed his wide physique, giving him an Adonis look. "Staying here every night, taking care of me, cooking for me tells me you want this relationship to step up a notch."

"You opened the door to me. That tells me you're ready for the next level."

"Beyond ready." He thrust his chin upward before a lopsided grin consumed his face.

Chapter 35

Joseph's nerves wore thin during the drive to Dr. Bennis's office. If not for Kendall's soft words and calming nature his nervousness would have spawned road rage. Remembering her not-long-ago fear of cars, he relaxed and eased off the accelerator. When they arrived at Dr. Bennis's office the nurse asked Joseph to sit in the lobby for thirty minutes before checking his blood pressure.

Joseph sat forward, elbows pressed into his knees. His foot tapped rapidly against the carpet. "What's taking so long? Has it been thirty minutes?"

Kendall's soothing touch found his back and he instantly relaxed. "Joseph, the nurse wants you to have time for the stress of the drive to subside."

He sat back, taking her hand in his. "Doesn't she understand that waiting makes it worse? I'm going to find out what's going on."

"Joseph," Kendall said sharply, "sit down and relax. If you keep this up your blood pressure will be through the roof."

Joseph exhaled deeply. "I'm glad you came."

Kendall laid her arm across his broad shoulders. "This is going to be okay. Just think, in a few minutes you'll be cleared to fly again."

Joseph smiled. It was a real possibility.

"Captain Stewart," the nurse called.

Joseph stood, pulling Kendall up with him. "Come back with me."

"Will they let me?" Kendall looked to the nurse.

"It's fine if Captain Stewart doesn't mind."

Inside the aesthetic exam room, Kendall took the chair, Joseph the gurney.

"This is my girlfriend, Kendall Masterson." Joseph proudly introduced the classy beauty escorting him to his doctor's appointment.

"Nice to meet you." The nurse made benign conversation with Kendall while leafing through his chart and reviewing the data. She went on to question Joseph about any symptoms he was experiencing.

"None."

"Very good," the nurse remarked.

"Kendall has been taking good care of me."

"So it seems. Is she seeing to it that you take your medications as prescribed?"

Joseph answered in the affirmative, listing the medications he was actively taking. They reviewed his diet and exercise regimen, discussed any unusual stress in his life.

The nurse approached the gurney and Joseph's arm shot out.

"Not yet, Captain Stewart. I'd like to check your weight first."

Joseph left Kendall in the exam room with a wink as he followed the nurse back out into the corridor. Height and weight confirmed, they returned. Kendall now looked as anxious as he had in the lobby.

Joseph locked his gaze on Kendall as the nurse wheeled the mechanical blood pressure machine over to him. The cuff tightened. The machine beeped.

"We'll have to take it again, Captain Stewart. The battery's dead."

Joseph wanted to jump off the gurney and scream. He'd waited a month for this moment, couldn't she have checked the battery before calling him into the room? The nurse climbed between the wall and the gurney and plugged in the machine. After a series of beeps, she hit the button that inflated the cuff again.

Joseph held his breath.

Kendall mouthed, "Breathe, Joseph, breathe," and smiled.

He exhaled in synchronization with the end signal and deflation of the cuff.

The nurse grinned. "Looks good, Captain Stewart. Much better than the last time you were here." She pulled the cuff, the sound of Velcro ripping away filling the small room. "The doctor wants manual checks of right and left arm also."

Joseph breathed easier. "No problem."

After checking the blood pressures manually, the nurse left the room to retrieve Dr. Bennis.

"This is good?" Kendall asked.

"So far, so good," Joseph answered cautiously. Until Dr. Bennis gave the okay, he didn't want to chance jinxing himself. He was very close to having his career back.

Dr. Bennis entered the room, hand extended. "Joseph, the nurse tells me there's good news."

"I certainly hope so. Dr. Bennis, this is my girlfriend, Kendall Masterson."

They exchanged pleasantries. Watching the exchange, Joseph still couldn't believe a woman as young, intelligent, and beautiful as Kendall wanted anything to do with an old man whose health wasn't 100 percent. He realized how lucky he had been to find her and he would make sure not a minute passed that she didn't feel his appreciation.

Dr. Bennis took a seat on a rolling stool and reviewed

his chart. When he finished he slipped his hands down on his knees. "What are you doing in my office? Get to work."

Joseph jumped off the gurney. "Really?"

Dr. Bennis stood. "Really. I'll clear you to fly immediately, but I want you to stay on the diet, keep exercising, and stick with your medications. If any symptoms arise see me immediately. Don't wait for an appointment, just walk in."

"Thank you, Dr. Bennis." Joseph shook his hand vigorously, laughing.

"You did it. Not me. See you in one month for a recheck." He lifted his hand in good-bye and left the room.

Joseph turned to Kendall. She sat in the hard plastic chair, hands clamped to her mouth, tears glistening. He opened his arms wide. "Come here, princess."

Slowly, Kendall rose.

"I couldn't have done this without you." He took her up in his arms and swung her around in circles, releasing his tension in a loud howl. The nurse barged into the room to investigate but quietly backed out when she saw Joseph devouring Kendall's lips.

Kendall looked down atop Joseph's head. He kneeled at her feet in a chocolate suit, massaging her hand. His sure strokes were accompanied by words of support. His cologne floated up to her and she inhaled deeply, knowing it would help to calm her.

The spasms had started as Kendall was dressing for dinner.

"Is that better, princess?" Joseph grinned up at her, his good mood still intact. The entire drive from the doctor's office he had talked about his happiness about being able to fly again. He thanked her over and over for giving him back an important piece of his world.

As Kendall sat on the edge of her bed, she didn't feel worthy of his praise. She worried she'd fall apart before they even arrived at her father's house. These were her parents, why was she so afraid? *Because you killed their daughter.* She looked at Joseph with earnest eyes. "I don't think I can go through with this. I'm going to call my father."

Joseph steadied the hand reaching for the phone. "And tell him what? He's opened the door to repairing your family. Are you going to deny him this?"

Kendall looked away from the clean-shaven, mocha face of her conscience. "I guess I can't do that?"

"No, you can't." Joseph sat next to her on the bed. "I'll be right there beside you. Give it an honest try, but if at any time you want to leave, we go. No explanation needed. You say to me you're ready to leave and I drive you home."

"Ohhh," Kendall moaned, dropping her head against his chest. "I'm scared to death."

"This is a big deal. You'll get through it."

Kendall looked up into his dark, knowing eyes. She would get through it.

It started off badly.

Helen waved hello from across the room to the daughter she hadn't seen in a year. Frank was distantly polite to Joseph as he showed everyone into the picture-perfect living room. He and his wife had hardly used this room when she lived there; he didn't use it all since she'd left him. The television and stereo were in the extra bedroom-turned-den and that's where Frank lived out the lonely days of his life. Missing his daughter and aching for his wife's love.

Kendall and Joseph sat together on the love seat. They

looked the storybook couple. Joseph handsome in his chocolate suit, Kendall beautiful in the tan pantsuit and pumps. Dressy, but conservative enough for dinner with her parents, they sat stiffly, both uncomfortable about what lay ahead.

Helen and Frank sat at opposite ends of the sofa, but could have been separated by a room. Kendall watched her parents, acting like strangers. She glanced over at Joseph. His fingers snaked around hers, giving a reassuring squeeze.

"Dinner will be ready in ten minutes," Frank announced, breaking an awkward silence.

"Captain Stewart, how did you meet my daughter?" Dressed in a form-fitting black dress, Helen looked more like Kendall's older sister than her mother.

"Joseph, please. I first saw Kendall up onstage at the African-American Museum. I tracked her down and couldn't stay away after that."

Kendall looked surprised.

Helen noticed. "She didn't know that?"

Joseph answered, "Not until this minute."

Silence invaded the room.

Frank stood. "I'll check on dinner." When he returned, Joseph was talking about his job as a pilot. Kendall's eyes were cast down on her lap. Helen listened, nodding at Joseph's every word.

"Dinner's ready," Frank announced as the doorbell rang. "Everyone go to the dining room." He hurried off to answer the door.

"Whose Mercedes is that out front, Frank?"

Kendall's stomach sank lower than the heels on her pumps. She squeezed Joseph's hand under the table. She would kill her father. As if the evening wasn't awkward enough between her and her mother, he had to throw Darren into the mix.

They couldn't hear Frank's response from the dining room.

Kendall's eyes dropped to her empty plate when Darren walked into the dining room behind her father. Wearing dress slacks, a white shirt, and a tie, he looked as if he had just come from church.

Helen jumped up from the table. "Darren." She rushed into his arms, giving him a warm hug much more welcoming than the curt wave Kendall had received. "You're a sight for sore eyes." She stepped back and examined him from head to toe. "Still as handsome as ever. Are you staying?"

Joseph's hand slipped free from Kendall's. She glanced over and didn't like the stoic expression on his face or the way his eyes burred into Darren.

Darren's eyes finally met Kendall's. "Hi, Kendall."

"Hi, Darren."

"Well, are you staying? You're part of this family, too." Helen scowled at Frank.

"No." Darren tried to beg out. "I was in the neighborhood and stopped by to say hey to Frank. I didn't know you were having dinner."

"Now you know. Sit down." Helen took charge of the house as if she had never run off with another man—and Frank gladly let her. "Frank, get another chair for me. Darren, you sit here in my seat. I'll get a place setting."

Kendall watched her mother and father scurry off to accommodate Darren. A man they once both believed was not good enough for her.

Joseph stood, careful not to let the linen napkin hit the floor. He extended a hand to Darren. "I'm Joseph Stewart, Kendall's date."

Darren's eyes flashed in her direction. The last drop

of hope drained from his face. Slowly, Darren accepted Joseph's hand.

Joseph sat down, angry eyes on Kendall. "Since no one was going to introduce us."

Kendall sat stunned. Her mother virtually ignored her. Her father ran around trying to please her mother. Darren couldn't keep his eyes off her. Joseph was burning up her profile with unasked questions. She wanted to go home and climb under the covers until it all passed. She'd jumped many hurdles only to find she hadn't traveled any distance.

Dinner was served and eaten in uneasy silence. No small talk. Only polite requests to pass the butter, salt and pepper. Kendall pushed the food around on her plate, unable to lift the fork to her lips. The tension was thick. Too many unresolved problems going ignored.

Feeling as if she might break at any moment, Kendall jumped in with both feet. "Mom, I didn't kill Raven on purpose. It was an accident. If I could take it back, I would."

"Kendall!" Frank obviously wanted to handle things more delicately.

Helen erupted as violently as her daughter. "Who told you not to try to go to that stupid concert, Kendall? Didn't I say the weather was too bad to try to drive on the wet streets with these idiots that can't control their speed on a sunny day? Didn't I say to wait until next time?"

"But I didn't want to. And neither did Raven. We both wanted to go to the concert. I didn't do it on purpose."

"Ladies." Frank's fist pounded the table, water glasses jiggling, the women instantly silencing. "You are sitting at my dinner table. You'll talk to each other with respect. Now we're going to work everything out or no one's leaving, but I won't have this tone at my table."

Kendall's anger and hurt would not be deterred. "Daddy, why is Darren here?"

Darren's eyes went to her like magnets and Kendall immediately regretted her words.

"Darren explained that, baby."

"He just happened by? Don't give me that."

Frank pounded the table again. "Watch your tone with me."

Darren stood. "I better go."

"Good idea," Joseph piped in.

"I have more right to be here than you," Darren rebutted.

Joseph rose to surpass Darren's towering height. "And why do you feel that way?"

"Sit down," Frank shouted. "Both of you. Sit down."

Frank's piercing gaze never left Kendall. "Nobody's leaving until this is resolved."

"And how are we going to do that, Daddy? Mom won't even look at me. She gave Darren more of a welcome than she gave me."

All eyes went to Helen.

Joseph found Kendall's hand underneath the table. She wanted to curl up in his lap and let him shield her from the pain.

"Helen." Frank's voice was calm, all signs of his anger gone. "Tell your daughter that you love her."

Helen's eyes cut into him.

"You're about to lose your daughter forever. Tell her how you feel, damn it."

"Kendall knows I love her," Helen snapped.

"No." Kendall's voice wavered. "No, I don't."

Helen struggled to meet her eyes. "I love you, Kendall."

"But you blame me."

No response.

Darren tried to ease the tension. "It was a hard time for us all, Kendall."

"You starting in on me too, Darren?"

Joseph answered, "No, he's not." The warning loud and clear.

Darren scowled at Joseph before focusing on Kendall. "It was a terrible, terrible accident. We all loved Raven. I loved her as a little sister. You know that, Kendall. I'm saying we needed to come together and you pushed us all away."

Frank interjected. "That's the past and we need to work this out, become a family again."

"Daddy, Mom blames me. She can't stand to look at me. She wouldn't dare touch me. How can we be a happy family again?"

Helen jumped up from the table. "Everybody stop trying to speak for me. I can speak for myself." She smoothed her dress before going on. "Kendall, all I know is that my little girl is gone."

Joseph's hand went around Kendall's trembling shoulders. If not for his support and unwavering strength, she would have fallen from her chair an hour ago. No matter what happened, Joseph would be there for her. Knowing that, Kendall braced for the unveiling of the truth.

Helen went on. "I did blame you for Raven's death. But despite that I tried to embrace you and help you through your pain. You pushed me away. You might as well have spit in my face. I couldn't keep banging my head against a brick wall."

"Helen—"

"No, Frank. You want us to work it out. Let's start with being truthful to one another."

Kendall's stomach twisted. She felt shaky and out of control. "Joseph, I want to go now."

Joseph leaned into her, lending her his strength. He whispered, "Try to hear your mother out."

Helen continued. "I grew to hate you. *You* killed my daughter and then you had the nerve to turn on *me? Us?* I told Frank to leave it alone, but he wouldn't. He insisted on visiting you every day in the hospital—insisted on pulling me along. Kept saying you needed your mother. I can't stand the sight of Detroit Receiving Hospital to this day. Do you remember how you acted when we'd show up?"

Frank touched Helen's arm but she shook him off. "It tore Frank and me apart. Him supporting you. Me mourning Raven."

"I didn't mean to." Kendall's vision blurred with tears, her throat felt tight. "I couldn't take you glaring at me. I knew I had killed my sister. I knew you blamed me. I couldn't take your hatred on top of my guilt. The only thing worse was your support, Daddy. And your understanding, Darren. I needed to be alone to work through the pain. Can't you understand that, Mom?"

Helen dropped down in her chair. For the first time in a year, she really looked at her daughter. She shrank back at the pain she saw reflected back at her.

Kendall was crying. "I'm sorry. If I could take it back, I would. I can't bring Raven back, Mom. I'm trying to get myself together. I need you and Daddy in my life again."

No one spoke.

Kendall stood. "Joseph, take me home."

"Wait." Frank stood at the head of the table. With stiff movements, he turned to his wife. "Helen, I love you and I want you to come home."

Helen focused on Kendall, unshed tears threatening to fall.

"But no matter how much I love you, I don't want you in my house unless you can fix this with Kendall.

Everything that happened is in the past. We need to move on from this point and take care of the time we have on this earth together. Now I need to know if you want to be here or not."

Helen's eyes broke away from Kendall. "I never wanted to leave. I felt like I was smothering."

Frank waved his hand, dispersing the painful memories. "The past. Do you want to work this out with your daughter and your husband? Or do we go on living apart like strangers, the three of us?"

It didn't take long for Helen to answer. She burst into sobs that shook her body, reaching for Kendall across the table. Joseph released his hold on Kendall. The women met halfway and embraced in a hug so loving the men had to look away or shed a tear.

Chapter 36

"Twenty-one days, Joseph? This is our last night together for three weeks?" Kendall's eyes grew wide with sadness.

Joseph steered his SUV into Russ's driveway and parked behind Greg's Lincoln. He cut the engine and angled his body to face Kendall. "The airline expects me to pick up the extra flights. I'm one of the few pilots that isn't married and have never minded being away from home for long stretches. I was so glad to be going back to work I didn't put in a schedule request. I'm sorry. Now that you're in my life I'll let them know I can't do these stretches anymore, but I have to do this one."

"Twenty-one days. Where will you be?"

"I'll fly out in the morning to Atlanta and then do the Atlanta–San Antonio connection."

"You won't be in town even for a quick layover?"

"I'm afraid not. If you can be understanding this one time, I'll make sure it doesn't happen again."

Kendall's eyes dropped to her lap. "It's just that I'm starting to get my life back and my mother comes back to town and now you're leaving for three weeks. I don't know if I can do it."

"I'm going to miss you too, princess. I'll call you every night."

"I'll miss you."

"It'll work out. After dinner, we'll go back to your house and talk. Now, smile and let's go have some fun. Your boss and his wife are waiting. I want you to get to know Russ and Sara; Russ is a good guy, my good friend."

Kendall and Joseph were the last dinner guests to arrive and were greeted with smiles and hugs. Greg and his wife, Madge, were seated in the living room having a glass of wine.

"Russ, tell Joseph to get Kendall a drink."

Russ tipped his wineglass to Joseph without the usual humor they shared at Sara's unique communication style.

Joseph poured himself a glass of wine and Kendall a glass of punch. "Everything all right, Russ?"

"Yeah, why do you ask?" He remained distracted.

"We were supposed to go to a baseball game before I returned to work—"

"I'll have to make that up to you, buddy." He tossed back the last of his wine. "I've been tired—picking up a lot of extra flights."

"Do you need to talk? We could go outside—"

"No." Russ clasped Joseph's shoulder. "No, buddy, everything is fine."

Sara spared no expense on Joseph's celebration dinner, having hired a caterer for the small affair. She loved to host a party, dragging Russ along every step of the way. Tonight, she mingled between her guests, comfortable in her role as host. Joseph noticed Russ's aloofness, his natural sense of humor flat. More was bothering him than being overworked.

The caterer announced dinner, and the dinner party of six took their assigned seats at the elegantly decorated table. A brilliant floral centerpiece, bursting with cool summer colors, was subtly woven into the pattern of the china. Before the tomato, red onion, and basil salad was

served, Joseph thanked his host and hostess for both
their friendship and giving the party. Mindful of Joseph's
diet restrictions, Sara had chosen a menu that would be
suitable for all without skimping on taste. The main
course consisted of beautifully presented grilled salmon,
couscous with yellow squash, and asparagus. Everyone at
the table had met under more formal circumstances, but
lively conversations turned the acquaintances into
instant friendships.

Sara tapped her water glass with her butter knife.
"Let's move to the recreation room for coffee and
dessert." She stood, ushering her guests to the back of
the house, keeping the party flowing.

Kendall admired Sara. Everything in her life flowed as
smoothly as she ran the dinner party. She was known in
the art world for being *the one* to arrange all fund-raisers.
She kept a beautiful house. Her marriage to Russ was
going on fifteen years. Never a hair out of place, she appeared regal, but was down-to-earth and had a knack for
making others comfortable. As Kendall observed the in-
teractions between Sara and Russ, Madge and Greg, she
wished that one day her turn would come to host a dinner party for her new friends with her husband, Joseph.

After everyone had finished the dessert of angel food
cake covered with minty mixed melon topping, Russ
challenged Greg in a game of pool. Kendall encouraged
Joseph to join them while Sara insisted on teaching her
how to play Parcheesi. Although everyone was a bit older
than Kendall, she felt comfortable and enjoyed the
group's company.

She wanted to be alone with Joseph, but understood
how important the dinner was to him. He looked as tan-
talizing as usual, laughing with his friends. She studied
his iron thighs and tight buns as he bent over the pool
table. They should be alone, under the skylights in his

bedroom, spending their last night together making love. He stood, the muscles of his back flexing. She pictured her caramel mixing with his mocha and had to restrain herself from tackling him on top of the pool table.

Kendall had just gotten the gist of Parcheesi when the ruckus began. Gabrielle stormed into the recreation room, one of the catering employees following. Tall with flowing golden hair, her green eyes glowed jade with contempt. She stopped in the doorway, speaking to no one in particular when she announced, "I'm pregnant and you will not turn your back on me."

The room fell silent. Everyone froze, all contemplating exactly why it mattered to him or her.

Gabrielle's cruel stare hit everyone in the room, one by one. Horrified by the interruption of her perfect dinner party, Sara was the first to speak. "Russ, ask this creature what she means by storming into our home with an announcement that is insignificant to all of us."

Russ gripped his pool cue but did not speak.

"It's very significant to *one* of you in this room because he's the father."

Panic washed over the three men standing around the pool table. Kendall could feel anger as a palpable thing, humming between the three women sitting at the Parcheesi table.

"You all sit here in this big, fancy house laughing when I am alone and with child. I tell you, I will not stand for this. I will not be used and tossed aside." Gabrielle's Italian accent grew thicker with each angry word until she was speaking completely in the language no one understood—except Joseph.

"Gabrielle," Joseph said sharply, stepping forward. He continued the conversation in Italian.

Kendall had a juvenile vision. Lining up in elementary

school, the teacher asking the guilty party of a silly prank to step forward and accept their punishment.

The exchange between Joseph and Gabrielle became a heated argument. The words came fast with jabbing hand gestures. Gabrielle rolled her head and tossed her hair. Joseph scowled, his mustache twitching with every angry foreign word. Everyone stood quietly waiting for the outcome. Why had Gabrielle stormed the house with this announcement? Could she be pregnant by one of the men, who only moments before had lovingly enjoyed dinner with his wife or girlfriend?

Heat crept up Kendall's neck, reddening her face as she recalled Gabrielle draped over Joseph's sofa. The night of the ringing phone. The fingers on Kendall's right hand began to tingle as she watched Joseph chase after Gabrielle, heated words attaching them by an invisible string.

Everyone turned to Kendall. She couldn't take the harsh assessment, the questions obviously burning their tongues.

"I'm sorry," she apologized to Sara. Embarrassment moved her to the door.

Greg accosted Kendall in the foyer. "Madge and I will drive you home."

"No, I'm leaving the way I came." Kendall leaned over to place a kiss on his puffy cheek. She appreciated the tight hug he gave her in return.

"I'll check on you in the morning," Greg said as Kendall headed toward the scene on the lawn.

Joseph grabbed Gabrielle's arm and pulled her to the curb. He flung open the door to her compact car and placed her inside against her resistance. Kendall listened to more angry words fly between them. She had never seen Joseph this out of control. His calm, cool exterior was more than ruffled. His hands were balled at his sides, his Italian words harsh, his eyes blazing with anger.

When Joseph reached the SUV he opened the door for Kendall, still muttering. He mixed Italian, Japanese, and French into a language for the furious. His touch was gentle as he helped Kendall inside and took the driver's seat. They were well into the drive before Joseph was calm enough to speak. "I'm sorry you had to see that. Gabrielle is getting out of control."

Bubbling with anger, Kendall didn't comment. Before Joseph placed the SUV in park, she jumped out and raced up to her porch. He hurried after her, stopping the door with the girth of his body.

"Are you angry with me?"

"What?" Kendall knew he couldn't be that dense. "Gabrielle stormed into your celebration dinner and announced she's having your baby."

"What?" Joseph shouted. "Gabrielle's not having *my* baby."

"I'm younger than you, but I'm not stupid. I saw what everyone else saw tonight. Gabrielle announces she's pregnant and *you* step up to take credit. *You* get into a big fight with her and follow her outside. Greg's never met Gabrielle. Russ is married. Even a *child* as naive as me can piece that mystery together."

Joseph took a long step back and away from her.

Kendall didn't understand why he looked hurt or why she felt guilty.

Joseph spoke in a deceivingly low, steady voice. "I'm disappointed. I thought what we had was stronger than this. Gabrielle busts into Russ's house with her craziness and you automatically finger me? You doubt how I feel about you? You question my integrity and the promises I've made to you? With one vague accusation?"

Kendall only needed to look into his eyes to feel foolish.

"You didn't even ask—just jumped to conclusions."
He turned his back on her. "Good night."

"Joseph, wait."

He threw a hand up, kept walking.

Tears were falling by the time Joseph closed his car
door. Kendall went inside and then he drove away. She
peeled off her clothes and crawled into bed. When
would things go smoothly for her and Joseph? The attraction between them blazed, but outside forces always
interfered with their contentment. He should be lying
beside her, kissing her, stroking her—sharing this last
night together making love before his grueling work
schedule started. She should be moaning his name in
pleasure instead of groaning it in pain.

Joseph supported her in all things. He placed her
needs before his own. He was jealous of her friendship
with a gay man, for goodness' sake. She relived Gabrielle's
scene. She remembered how quickly Joseph took responsibility for his wrong actions, apologized to Max the next
time he saw him. And the scene with Gabrielle at his
house. He hadn't denied or covered up anything. Joseph
protected his integrity as if it were a precious jewel.

Honor and honesty were very important to Joseph. He
wouldn't lie to her. He wouldn't walk away from his responsibilities. Wouldn't he be honorable and step up if
he had fathered a child?

But still, Kendall couldn't ignore Gabrielle's tirade.
Gabrielle's phone calls all during the night on Kendall's
last visit to Joseph's home—disturbing their tender moments of kissing and caressing. And then there were the
people who loved her most. Greg, Max, and her father's
warnings clouded her mind. She hadn't wanted to believe
their assessment of Joseph, but things kept happening that
made her suspicious they might be right.

Kendall tossed and turned while she sorted it all out.

She had to rely on her gut feeling. She knew Greg, Max, and her father only wanted to protect her. Gabrielle was obsessed with Joseph, angry he didn't return the feelings. That Kendall was even considering Joseph's innocence said volumes. When she looked into Joseph's eyes and saw the hurt caused by her doubt of his commitment to her, she knew she had wrongly accused him.

Chapter 37

Gabrielle showed up at Russ's house to announce her pregnancy and point an accusing finger at the father of her child.

That was no coincidence.

Russ wasn't available to take Joseph's telephone call the next morning.

That was no coincidence.

Gabrielle was scheduled to work Joseph's flight from Detroit Wayne Metropolitan Airport to Atlanta.

That was no coincidence.

Captain Joseph Stewart pulled his luggage-on-wheels behind him as he made his way through the crowd to his aircraft. He looked regal, chest puffed up, in his crisp uniform and shiny shoes. Inside, his heart ached, not knowing what would happen to his relationship with Kendall.

Kendall's accusing eyes and quivering voice made Joseph feel guilty for something he hadn't done. He should have stayed and tried to convince her of his innocence. He had been badly hurt by the easiness with which she believed him to be a cheat and a liar. Even when the ex-boyfriend showed up with a box of history, Joseph had given her the benefit of the doubt—and time—to make her choice. Hadn't he done everything he could to prove himself? Hadn't he been understanding of her issues? Supported her through her problems?

Given her anything she asked to keep her happy? Not pummeled Darren when the light-skinned pretty boy sat down for dinner at the most intimate time Kendall had shared with her family in a year?

No, Kendall's behavior was as unacceptable as Gabrielle's.

Joseph thrust his chin outward. Stoic. Always about business. That was how he had lived until Kendall crashed through his walls and showed him how to have fun. Young and vibrant, she made him smile and find pleasure in simple things. She showed him there was life outside the airport.

They were good together. How could she throw it all away?

"Joseph!"

He froze, searching the crowd.

"Joseph!"

He'd know the singsong way Kendall called him over the noise in a crowd double this size.

"Joseph!"

He swung around to see Kendall making her way through the throng of harried travelers. She bounded up to him, wrapping her arms around his tapered waist. "I should have believed in you, I'm sorry. I didn't want you to leave for three weeks without knowing that."

Joseph saw the inquisitive stares of his coworkers. Never had they seen him express emotions. Calm in crises, reserved in social settings, Captain Stewart was a model for propriety.

Kendall looked up at him with the wide eyes of a doll. "Do you forgive me?"

"Of course." He released the handle of his suitcase and embraced Kendall, lifting her to meet his lips. Amongst stunned watchers, he kissed Kendall like never before.

After several minutes of providing a spectacle and ac-

cepting congratulations from fellow pilots, Joseph set
Kendall upon her feet.

"I should have listened last night. I ruined our
evening together. I know you would never break your
promise to me."

Joseph cradled her chin. "I should have made you feel
more confident in my innocence. We were both stub-
born, but it's forgotten. I'll tell you one last time. There
is nothing—never has been, never will be—between
Gabrielle and me."

"I know." She clutched her chest. "In my heart, I know."

A man dressed in a matching uniform with fewer em-
blems passed by. "Time to board, Captain Stewart."

Joseph acknowledged him by placing a hand to the
bill of his cap. "How'd you get here?"

"Max is out front waiting. He's going to take me to
work from here."

Good. He didn't want her trying to navigate the crazy
airport traffic. It would surely cause a setback in her
progress.

"I have to board."

"I'm proud of you." Kendall smiled. "I'll watch you
take off."

Joseph's face filled with pride. He could showboat his
greatest talent for the woman he—

"I love you, Kendall."

Shock and then relief flashed in Kendall's smile. "I
love you too, Captain Stewart."

Joseph kissed her cheeks, her lips. "Stand at that window." He pointed it out. "You won't leave until I'm in the
air?"

"Not until I can't see you anymore."

"I'll call you tonight." Joseph secured his luggage and
started off. He stopped, turned around. "I love you," he
called across the bustling airport.

* * *

Greg escorted Kendall through the Detroit Institute of Art's annual high school artist showcase. She admired the up-and-coming artists, leaving them with encouraging words that made their parents glow with pride. She wandered the halls side by side with Greg, but her mind was on Joseph.

She missed him terribly. The nightly phone calls were not enough. She needed to see him, touch him, kiss him. Replenish her soul and make their love a tangible thing again.

"You're very quiet." Greg's suit made him look ten pounds lighter.

"Missing Joseph." She wrapped her arms around his and rested her head on his shoulder.

"I didn't want to say anything—"

"Then don't. Please."

"I met Gabrielle once. I didn't remember it until Madge cornered me the night of her revelation."

"Greg," Kendall warned.

"Hear me out." He steered her out the door into the parking lot. "Madge knows a bit of Italian. She traveled extensively before we married. She couldn't understand it all, but what she did get—"

Kendall stopped, pulling her arm from his. "I don't want to hear it. I trust Joseph and he said he's not responsible."

"And I believe him. Even before my wife tried to translate."

Greg's support meant a great deal to Kendall.

"The question is," Greg continued, "why didn't Russ stand up? He let Joseph take the fall. And Joseph stepped in, trying to diffuse the situation all the while making himself look guilty."

"I've told you, Greg. Joseph is a good man."

* * *

Joseph spotted Russ across the bar. A little switching of assignments and Russ was able to meet him in Atlanta.

"Does Sara know?" Joseph asked, very direct.

Russ shook his head no. His shoulders slumped over the bar while he twirled a shot glass in quick circles.

"I'm not going to take the fall for this."

Russ's head shot up. "This will end my marriage."

"You should have thought about that before you slept with Gabrielle. God, Russ. Gabrielle? You know how clingy she is. You know she's been hitting on me for months. Didn't you think she might be using our friendship to get to me?"

Russ became angry, pushing his glass down the bar with the back of his hand. The bartender shied away. "Did you think Gabrielle might really be attracted to me, Joe? You walk through the airport with your nose in the air fighting off the women. Look at me. Look at my life. I needed Gabrielle to want me."

Joseph kept an even tone. "Why don't *you* take a good look at your life? You have a good career, a nice home, and a loving wife. Why do you need a 'Gabrielle' in your life to jeopardize it all?"

Russ's voice rang with sadness. "It gets old."

Joseph wouldn't accept the lame excuse. "Then make it new again."

Russ signaled the bartender.

"Are you flying?"

"Tomorrow afternoon. Back home."

"Russ, you are a good friend. So is Sara. I can't take the fall for you on this. I love Kendall. I have a commitment to her. Gabrielle has caused enough trouble between us—I won't let her, or you, break us apart."

"I need a little more time," Russ pleaded.

"I'm sorry. I won't humiliate the woman I love over this foolishness. You made a mistake—own up to it. Fix this with Sara; do right by the baby."

"You'd end our friendship over a woman?"

Joseph stood, seeing his friend in a new light. "Did you hear me? I love Kendall. I won't ruin what I have with her because of your mistake. If you want to end our friendship because I respect my woman, so be it."

Joseph left the bar knowing he would never speak to Russ or Sara again.

"It's Russ's baby."

"Joseph?"

A long sigh into the phone.

"Why are you telling me this?" Kendall asked. Already in bed for the night she checked the time—after three in the morning. Joseph's conscience was bothering him.

"The mistrust you had in your eyes . . . I wanted you to know the truth. I told Russ I wouldn't keep quiet if Sara questioned me."

"Joseph, we settled this before you left. I know you had nothing to do with Gabrielle getting pregnant."

"I needed to tell you. Share my trust with you."

Kendall gripped the receiver. His decision was tearing him apart. "You sound down."

"This ended my friendship with Russ."

Kendall didn't know what to say.

"And I miss you more than I imagined I would."

"I miss you too, Joseph."

Joseph sighed again. "There's more."

Kendall braced herself, not ready for "more." She wanted easy. She needed Joseph in her arms, helping her to fight the injustices of the world. Supporting her as she mended the wounds of her splintered family. Encouraging her to drive again. She needed him strong and powerful, focusing all his energy on her. Feeling his hurt, his turmoil, miles away split her heart in two.

After a short time, Joseph went on. "Gabrielle asked me to help her."

"Help her how?" But Kendall knew. And she also knew Joseph would spare those details to save her from the hurt. Gabrielle wanted Joseph to complete her instant family.

"She asked me to take Russ's place. When I refused, she asked me to talk to Russ, which I did, to no avail. Then she asked me to escort her to a clinic." The words were painful for Joseph to speak.

"What did you say?"

"I told her no for many reasons. I'm not letting her come between us. I'm not taking the fall for Russ; Sara is a good friend to me. I don't agree with what she's thinking of doing. And I don't want to be a part of this. It isn't my mess, I don't want this integrated into my life; I don't want Gabrielle or Russ coming to me with their problems."

"Joseph, you can't feel guilty about your decision. This *is* between Russ, Sara, and Gabrielle. You did the right thing."

"I feel better knowing you don't think badly of me."

"Never."

"Did I tell you I miss you?"

Kendall smiled. "Yes, but you can tell me again."

"No, but I'll tell you I love you. I love you very much, Kendall."

Saturday morning, Kendall cut, chopped, and marinated for the backyard party. A coming-out party for her. A remembrance party for Raven. All her family had accepted her invitation. Most because they missed her, some because of curiosity. As the morning wore on, nervousness gave way to excitement.

Kendall felt whole, her old self again. There were still hurdles. She hadn't ventured onto the freeway and she didn't drive long distances, but she was making great strides. The relationship with her mother was getting better. They were taking slow steps toward a friendship. Her father was overjoyed to have her back in his life and ecstatic to have his wife at home again. She thought of Gabrielle but pushed away the pity; Gabrielle had made her own choices and had to live with the consequences. Kendall hoped the baby would be given the chance to have a good life. Her heart went out to Sara. She couldn't imagine the effects of such a betrayal and thanked her stars for Joseph.

Kendall watched Max out back struggling to erect a canopy. She pressed her hand to her mouth, then pulled it away and let the laughter flow freely. She wouldn't deny herself happiness.

Joseph.

Kendall missed him. Being apart for three weeks was unbearable. She passed her days with work and tango class, but when she crawled into bed at night, she craved Joseph's touch. Months ago, she had barricaded herself inside the duplex. With his encouragement, she was driving and riding motorcycles.

The doorbell rang. Kendall checked the time—there was another hour before guests were to arrive. Drying her hands, she hurried to the door. On the stoop, her father stood with his arm woven around her mother's waist.

Helen smiled. "I thought you might need help getting ready for your guests."

"I'd like that." Kendall stepped aside, allowing her parents to walk back into her life. "I'd like that a lot."

Chapter 38

Kendall set her clock for six in the morning. She had planned the day a week ago, rerunning every detail in her mind until she knew it better than her own name. She'd taken care of everything. Covertly found out that Joseph never drove to the airport when he had a long stretch of flights because of the hassle of parking his car. Checked and double-checked the time his flight would land at Detroit Wayne Metro Airport and what time his duties would end. She planned out every second of his weeklong layover. She'd spent the day at the beauty salon getting her mane curled and sculpted into a style that made her look sexy. With the new look, she needed a new outfit. Passing a lingerie boutique she picked up a little something in red to light Joseph's fire. Calling herself a scamp, she smiled as she pranced through the mall, imagining how Joseph would remove the skimpy piece of material.

At six in the morning, to settle her nerves, Kendall took a long, lavish bath accentuated with a heady floral fragrance. She dressed in her new blue knit halter and denim shorts, slipping her manicured feet into yellow sandals. No, she didn't care if the world could see the scars on her right shoulder. Joseph thought she was sexy and this outfit had been purchased with him in mind. She kept her makeup light, as the hot summer day warranted, applying a sheer lip gloss and a dusting of pink

color to her eyes. Playful, but sexy; revealing, but taste-
ful, she was showing Joseph a side of her he had never
seen. A side he would appreciate.

Kendall left home in plenty of time to get to the airport. She tossed her overnight bag in the trunk of her
Honda. With confidence, she drove to the airport. She
avoided the freeways, but her car no longer weaved between lanes and she didn't stop along the way.

Kendall was sitting at the gate where Joseph would land
the 747, thirty minutes before he was due to arrive. She visited the sundries shop and purchased an art industry
magazine and a "just to say I love you" card for her parents.
Standing at the register to pay for her purchases, she spotted the cover of the local African-American paper. On the
cover of the *Michigan Chronicle* was a picture of Darren, his
arms folded across his chest. The caption dubbed him THE
LAST HONEST AUTO MECHANIC. She purchased the paper and
read about his business growing dramatically because of
the charismatic owner and his superb customer-satisfaction
policies. Happy things were going well for Darren, Kendall
handed the paper to a waiting passenger and leafed
through an art industry magazine, contemplating her next
project at the gallery until time for Joseph's plane.

Kendall stood at the window watching Joseph land the
huge aircraft. The plane glided to the ground, mocking
a paper airplane. He steered the mammoth jet down the
tarmac and eased into the gate. Kendall didn't realize
her nose pressed the glass until a woman addressed her.

"Smooth landing," the woman commented.

"My boyfriend is the pilot." Pride made Kendall's heart
leap.

It seemed like hours before the plane emptied. Passengers ran to their loved ones, sharing hugs and tears.
The flight attendants exited next. Kendall moved closer,
anticipation making her light-headed.

And then she saw Joseph. Walking between his copilots, tall, dark, and handsome. Kendall felt her knees buckle. She hadn't seen him in three weeks. She couldn't wait one more second to fall into his arms.

"Joseph." Kendall waved her arms above her head.

Joseph's head snapped up. His mustache lifted in a smile beneath his cap. He lowered his sunglasses, revealing smoldering eyes with their own seductive purpose.

Joseph's sexy eyes were Kendall's undoing. Ignoring the gatekeeper, she ran to meet him. He hurried to her, leaving his luggage-on-wheels behind.

The copilots grinned, a bit mystified by the woman who had accomplished what no other woman had ever been able to do: make Joseph love her. More talkative than usual during the flight, the pilot had grumbled several times about landing on time because he missed his girlfriend. They watched as the stoic, always-about-business pilot lost his cool, rushing to meet the beautiful woman.

Kendall jumped into Joseph's arms, knocking his cap to the ground as she smothered him in kisses. When standing near the deserted gate, embraced in kisses, became shameful, Joseph broke away from Kendall. "You didn't tell me you were coming."

"I wanted to surprise you."

"Where's Max?" Joseph grabbed his luggage and guided Kendall through the airport crowd.

"Don't worry about Max." She clenched his waist, burying her head in his chest. "I missed you too much to wait for you to get to my place."

Joseph laughed, male pride—a little arrogance—engulfed in the deep rumble. Those that knew him watched as he crossed the airport openly displaying his emotions. He kept Kendall at his side, introducing her to his coworkers as he completed his work and checked out for the week.

They were headed out of the airport when Kendall shared her next surprise. "I drove to the airport."

Concerned with her safety, Joseph froze. "You drove? Alone? Are you all right?"

"Don't I look all right?"

His eyes flashed heated signals. "You look better than all right." He cupped her cheek. "You did it?"

"I did it."

"This calls for a celebration. I'm taking you to the most exclusive restaurant in Detroit. I'll check the play-bill and we'll see a show—"

"Joseph," Kendall softly interrupted, "the only cele-brating I want to do is in your arms."

"I like the sound of that." Joseph wrapped his arm around her waist and pulled her near as they cleared the crowd.

In the parking lot, Kendall smiled. "I'll drive."

Kendall never needed the clothing packed in her overnight bag. Except for the lingerie—Joseph put that to good use.

Having taken the week off from the gallery, Kendall spent the entire time of Joseph's layover secluded in his home. They made big plans, but could never bring themselves to leave the privacy of his country cottage. For one week, they lived as a married couple would live. Doing the routine things that life required. Somehow, doing the routine with Joseph always turned into a very nonroutine session of making passionate love. By the last day of his layover, every room in his enormous home had been used to express their love.

Kendall lay cheek-to-chest with Joseph, their bodies heaving and wet, watching the heavy rain beat against the skylights above Joseph's bed. "You leave again in the morning."

"Yes." His breathing had evened out, he sounded in control as usual.

"Where to?"

"Detroit-Atlanta."

Kendall's voice quavered, betraying her. "How long?"

Joseph threaded his fingers through her hair. "Nine days."

Kendall's hand slid across his rippled abdomen. "But it's Detroit-Atlanta so you'll be in town, right?"

"I might be able to pull one or two overnights in the middle of the schedule."

"Right about the time I'll be away with Greg bidding on the new artwork?"

Joseph didn't answer. His hand slid down her neck and rested around her shoulders.

Kendall lifted her head, capturing his eyes, needing to convey the truthfulness of her words. "Joseph, I don't know if I can stand being away from you for nine more days."

"Princess." He held her tightly. "It won't be that bad."

"You don't think so?"

Joseph looked away from her pain.

"Will it always be this way? You away for long periods of time, me here alone. I can't take a week off work every time you're in town."

Joseph sat up against the headboard. "This has been on my mind, too, Kendall."

"Well?" Kendall sat up, facing him.

"Well, what?"

"How long do you think we'll be able to go on like this?"

The discussion made Joseph edgy and his tone couldn't hide that fact. "Are you thinking about replacing me?"

No, no, she wasn't. Never. But how long before that became an issue too? How many days did they need to see each other to keep their feelings alive? It was possible, probable that one of them would be become restless and need to be held. Having newly rediscovered life, Kendall didn't want to give it up; return to sitting at home alone every night, unable to enjoy the culturally rich city. And Joseph had a voracious sexual appetite. How long would it be before—

"Kendall, are you seeing someone else?"

"No, Joseph. Of course not."

He scanned her face, his gaze moving across her body, searching for the fingerprints of another man. "You promised me no other man would ever touch you in the way I do. Ever."

"I keep my promises."

"Good." It sounded like a warning.

"But how long—"

"Forever."

Kendall wished declaring something made it true.

Melancholy settled on Kendall's shoulders when Joseph kissed her good-bye at his front door the next morning. She couldn't adequately describe the loneliness to Max when she met him for lunch in the middle of the week.

As good and powerful as her and Joseph's love was, she couldn't understand why its warmth didn't sustain her across the distance. They talked every day. He sent her postcards with *I love you* sprawled in his neat handwriting. Flowers arrived at the gallery. But every night, after hanging up the telephone, she cried herself to sleep.

On day five of Joseph's absence, the UPS man stood on her porch in a brown shirt and matching shorts. She signed and he handed her a flat envelope. Inside the envelope was a round-trip ticket to Atlanta. She rushed to the telephone and dialed the hotel where Joseph stayed while in Atlanta. Knowing he was in the air, she left him a simple message. "Captain Stewart, I'll see you next weekend."

* * *

Two days later, she stood in the middle of Atlanta's superbusy airport searching the crowd for Joseph. Instead she found an airport employee holding a sign with her name on it.

"I'm Kendall Masterson."

"Hello, Ms. Masterson. I'm Lila. Captain Stewart has been delayed. He called ahead and asked that we get you to the hotel. He shouldn't be more than a couple of hours off schedule."

Kendall wrestled with disappointment. She wanted to see Joseph's smiling face when she stepped off the aircraft. She focused on the positive. She was in Atlanta, one of her favorite cities, and she'd be in Joseph's arms in a matter of hours.

A short time later, Kendall emerged from the shower in Joseph's hotel suite wearing a silky black negligee that fell to her ankles but provided seductive peeks of the swell of her breasts. Dressed in full uniform, Captain Joseph Stewart stood waiting. She took in every inch of his fine mocha body. His recently trimmed mustache and close-cut hairstyle with the gray specks at the temples were distinguishingly sexy. From the dark uniform cap to the shiny black patent leather shoes, Joseph was a picture of perfection.

With forced composure, Kendall sashayed up to him. "Captain Stewart."

"Ms. Masterson, sorry I wasn't able to meet you at the airport. It couldn't be avoided."

Her fingertips glided over the gold wings gracing his lapel. "I'm sure."

Evident in the stress of his jaw, Joseph hung on to his composure by a thin thread. "I'm happy you could fly out to be with me."

Huskily, "I'm sure."

"My layover—"

"Layover," Kendall repeated, a true temptress as she whispered the word. Her tone made Joseph's lips part, but he could find no words. She loosened the knot of his tie. The dark jacket was easily removed. Crumpling the starched white shirt wasn't an issue as Kendall tore away at the buttons.

All feigned composure was lost as they ripped off the offending clothing that separated their bodies. When both were naked, Joseph effortlessly scooped Kendall up and placed her on his bed. Kendall knew to search underneath the pillows for the protective barrier. For the first time, she applied it, Joseph panting and shaking while her fingers performed the deed. She had worked him into a frenzy by the time the barrier was secured and he entered her without formality. Long minutes passed afterward before Joseph was able to speak.

"I can't believe how you've changed," Joseph mused, emerging from the bathroom.

"Good or bad?"

The mattress dipped under his weight. He laid Kendall's leg across his thigh and used slow motions with a warm cloth to soothe his aggressiveness. "Better." He gave her a devilish grin. "You never would have asked me to do that before. Did I hurt you?" He pulled the cloth away to inspect.

"No."

No. He would never hurt her. No matter how desperately he needed her body. Love would always rein him in.

Joseph had slipped into evergreen pajama pants and Kendall back into her gown when he turned on the stereo. He approached the bed, extending his hand. "Can I have this dance?"

Kendall's brow arched upward. A familiar tone used

to dance the tango filled the room. She watched the lift of his mustache as she placed her hand inside his. With flare, he led her to the middle of the suite. In one crisp movement, he pulled her into his chest—the routine starting stance for the tango.

"Joseph?" Kendall questioned, delighted by the possibility they could share her love of the dance.

A serious expression covered his face as he let the rhythm of the music choose his steps and set the pace of his timing. Impressed by his advancement since their last dance at the beach picnic, Kendall responded with her own interpretative energy. Fueled by their intense love for each other, their movements were intimate, beautiful. Joseph led them in a left and right promenade, Kendall feeling free and possessed simultaneously. Corte, backward and forward, their bodies too close to fit a sheet of paper between them. Step quick-quick, slow, Joseph lunged forward, Kendall bending backward, arching her breasts against his bare chest. The figure-eight step leading into an open fan variation, he flawlessly completed advanced steps of the tango with sensual grace. Joseph finished by dipping Kendall backward, the final note of the music finding her on her back on the carpet, Joseph's hands swallowing hers from above. Her black negligee framed her body, dipping into deep curves.

Silence.

"How did you learn to do that?" Kendall asked.

Joseph kneeled beside her. "You told me about the tango classes here when we first met. I started taking lessons as soon as I was released to fly. I wanted to learn how to tango. I wanted you to be able to share the thing you love with me."

"That was incredible."

"You are incredible. Marry me."

"No." Shocked, Kendall answered too quickly.

"No?"

Kendall's heart thumped. Her throat closed. Tears threatened. Overwhelmed with happiness, she couldn't process the moment.

"Have my babies."

She shook her head. Surely the intimacy of the dance had altered Joseph's judgment. He couldn't love her enough to spend a lifetime with her.

"I want six kids."

"No."

Joseph straddled her waist. "I want to marry you and have a family."

"No," Kendall heard herself say when she wanted to scream, "Yes." But she couldn't give in to the cruel joke. After all the ups and downs of the last year, happiness couldn't come this easily. Saying yes would make it all disappear. She'd wake up from her dream.

Joseph's fingers massaged her scalp. "I can't stand being away from you. It's only been seven days since we were together, but a piece of me died each day I couldn't see you." He kissed her forehead. "Touch you." He kissed the tip of her nose. "Kiss you." His lips found hers. "Make love to you. I won't be separated from you again. I took an early retirement from the airlines."

Kendall managed two words. "You can't."

"I did. Today was my last flight. There's an abandoned private airport I've been thinking about. I have a meeting scheduled to look it over Monday. It'll cost me a chunk of my retirement, but if I like it, I'll start a flight school. If not, I'll find another. Whatever, I won't be leaving you again. I need to be at home with my wife and kids."

In the thickening haze of Joseph's emotional words, Kendall became light-headed. She closed her eyes. He encouraged her to open them with kisses to her lids.

"I'm forty years old and I want six kids." He pulled the

string of his pajama bottoms, pushing them down his iron thighs to expose his readiness. "We need to get started as soon as possible."

"No." Kendall wanted to explain her refusal. She wanted to tell him she loved him more than air, but he was pushing her gown over her hips, shoving her thighs apart, and overwhelming her with his expertise at controlling her body. Lovingly, he kissed her lips and marked her neck. His entrance was different, raw, packed with emotions words could never identify. The friction of their joining stifled the words she wanted to use to tell him having his children would be a joy.

"Will you have my babies, Kendall?" Joseph whispered in her ear.

The tears ran freely. "No."

"Will you marry me?"

"No."

Joseph cupped her face, his smoldering eyes locked on to her soul. His stroke was sure, ignoring the nonsensical words she uttered. With every flex of his hips he demonstrated his love and accentuated his purpose of making a baby.

Kendall felt sanity slipping away. She strained to control her body, keep her heart in check. Not lose the dream to reality.

"I love you, princess. Marry me," Joseph insisted.

"No," Kendall whimpered. Emotional happiness so wonderful it hurt. Physical pleasure so satiating it was painful.

"Woman, stop telling me no." With an arrogantly satisfying stroke, Joseph asked again, "Will you marry me, Kendall?"

This time, as her body exploded, she could only scream the truth. "Yes, I'll marry you. I love you, Joseph."

Dear Readers:

I was about halfway through the first draft of *Tango* when Aaliyah's plane crashed. I had reached the end when America was devastated by the September 11 tragedy. I wasn't sure how to handle these disasters, or if I should finish the book at all. I decided to tell Joseph and Kendall's story, but omit these events. To mention them in passing would demean the pain of the families affected, and I could find no way to do justice to anyone by adding them. Remember the victims and their families in your heart, and take pleasure in the carefree time Kendall and Joseph are able to spend together.

If you, the reader didn't support my efforts, I wouldn't be able to continue writing for you. Enjoy, and I can't wait to continue the lively discussions on the book signing circuit. Keep writing: P.O. Box 672, Novi, MI 48376, or: kwhite_writer@hotmail.com